TIME DOGS

SEAMAN AND THE GREAT NORTHERN ADVENTURE

TIME DOGS

SEAMAN AND THE GREAT NORTHERN ADVENTURE

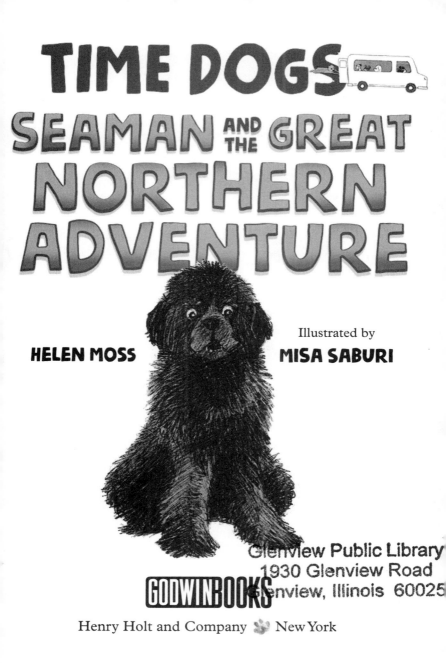

HELEN MOSS

Illustrated by
MISA SABURI

GODWINBOOKS

Henry Holt and Company 🐾 New York

Henry Holt and Company, *Publishers since 1866*
Henry Holt® is a registered trademark of Macmillan Publishing Group, LLC
175 Fifth Avenue, New York, NY 10010 • mackids.com

Library of Congress Control Number: 2018955698
ISBN 978-1-250-18635-5

Our books may be purchased in bulk for promotional, educational,
or business use. Please contact your local bookseller or the Macmillan
Corporate and Premium Sales Department at (800) 221-7945 ext. 5442
or by email at MacmillanSpecialMarkets@macmillan.com.

First edition, 2019 / Designed by April Ward
Printed in the United States of America by LSC Communications,
Harrisonburg, Virginia

1 3 5 7 9 10 8 6 4 2

TO MUM AND DAD

1

THE SQUEAKY, FREAKY FLYING MACHINE

I was woken by the whiff of rotting tuna.

I sat up and sniffed. The tuna smell was old cat food. I was also picking up hot sauce, wet carpet, and chicken poop. I may not be as quick on my paws as I used to be, but my nose is as sharp as ever.

Clatter, bang, clatter.

The noise was coming from the dog flap in the back door. I did a quick head count.

Baxter, Maia, and Newton were all with me on the rug by the fire. "Security alert!" I barked. "Action! Action!"

Baxter grunted in his sleep.

Maia opened one eye.

Newton didn't do anything. He's a little deaf these days.

I gave up and raced down the hall. "Stop right where you are!" I shouted. I slipped on the wooden floor. Scooting to a stop, I found myself nose-to-nose with Titch.

I should have known from the smell!

Titch is a stray, but she turns up at Happy Paws Farm most days. Usually around mealtimes. Right now, she was halfway through the dog flap. "What's up, Trevor?" she barked, almost knocking me out cold with a blast of tuna breath.

"What's up? *What's up* is that I was

having a nice quiet nap. Then *someone* started breaking the door down."

"Not my fault they make these dumb flaps so small!" Titch wiggled her huge head. Her raggedy ears bobbed up and down, but she was still stuck. The dog flap flipped up and smacked my nose. "I'm going on a road trip," she said. "Any of you old-timers want to tag along?"

Maia, Baxter, and Newton padded sleepily into the hall. About time! The house could have been invaded by pests by now; rats or raccoons, or—even worse—a *cat*.

"No, *thank you!*" Maia yawned. "We do *not* want to ride the garbage truck with you again, Titch."

"Relax, Princess Fluffybutt!" Titch laughed. "No garbage trucks this time. I'm talking about the squeaky, freaky flying machine."

Baxter's ears drooped. "You mean the *van*?"

"Speak up!" barked Newton. "Did someone say *van*? Have you forgotten what happened last time?"

By jiminy! How could any of us forget? Baxter had only climbed into the old van to look for his favorite tennis ball. The van started beeping and wobbling. I called the pack to action. We jumped aboard to rescue him. Next thing we knew, we were zooming into the sky . . .

"Aw, come on!" said Titch, bits of cat food spraying from her mouth. "What else do you have planned? An action-packed afternoon of dribbling in your sleep?"

Titch had a point. It was one of those long, rainy days when nothing much happens. Last time, the van took us to a place called Alaska, where we joined a team of sled dogs on a life-or-death mission. My tail sprang up. I was ready for another adventure. But then I remembered. Old Jim would be coming to fetch me soon. I couldn't gallivant off and leave my human all alone.

Newton tipped his head to one side, thinking. He's a border collie. He's the brains of the pack and he does a lot of thinking. "It *would* be interesting to see Balto and the team again," he said.

Baxter's ears perked up again. "And play in the snow . . ."

Maia did a little prance. "I have a dance class with Ayesha tonight, but I could squeeze in a short visit."

I made a pack decision. "Count us in," I told Titch. "As long as we're home by pickup time."

2

NO DOGS ALLOWED

Road trip!" whooped Titch. "Let's go!" Then she remembered she was stuck in the dog flap. "Can someone help me out here?"

Baxter gave a shove.
With a *clatter-flap-clatter*
and a loud grunt, Titch
shot back and fell over
on the doorstep. She's
missing a back leg;

balance is not her strong point. We all jumped through after her and dashed and splashed across the yard to the barn. The van was parked inside with the back doors wide open.

We scrambled aboard.

Newton made for the driver's seat and ran his nose over the shiny box beside the steering wheel. The *control panel*, he calls it. Shaking raindrops from my fur, I jumped up beside him. All of a sudden, the control panel sparked into life. Lights flashed, buzzers beeped. The air crackled with the smell of thunderstorms.

The van lurched from side to side.

"Oh yeah!" yelled Titch. "The freaky flying machine is on the move!"

"Wait!" cried Maia. "Where's Baxter?"

I ran to the door and looked out. Baxter

was standing outside the barn like a startled squirrel. "All aboard!" I barked. "Remember the pack motto: Never Leave a Dog Behind!"

"I thought the van would be parked *outside*—like last time." Baxter's voice was muffled by the tennis ball in his mouth. Like most Labrador retrievers, he likes to chew stuff—especially when he gets scared.

And he gets scared a lot. "We're not *allowed* in the barn," he whimpered.

So that's what this was about! Baxter lives at Happy Paws Farm full-time. The rest of us just stay here when our humans are busy. Baxter's humans, Lucy and her grandma, make *inventions* in the barn. Mostly shiny things that beep and zap and give you the heebie-jeebies. Point is, the barn is strictly No Dogs Allowed.

"Baxter, buddy!" Titch hollered over my shoulder. "We're not *in* the barn. We're *in* the van. It's a totally different thing."

At last, Baxter sprinted across the barn—with his eyes closed, as if that meant he wasn't really there—and jumped into the van.

Just in time.

The van lifted off the ground. Higher

and higher we rose. Past the inventions hanging from racks on the walls. Past the pigeons roosting in the rafters . . . Suddenly

Newton looked up. "Ah, we probably should have thought this through," he murmured. "We're *inside* the barn. We're going to crash into the roof . . . any . . . second . . . now . . ."

I braced, ready for the smash of solid van against solid roof.

But it didn't come. No crashing or smashing. Just a fizz that rippled through my fur. Then, somehow, we were out of the barn and zooming up through a dark, shimmery sky.

The back of the van is kitted out with furniture. Maia sat on the bed. Titch tried to open the refrigerator. I checked the corners for rats. Then I curled up by the doors to wait. When I woke, the van was rattling and creaking—just like it did last time. We began to plummet, down, down, down, faster and faster. "Hold your positions!" I barked. I stood to attention, my ears and tail held high. I like to set a good example to the pack; otherwise they can panic. Especially Baxter.

We hit the ground at last. *Thud, bump, scrape.*

I turned to Maia. She may be a fluffy little papillon, with pink ribbons and a sparkly pink collar, but she's a lot tougher than she looks. She's also done agility training. Maia is my go-to dog for special operations—like opening doors. "I'm on it," she said, standing on her back legs and pressing the handle on one of the doors with her paw.

"Look out, Alaska, here we come!"

Titch dove out through the doors, just as they flew open. "Last one in the snow has to kiss a cat on the nose!"

No one moved. We just stared out after her. We didn't want to kiss a cat, of course.

It's just that there *was* no snow.

3

DUCKZILLA!

Titch picked herself up and shook mud from her fur.

By jiminy! I thought. *Alaska sure has changed!* We had landed beside a wide river. Sunshine sparkled on the water. Plains of long, golden grass stretched away on either side.

"Most peculiar," Newton murmured. "It's winter at home. But it's summer here."

He frowned at the control panel. The lights had settled into a pattern of glowing lines:

1805

"I wonder what that means . . ."

I jumped down from the van to assess the situation. Closing my eyes, I searched the air for the scent of Balto and the sled team. A million thrilling smells crowded into my nostrils. I forgot all about *assessing*. Dizzy with excitement, I raced along the riverbank. Life of every kind was bursting out all around. Flocks of geese and ducks flew low over the water. Herds of antelope and elk grazed on the plains. The air buzzed with bugs and the grass rustled with small scurrying creatures.

My legs felt so springy I couldn't help jumping like a grasshopper.

Maia danced in a cloud of yellow butterflies.

Baxter splashed through shoals of shimmering fish.

Titch rolled in a giant cow pie.

Even Newton quit *wondering* and joined the fun, rounding up rabbits, chipmunks, and squirrels.

All of a sudden, I remembered: this happened last time we came to Alaska, too. We had changed from "old-timers" to puppies again.

I wanted to explore everything at once. Nests, burrows, droppings, trails . . . But then something stopped me in my tracks. "Alert! Alert!" I called. "Attention All Pack!"

"You won't catch many rats making all that noise!" Newton laughed. Now that he was a puppy, his ears were working again. I guess everything sounded extra loud to him.

But it wasn't rats I was worried about. It was the trail of fresh paw prints. For a moment, I thought it was Balto. The prints smelled like *dog*. They looked like *dog* . . . and yet . . . Titch placed a huge front paw inside one of them. There was room to spare.

And it wasn't just the size of the prints that puzzled me. The shape was odd, too. The pads were kind of *joined together*.

Newton peered at them. "This dog appears to have *webbed* paws like a duck or a goose. Hmm . . . most interesting."

Titch's fur stood on end. "That's not *interesting*!" she shrieked. "That's a freak of nature. Half dog, half duck!" She bared her teeth and whipped around. "Where are you hiding, *Duckzilla*? You don't scare me!"

Baxter shrank away, looking around for his tennis ball, but he'd dropped it when he was splashing in the river. "It's a *m-m-monster*!" he wailed.

I had to get the pack under control. "Don't panic," I said. "There's no such thing as monst–*oomph*!"

That *oomph* was the sound I made as something very big, very black, and very shaggy leaped out from a thornbush and landed on top of me.

4

THE WRONG TRAIL

Aaagh!" I yelped.

"AAAGGH!" roared the thing, as it sprang away from me.

Baxter peeped out from behind Newton. "Is it going . . . to . . . eat . . . us?"

Newton shook his head. "It's just a dog!"

"Of course I'm a *dog*," said the giant dog in a deep, rumbly voice. "What did you think I was?"

Maia flicked her ears "A monst—"

"A monstrous *bear*," I cut in. This guy would take us for a bunch of nincompoops if he thought we believed in *monsters*. I bowed politely, trying to give a good first impression of my pack.

The dog began to sniff us over. Then he noticed we were all staring at his webbed paws. "You pups never met a Newfoundland before?" he asked. "Kings of the Water, they call us. We swim like fish, swift and strong."

"Show-off!" muttered Titch. She had no time for good impressions. "So, *Duckzilla*," she snarled. "What's the big idea? Leaping out at people like that?"

The Newfoundland shook his head. "*Duck-zilla?* Seems you've mistaken me for someone else. My name's Seaman. From the Lewis and Clark tribe. Who are you pups with? The Hidatsa? Arikara? One of the Sioux nations?"

Baxter and Maia stared at him, their mouths hanging open. Even Newton looked puzzled.

Titch broke off from scratching at a mosquito bite on her butt. "We're with the flying van, buddy."

"The *Fly-Ing-Van?*" Seaman repeated. "Nope, never heard of them. Well, anyways, sorry about jumping out at you." He sniffed suspiciously in Titch's direction. "Reckon I mistook you for a buffalo."

Titch growled at him. "Do I *look* like a buffalo?"

Seaman shrugged. "No, but you sure do smell like one."

Maia giggled. "So *that's* what the giant cow pie was!"

But Seaman was already heading off into the long grass. "Can't stand here shooting the breeze all day," he called back. "Work to do. One of my humans wandered off yesterday. Gotta find him."

I shouted after him, "Yesterday, you say?"

"Yup!" said Seaman, without turning around. "Went off hunting. Didn't come back."

"You're on the wrong trail, then! The scent you're following *is* human, but it's old." I sniffed the grass. "At least five days, I'd say."

Titch blocked Seaman's path, standing as firm as her three legs would allow. "So, here's the deal, Duckzilla," she said. "We help you find your human. You give us an all-you-can-eat dinner at your place."

Seaman pushed past her, but Titch didn't give up. "Go on, Trev. Do your thing."

I don't take orders from Titch, of course. But there's nothing I love more than a good tracking mission. Nose down, tail up, I set to work. It didn't take long to pick up another human scent. *Wood smoke. Gunpowder. Grease.* Less than a day old, too. I locked my nostrils onto the trail and pushed through the tangle of young willow trees along the riverbank. The others raced after me.

"Help!"

I looked around. A big round face was peeping out from the branches of a mighty cottonwood. A human face.

"Yup, that's York," said Seaman, pulling up next to me. "What the blazes is he doing up there?"

We soon found out. A creature the size of a truck burst out of the bushes and charged at the tree.

Suddenly it caught our scent and swung around to face us.

Fear and excitement chased each other up and down my spine.

This time it really was a bear.

5

NOW OR NEVER

Doggone it!" muttered Seaman. "It's a grizzly."

The grizzly bear snarled, showing us his yellow fangs. His small black eyes glinted with rage. But it was the human he wanted. He reared up, threw back his head, and roared. Then he smashed his front paws down onto the trunk of the cottonwood tree. Again and again, the grizzly struck. The tree swayed and creaked under the relentless attack.

A patch of dark blood matted the fur on the bear's shoulder. "Looks like York got a shot at him," said Seaman.

No wonder the bear was mad, I thought.

Newton pointed at a long wooden object lying in the grass. "He's dropped his gun."

A branch crashed to the ground. "HELP!" the man cried.

Seaman cussed under his breath and began creeping toward the bear. "I'm going in," he said.

I stood to attention. "We'll provide backup. It's our pack duty to help out a fellow dog."

"Are you totally *nuts*?" Titch snorted.

"That monster will chew you up and spit you out like one of Baxter's tennis balls."

"Wait!" said Newton. "I have an idea. We all charge at the bear from different directions at exactly the same time. He'll be so confused, it'll give the human time to jump down from the tree and get away."

"*Charge?*" Baxter gulped. "As in *run? Toward* the bear? That sounds s-s-scary."

"It's simple if you get the timing right," said Maia. "Just like a dance move."

Seaman stopped creeping. "All right. We'll give it a try. You pups get into position and wait for my signal."

It was a good plan. But who did Seaman think he was, giving orders to my pack? That was my job. I bit back my frustration and waited for his signal. *Crash!* Another branch broke. By jiminy! What was Seaman waiting for? It was now or never. "Pack, *attack*!" I barked. "Go! Go! Go!"

I charged at the bear.

Behind me I heard Seaman shout.
"No, not yet! I'm not ready!"
But there was no turning back now.
A giant paw was coming straight at me.

6

THE RIGHT MOMENT

I twisted away. Just in time. Claws as long as knives sliced tufts of fur from my side. The grizzly took another swipe. I tried to dodge again. I stumbled and fell. Those deadly claws were almost at my throat when I saw a flash of fluffiness racing toward me.

"Maia! Get back!" I yelled.

But the bear had seen her, too. At the last moment, the giant paw swerved away from me and batted Maia high into the air. Then it swept at me again. This time I was ready. I leaped onto the back of the paw. The bear roared and raised his paw to his mouth, trying to bite me.

I sprang past the long yellow fangs and landed on top of the bear's nose. Clinging on tight, I dug my teeth and claws into the soft flesh of his snout.

The bear squealed in pain. Blood filled my mouth. I didn't know whether it was mine or the bear's. I couldn't hold on much longer. But if this was the end, I would go out fighting.

And now, at last, the others were joining the battle. Newton, Baxter, and Seaman rushed in, barking and gnashing their teeth. The bear spun around, swatting them away like mosquitoes.

Crack! The gunshot split the sky in two. The man must have escaped from the tree and found his gun. He fired again. The smell of gunpowder filled the air. The shots missed, but the bear took fright. With a grunt of defeat, he dropped to all fours and lumbered away.

I jumped clear and rolled into a bush. When I opened my eyes, three faces were peering down at me. Newton and Baxter looked worried. Seaman looked furious. "You harebrained maniac!" he bellowed. "You could have gotten us all killed! I said *I'd* give the signal . . ."

"You were too slow," I snapped.

Seaman growled in frustration. "I was waiting for the right moment. You, young pup, should have done the same."

"It *was* the right moment. The moment *before* the bear shook the man from the tree and ate him for dinner!" I sat up and looked around. "Where's Maia?" I gasped, suddenly remembering the bear throwing her into the air . . .

"I'm right here!" Maia's voice came from near the tree. She was busy smoothing down her fur. "I did an awesome double backflip and landed on a branch." She sighed. "Don't tell me no one saw it."

"I was kind of busy," I muttered. I tried to sound mad at her. Really, I was just relieved.

"Don't fight, guys!" Baxter wagged his

tail. "Newton's genius plan worked. The bear has gone. The human is safe."

"Oh yeah! Go, us!" Titch strolled out from behind a rock.

"*Us?*" I spluttered. Now I really *was* mad. "Tell me. What exactly did *you* do?"

"Relax, Trev!" Titch tossed her head. "*Someone* had to keep a lookout. In case Old Grizzly's bear buddies showed up to join the fight."

I looked at Newton, Baxter, and Maia. We couldn't help laughing. If Titch had a pack motto, it would be Look After Number One.

I heard a noise and whipped around. But it was only the man, York. Water dripped from his clothes. He must have jumped in the river, in case the bear chased him.

"Goodboy!" he said, scooping me up in his arms. "You led the charge, didn't you?" Then he patted Seaman and the others. "Good job, everyone."

Titch butted her head against Seaman's shoulder. "We've kept our side of the deal," she said. "Now how about that dinner you owe us?"

GOODBOY, HERO

Seaman led us back along the riverbank. He'd stuck to the deal and agreed to give us a meal. But he was still furious. He marched ahead, swishing his tail like an angry cat.

All of a sudden, he caught sight of the van parked on the bank. He backed away, his ears clamped down in fright. Then, with a soft *pop*, the van turned into an old willow tree. By now, Seaman had a serious case of the heebie-jeebies. "What the blazes," he mumbled. "Your *Fly-Ing-Van* tribe sure has some *powerful* magic . . ."

"It's just camouflage," Newton explained. "The van changes to match the background. It was a snowy rock last time we came to Alaska. Now it's a tree . . ."

A pair of crows landed in the branches and cawed at us.

Seaman wrinkled his nose suspiciously. "It doesn't *smell* like a tree . . ."

He was right, of course. The van smelled exactly like a van.

"I've figured that part out," said Newton. "The van is a human invention. Humans can't smell. If it *looks* like a tree, they think it's a tree. The camouflage works. They don't notice the scent is wrong."

As if to prove the point, York walked right past the old willow without giving it a second glance.

A few more miles and we came to a bend in the river. "This is it!" said Seaman. "The Lewis and Clark camp."

We were looking down from a low cliff. Below us, on a wide beach of smooth, flat stones, humans were bustling in and out of small shelters made of long poles and elk and buffalo skins. A cloud of wood smoke swirled around them like fog. I thought at first that it was one big family. Then I saw that they were all adult males, but for one female. She knelt beside the fire, stirring a cooking pot and singing to the baby on her back.

Two of the men hurried to meet us. One clapped York on the shoulder. The other—a tall, thin man with a long nose and kind eyes—crouched next to Seaman. Seaman gazed up at him. "This is my human, Captain Lewis," he said proudly. "He's the leader." He looked over at the man talking to York. "And that's Captain Clark. Second-in-command."

York scooped me up again. "This little fellow saved my life." York was a big man

with a very loud voice, and he was bellow-
ing in my ear. But I could tell he was saying
good things about me, so I licked his nose.
"I'm going to call him Hero. Goodboy,
Hero."

Hero. York said that word so many times I realized he thought it was my name. "No, I'm Trevor," I barked. "Tre-vor!"

York laughed and said *Hero* again.

"He can call you Cat-Poop-Face for all I care," said Titch. "As long as we get some food."

The woman by the fire—Seaman told us her name was Sacagawea—seemed to understand. She called us over to a pile of buffalo bones and fat. Fighting off grizzly bears is hungry work. We fell on that meal like a pack of wolves—even Maia, the world's pickiest eater.

"*Yum,*" slurped Baxter.

"*Yum,*" slurped Newton.

"*Yum . . . yum . . . yum!*" slurped Titch. Grease dribbled from her jowls. "Just needs . . . *slurp* . . . a little . . . *slurp* . . . hot sauce."

Full at last, I flopped down to lick my whiskers clean. Then I sprang up again. Mosquitoes were dive-bombing me from every direction. I hopped about, flicking my ears and snapping my teeth. "Is that an after-dinner dance?" Seaman laughed. The meal had clearly put him in a better mood. "Lie down by the fire," he said. "Doggone bugs can't stand the smoke."

I moved so close that the flames scorched my fur. The others joined me. *We should start for home soon*, I thought. Our humans would be coming to pick us up from Happy Paws. But I could barely keep my eyes open. "Just a short nap," I murmured. "Then back . . . to . . . the . . . van."

When I woke, the birds were settling down to roost in the trees. The humans sat cleaning their guns and mending clothes.

There were no flashes or beeps. I guessed they'd left their electrical things at home. The woman was braiding Maia's fur with beads and shells. "We came to visit our friend Balto," Baxter was saying to Seaman. "You must know him. He's famous in Alaska."

"Nope, never heard of any Balto." Seaman nibbled at a thorn in his paw. "Nor Alaska, neither. It must be upriver a ways." He gazed toward the distant mountains, a dreamy look on his face. The setting sun painted the snowy peaks red and pink. "That's where we're heading. Up the Missouri River and over the mountains, all the way to"—Seaman lowered his voice dramatically, as if he was about to say something wild and crazy—"the *Pacific Ocean*."

"In *those* tubs?" Titch laughed, glancing at the row of big wooden canoes tied up along the shore. "Why don't you guys just jump on the freeway? You could be hitting the surf this time tomorrow."

"I was wondering the same thing." Newton tipped his head to one side. "Where have your humans parked their cars?"

"*Free-way? Cars?*" Seaman looked around nervously, as if strange objects might appear out of thin air. "Are those a part of your *Fly-Ing-Van* magic, too?"

Baxter's mouth dropped open. I knew how he felt. Seaman *had* to be joking. How could he not know about cars?

I was about to ask.

But my words were lost in a thunderous clamor of hooves.

8

DANGEROUS!

The hooves belonged to a herd of antelope.

The frightened animals were stampeding across the plain, heading straight for the river. One after another, they began to hurl themselves over the cliff.

"They're running from a wolf pack," shouted Seaman, over the thunder of hooves and the *splash-crash* of antelope hitting the water. They were some way upriver from the camp, but still the noise was deafening. "Let's have ourselves some fun!" he cried, leaping up and running off along the beach toward them. "We'll race them across the river."

Baxter bounded after him, whooping with glee. Newton followed. He's not much of a swimmer, but his border collie instincts couldn't resist the chance to round up all those antelope.

Titch didn't move. "Water! *Gross!* If dogs were meant to swim, we'd have fins!"

Maia agreed. "I don't want to get my new braids all tangled."

I prefer to keep my paws on dry land, too. The three of us climbed to the top of the cliff and settled down on a flat rock to watch the race. The antelope were swimming for their lives, their heads held high above the water. Baxter was not far behind them. Newton had barely made it out of the shallows.

But Seaman was the star of the show! He surged past Baxter, dove under him, popped up on the other side, twisted around, then dove again. Onshore, the Newfoundland was like a big woolly bear. In water, he was as swift and sleek as a seal.

Maia wagged her tail admiringly. "Wow, those webbed paws are really something."

But Titch just yawned. "What a show-off!"

With a bark of excitement, Seaman glided alongside a young antelope near the back of the herd. All of a sudden, dog and antelope both sank beneath the surface.

The water churned and frothed.

Swirls of blood billowed through it.

Maia gasped. "I thought this was a race. Why is Seaman *attacking* that antelope?"

Now, I'm a Jack Russell terrier. I'm a born hunter. But even I didn't think it was fair to bring down a terrified animal just for fun. It wasn't a pest, and we didn't need it for food.

But it wasn't Seaman who popped back

up through the bubbling water. It was the antelope. Eyes rolling in fear, long legs thrashing, it kept on swimming for shore.

I scanned the river for Seaman.

At last his nose broke up through the ripples. "Help!" he howled. "It bit me!"

"Bitten by an antelope?" Titch laughed. "Ooh, *dangerous*! If you're a blade of grass, that is."

But the blood was now a dark, spreading cloud.

And Seaman had disappeared beneath the water once more.

9

LOOK BEFORE YOU LEAP

I quickly assessed the situation. Luckily, Baxter was not far from the spot where the cloud of blood still swirled. "Baxter!" I shouted. "Danger! Danger! Seaman's in trouble."

"I'm on it!" barked Baxter, speeding to the place where Seaman had disappeared. He dove. He surfaced. "It's a beaver!" he yelled. "It's got hold of Seaman's leg."

Baxter dove again. When he came back up, he was dragging Seaman with him, his teeth clamped around the big dog's shaggy scruff.

Maia cheered. "Hooray for Baxter!"

I was proud of him, too. Baxter is scared of his own shadow, but he can be brave when it matters most. We learned that when we were helping the sled team in Alaska.

But it was too soon to celebrate. The water churned and Seaman vanished again. "The beaver won't let go," Baxter spluttered. "It keeps pulling him down."

I knew what I had to do. Baxter is the top dog for water-based rescue operations. But if it came down to a fight, he didn't stand a chance. Labradors are just too gentle for their own good. This was a job for a terrier. "Hang in there," I shouted. "I'm coming!" I ran along the cliff top to the point where the beach below narrowed to a thin strip. I could jump straight into the water from here. Maia was right behind me, ready to dive in, too, but I had a better idea. "Go alert the humans," I told her. "We might need them."

As always in a crisis, Titch was nowhere to be seen.

I looked down at the river below. It ran deep and swift and fierce. I gritted my teeth and closed my eyes. *Never Leave a Dog Behind*, I told myself. *Even if that dog did call you a harebrained maniac . . .*

"Wait!"

I opened my eyes. Newton was paddling toward Baxter and Seaman. "Look before you leap!" he shouted up at me. "The current has caught them . . . it's bringing them . . . closer to you." Newton panted out the words as he battled upriver. "If you time it right . . . you can land . . . next to them."

I looked back to where I'd last sighted Baxter. When his head appeared again, he was still clinging onto Seaman's scruff. All my instincts told me to leap into action. But Newton was right. They were drifting closer, blood trailing after them like a banner. Soon they would be right below me. I could dive-bomb the beaver. Take it by surprise.

I forced myself to wait . . .

and wait . . .

and then I leaped.

There was a moment of confusion; frothing water, thrashing paws, choking, spluttering. Then I felt something solid beneath me. Had I landed on a rock? But no, it was moving. I was on the beaver's back! It was a female, and even through the water, I could smell her fear and rage. Without stopping to think, or even breathe, I sank my teeth into her thick leathery tail and shook it for all I was worth.

Blood and water rushed up my nose and

into my throat. I hung on tight. The beaver flailed her tail so hard I thought my jaws would snap. Just when I thought I couldn't hold on another moment, the beaver let go of Seaman's leg.

But the danger wasn't over. Ripping her tail from my jaws, she surged back up at me from below, aiming her huge bloodred teeth at my belly.

I kicked out hard and knocked her back.

The beaver gave up the fight at last. She rolled over and swam away.

I broke through the surface, gasping for air. Baxter was still holding Seaman up by his scruff. Newton had reached us now, too. We both grabbed some loose fur in our teeth to help Baxter. Seaman's eyes were closed. I wasn't even sure he was alive.

Baxter didn't look much better. "Keep swimming!" I mumbled. "Gotta . . . swim . . . to the shore . . ."

"It's no good," Newton panted. "The current's too powerful. It keeps sucking us back into the middle of the river."

10

NO OTHER OPTIONS

Seaman's eyes fluttered open. "*Snag . . . ,*" he murmured. "*Snag . . . current . . .*"

I did a furious snort that Titch would have been proud of. We'd been savaged half to death by a blood-crazed beaver, and now we were about to drown. This was more than a snag. It was a major crisis.

"*Snag . . . current . . . rock . . . willow . . .*"

Seaman had clearly lost his mind.

But suddenly Newton barked. "Of course! I know what Seaman's trying to say. He's telling us to work *with* the current. See those rocks in the middle of the river? If we steer that way, the current will carry us through the gap between them. It's like a mini waterfall. It comes out just above a big willow that's fallen across the river. I saw it earlier. That's what he means by a *snag*. It's a fallen tree. He reckons it will catch us."

"Will it work?" Baxter's voice was muffled by soggy fur.

Newton took a long time to reply. "Probably . . ."

I didn't like that word. What would happen if the snag *didn't* catch us? We would *probably* be swept miles downriver. We would *probably* drown. But there were no other options. I gave the order. "Hold tight and head for the rocks!"

Clinging on to Seaman's scruff, we paddled toward the middle of the Missouri with all the strength we had left. Soon the current had us in its grasp, flinging us at the rocks. Somehow, we made it through the narrow gap. Round and round we spun, water crashing over us, rocks bashing into us, as we tumbled along on the torrent. At last I heard Maia's voice. "Over here!" she barked. "This way!"

I heard Sacagawea shouting, too. "Seaman! Hero!"

I glimpsed them standing on the fallen willow trunk. Then I was underwater again. Something hit me across the back. We had washed up against the snag. We'd made it!

I heard a splintering crack.

A splash. The cry of a human pup.

The tree trunk had broken.

BAD ATTITUDE

I opened my eyes to darkness filled with the sounds and smells of sleeping humans and dogs. I was inside one of the shelters in the camp, tucked up on a warm blanket. But how did I get here? Where was my pack? Had I checked the corners for rats? "What happened?" I murmured.

The others were curled up next to me. Maia spoke softly. "Don't you remember,

Trevor? Seaman was bitten by a beaver . . ."

The memories flooded back. The current, the rocks, the snag. The terrible crack as the willow trunk broke.

"The humans got there just in time," said Newton. "They waded into the river and fished us out."

Baxter laughed. "We were like a bunch of big furry salmon! What a catch!"

Everyone was safe! Relief washed over me. But there was someone missing! "Where's Seaman?" I asked. "Did he make it?"

"Come and see." Newton led the way to the back of the tent. Seaman was lying on a pile of furs near Captain Lewis's bed. His injured back leg was wrapped in bandages, but his chest rose and fell with slow, wheezy breaths. He was alive!

"Captain Lewis carried him out of the water," whispered Baxter. As if hearing his name, Lewis stirred in his sleep. He reached out and patted Seaman's side.

I wagged my tail, even though it hurt. "We did a good job today, pack!" I said proudly. "Baxter, Newton, awesome rescue work. And Maia, too. You fetched the humans just in time."

Maia looked down. "But I didn't," she mumbled. "I shouted at them like crazy. But only Sacagawea followed me to the river. The men just hollered at me to be quiet."

"Can't say I blame them." Titch had appeared out of nowhere, a buffalo leg bone held in her jaws. "No offense, Princess Fluffybutt, but you do have an annoying, yappy little bark."

I should have been used to Titch and her bad attitude by now, but this was too much. "What is it with you, Titch?" I snarled. "I know you're not an official pack member. But you could help out once in a while! We could all have drowned. And where were you? *Looking After Number One* as usual."

Maia gently cuffed my nose with her paw. "But Titch *did* help out this time."

I gaped at her in surprise.

"That's right." Titch looked up from gnawing on the bone. "You tell Captain Hero. It was me who fetched the men."

Baxter laughed. "Well, you do have a *very* loud bark."

"I didn't just bark at them, buddy. I used the old Swipe and Run trick."

"The Swipe and Run trick?" I couldn't help asking.

Titch grinned. "You run off with one of the humans' favorite toys. Gets their attention every time. I usually go for those phone things they all love, but they don't have them here. So I swiped York's gun. You should have seen him sprint after me. All the way to the riverbank. He saw you goofballs in the water, and the woman with the baby standing on the willow trunk. He

71

called the other men . . ." Titch paused, crunching the bone in half. "They got there just as the snag broke."

I suddenly remembered the splash and the human cry. "The baby! He fell in the water!"

Newton nodded. "You won't believe this! Titch rescued him, too."

Titch shrugged. "No big deal. I was standing in the shallows watching all the drama, when the human pup just about landed on top of me. I picked it up and dropped it on the bank. Wriggly, squeaky little thing it is, too!"

There was a low groan. Seaman was opening his eyes. "Thank you," he murmured sleepily. "All of you." He lifted his head. "Trevor, I'm sorry I chewed you out before about charging at the bear. I'm *glad* you rushed in like a harebrained maniac this time. You saved my life."

Seaman was wrong, of course. I *hadn't* rushed in. I had wanted to. I was about to leap straight into the river. But I had listened to Newton's advice. I hung tight on the rock until Seaman and Baxter and the beaver were right below me. "I didn't exactly rush in," I said. "Thanks to Newton, I waited for the right moment. Just like you told me."

Seaman nodded seriously. "Well, I guess there are times to rush in, and times to hold back. The hard part is knowing which is which."

"Wise words, Duckzilla," said Titch. "And there are times *not* to show off by racing antelope too close to a beaver dam."

Seaman laughed. "That's the best advice I've heard in a long time." Then he winced in pain. "I thought I had lost this leg. Doggone beaver just about bit right through it. But Captain Lewis used his magic medicine, and he sewed it right up."

I was drifting off to sleep again. We would leave at first light, I decided. Head back to the van . . . and home . . .

But Seaman's next words jolted me awake. "How would you pups feel about staying to help take care of my humans while my leg heals?"

12

TALL TALES

Newton, Baxter, and Maia were not keen on staying. Newton has a big human family with a new baby to look after. Baxter has his girl, Lucy, and all of Happy Paws Farm to protect. Maia's human lady, Ayesha, can't manage without her.

I felt the same way. Old Jim's mate, Brenda, died last year, and he needs me more than ever. But Seaman had asked for our help. It was our pack duty to do what we could. "How about two days?" I said. "Three, max."

"I'll hang around as long as you like," said Titch. "Buffalo meat is awesome."

Seaman looked up at me. "Thank you. I reckon three days will be time enough to rest my leg. Then you can return to your *Fly-Ing-Van* people."

"It's a deal," I said.

Next morning, after an early breakfast, Captain Lewis gave orders for the men to pack up camp. Then we set off. Some of the humans rode in the boats, while others hiked along the riverbank.

We soon settled into our new jobs. Maia

kept watch over Sacagawea and the baby. Newton worked with Captain Clark, scouting out the trail ahead. Baxter took Seaman's place alongside Captain Lewis, happily diving into the river to fetch the ducks and geese that he shot. I teamed up with York, who also loved to hunt. We tracked down everything from prairie dogs to porcupines. I was having so much fun as Hero I almost forgot my old life as Trevor.

Titch didn't help out at all, of course. "Humans are seriously overrated," she said. Instead, she rode in one of the canoes, with Seaman. To my surprise, they quickly became firm friends. They called themselves the Three-Legged Club and spent all day swapping stories. Before he met Captain Lewis, Seaman was a ship's dog. Titch had also been to sea—as a stowaway on a cruise ship. Now and then, I listened in to their tall tales. Seaman, it seemed, had fought off pirates and ferocious sea monsters. Titch had chased mermaids and been half eaten by a giant shark.

The rest of us had no time for stories. We were too busy trying to keep the humans alive.

There was danger everywhere. The very next night a startled buffalo charged toward the camp. It would have crushed the men who were sleeping outside by the fire, if I hadn't raised the alarm. We barked and growled at that buffalo until, at the last moment, it changed direction and galloped away into the night.

Then there was the wildcat. A huge, ferocious beast with a spotted coat and tufted ears. It leaped from a tree and landed on York, savagely clawing his back. I soon scared it off by biting its tail. There were narrow escapes from coyotes, wolves, and rattlesnakes, too.

Wild animals were not the only hazards. There were grass fires on the plains and mudslides on the cliffs. There were hailstones the size of coconuts. Late on the second day, a strong wind began to blow, whipping the river into foaming waves. The men put up sails and the canoes raced along on the breeze. All of a sudden, a gust of wind caught the boat that Titch and Seaman were riding in and spun it around.

The boat hit a wave side-on. It lurched and swayed and almost flipped right over.

Somehow the boat stayed upright.

But it was filling with water and sinking fast.

13

THE MAGIC NOSE

Hearing the commotion, York and I ran to the riverbank.

The two brave sea dogs of the Three-Legged Club were clinging to the sinking canoe, howling for help. Seaman couldn't swim with his bandaged leg, and I suspect that Titch—for all her tales of chasing mermaids and fighting sharks—could not swim at all.

Some of the men on the boat began bailing out the water with pots and pans. Others rowed frantically for the shore. Newton and Maia were on board, too, along with Sacagawea. Maia helped her grab the boxes of supplies that were being washed away, while Newton kept a tight hold on the baby.

Baxter and Captain Lewis hurried along the cliff top to join us. "The compass!" cried Lewis. "Save the compass!"

I didn't understand the human words, but Lewis was pointing at a small flat wooden box in the water below. Maia balanced on the bow of the boat and reached down to scoop it up, but a wave snatched it out of her mouth. Up and up it flew. Down it dropped, toward the bottom of the cliff.

If the little box landed on the rocks, it would surely smash to pieces.

But instead of a smash, we heard a soft thud and a startled honk.

The box had fallen into the nest of a very angry goose.

Captain Lewis began to climb down the cliff.

"Come back!" Baxter barked at him in alarm. "The cliff's not safe. It's crumbling."

But it was too late. Lewis was already slipping. He slid to a stop on a narrow ledge, stones tumbling down all around him. One wrong move and he would plummet onto the rocks below. York took a coil of rope from his belt and began to lower it down the cliff.

Meanwhile, the goose had pushed the little box out of the nest and was nudging it toward the water with his beak. I scrambled down the cliff and onto the rocks. "Hand over the box!" I barked. "It belongs to my humans."

The furious goose honked rude words at me. He also flapped his wings and stabbed at me with his beak. Titch had named Seaman Duckzilla, but this was *Goose*zilla. Dodging the deadly beak, I snatched up the box in my teeth and ran for my life.

I sped back up the cliff, just in time to see York and Baxter pull Captain Lewis up over the edge. Lewis flopped onto the grass. "The compass!" he groaned, thumping his head in frustration.

I dropped the wooden box onto his chest. Captain Lewis grabbed it, flipped the top open, and looked inside. He tapped it a few times and then laughed.

I could tell the man was happy, so I wagged my tail. York knelt and stroked my ears. "Goodboy, Hero!"

I wagged my tail even more.

Later, when the boat was safely on dry land and we were all sitting by the fire, I asked Seaman why that little wooden box was so important to the humans.

"It contains the Magic Nose," he said.

"*Magic Nose?*" I repeated in surprise. I was learning that Seaman saw magic just about everywhere.

Seaman nodded. "That's right. You know how humans can't smell? When they want to figure out which way to go, they can't just pick up a scent the way we do. Well, Captain Lewis uses the Magic Nose to sniff the air and find scents for him. He checks it just about every time we set off."

"Oh, I get it. It's a *compass*!" Newton laughed. "My humans use one when we go for hikes." He shook his head at Seaman. "It's not really magic. It's a kind of human invention."

Baxter's ears suddenly drooped. I could tell that the word *invention* had reminded him of his girl, Lucy, and her grandma. He was missing them.

I was missing home, too. I loved being Hero, out hunting all day with York. But I needed a rest. I was ready to be Trevor again, snoozing with Old Jim in our favorite armchair. I nudged Baxter's nose with mine. "Seaman's leg is healing fast. We'll go home soon."

Newton wagged his tail. "Good. This place is too dangerous. It's life or death every other moment. I'm a nervous wreck!"

"Protecting these humans is a full-time

job," said Maia. "I'm ready to go home to Ayesha." She scratched at a bead in her fur. "And I miss my coconut shampoo. These braids are starting to itch."

We didn't know that the biggest danger still lay ahead.

And it came from the humans themselves.

14

NOTHING BUT TROUBLE

The next day, some miles upriver from the Magic Nose Rescue, a small group of men on horseback came galloping up behind us, followed by a ragtag pack of skinny dogs. The men slid down from their horses and walked along the bank to talk to our humans, who were tying up the boats for the night.

While Seaman stuck to Captain Lewis's

side, I hurried over to the new dogs to carry out a security check. They were already scarfing down a pile of fish guts our men had dumped in the shallow water. "State your names and your business here," I barked, raising my tail high to show them I was in charge.

Their leader was an old mud-brown female with even more bits missing than Titch. "Back off!" she snarled, crouching over the fish guts, her hackles flicking up

like knives. Her teeth were as thin and jagged as those of an eel.

I yelped. In pain, not in fear. Baxter was hiding behind me and had started chewing nervously on my tail.

Another dog pushed forward. "Hey! They're just a bunch of puppies playing at being tough guys!" They all laughed, fish blood spraying from their long, pointed muzzles.

"I'm Fang, if you must know," said the leader. "We're not here to make trouble, kid. Seems to me you have more than enough food to go around." She aimed a look at Baxter. He'd eaten a large elk steak for lunch, and his belly was as round as a barrel.

Titch growled. "Just keep your gnashers off the buffalo meat. That's ours!"

"What about your humans?" Maia chipped in, before Titch could start a fight. "Are they good men?"

"*Good?* How should I know? We're wild dogs, not *pets*." Fang sneered at Maia's beads and feathers and her pink collar. "We're just tagging along with them awhile for the free food." She glanced at the new pack of men. "That tall one with the beard is their boss, Larocque. From what we can pick up from the horses, they've been trading in all the villages along the river. For beaver furs, mainly. They're heading home, way over the plains to the north."

"North?" said Newton hopefully. "Not Alaska, by any chance?"

Fang shrugged. "Never heard of it."

"All clear! The humans have made

friends," said Seaman, strolling over to join us. "Captain Lewis has invited them to stay the night in our camp." He looked down at Fang. "We're on a mission to find the Pacific Ocean," he barked importantly.

"Whatever!" Fang buried her nose in the fish guts again. "We're on a mission to eat this lot before the rats show up."

That evening the humans threw a party. They built a big fire and sat around eating mountains of buffalo meat, which smelled delicious, and drinking whiskey, which did not. They talked and laughed and played cards. Some took out fiddles and made the screechy noises humans seem to like so much.

We settled down to the never-ending

task of removing grass seeds from our fur. I invited Fang and her pack to join us by the fire. Although it was summer, the night air was crisp and cold. But the wild dogs refused to set paw inside the camp. "You shouldn't get too cozy with humans, kid," warned Fang. "They are nothing but trouble."

Looking back, maybe she had a point.

But it wasn't the visitors who started it. It was men from our own pack. Reed and Newman had been helping themselves to extra rations from the whiskey barrel. Seaman groaned. "Uh-oh! I've seen what happens when they drink too much whiskey. They barge about, complaining and picking fights."

Sounds just like Titch, I thought. But I didn't say it, even though she was scratching fleas out of her ears and flicking them all over my tail.

Reed staggered through the camp and began hollering at Captain Lewis. Newman shoved Captain Clark so hard he almost fell in the fire.

"Don't let those young pups challenge your authority!" I barked at Lewis. "You're pack leader, by jiminy! Show them who's boss."

Lewis seemed to get the message and ordered the troublemakers out of the camp. But just when the situation seemed to be under control, two of Larocque's men stormed up to their leader, pushing Reed and Newman ahead of them. "Just caught these scoundrels red-handed," one of them shouted. He was waving a bundle of furs and a pouch of coins.

It was clear those troublemakers had been caught stealing.

All of a sudden, Reed lunged forward and punched Captain Lewis. York jumped up and pulled him to the ground. One of Larocque's men took a swipe at Newman. He missed and hit his friend on the nose. Suddenly all the men in both packs were on their feet. Some threw punches. Others threw cups or plates or rocks. The stink of rage swirled in the air with the whiskey fumes. It made my fur prickle. Seaman flew to Lewis's side and growled fiercely at Reed. I ran to join York. I couldn't make sense of this fight, but York was my human now. It was my duty to protect him. I snarled at anyone who came too close.

"Stop!" Maia hissed at Seaman. "You're

making it worse. You should take your own advice, mister. The part about knowing when to hold back." She cuffed my ear with her paw. "You too, Trevor! You can't solve *every* problem by rushing in and biting things."

I heard Titch's voice behind me. "Biting things usually works for me, Princess Fluffybutt. Although, I must admit, biting *humans* never ends well. Believe me, I've been there."

"Maia's right," Newton shouted over the clamor. "We should be using our brains, not our teeth."

I wasn't so sure. Some of the men were reaching for their guns and knives.

How were *brains* going to stop bullets and blades?

SHADOWS ON THE WALL

We need to make the humans forget about fighting," said Newton. "We need a *distraction*."

"My point exactly," said Maia. "One distraction coming right up." She flipped up onto her back legs and began to skip and twirl. The beads and shells and feathers that Sacagawea had braided into her fur jangled and fluttered as she moved. A few of the men stopped to watch. One or two picked up their fiddles and began to play again. But others were still brawling.

"Come on!" Maia called to us. "Join in!"

Titch snorted. "Do I *look* like a dancer?"

Maia did another leaping twirl. "You don't have to dance. Just lie down in a row."

We all did as we were told. Even Baxter, who was quivering like a rattlesnake tail.

Maia jumped over us. Once, twice, then again, backward. "Now, on your backs with your paws in the air," she said. She hopped from one to the next, using us as stepping-stones. When she got to Seaman's big webbed paws, she did a backflip.

The distraction was working. The fiddle players struck up another tune. Most of the men had begun to laugh and clap along. But a few of the younger ones were still brandishing their guns and knives. We needed a showstopper . . .

But what could we do? I stared at Maia, frantically trying to think of something. As she danced and pranced in the firelight, so did her long, flickering shadow on the buffalo-skin wall of the tent behind her. That's what gave me my idea. I whispered the plan to Seaman. He agreed. I quickly dragged a branch from the stack of firewood and dropped it at York's feet. It took a while, but at last he understood. He climbed up on the branch.

Seaman reared up on his back legs beside him.

"Help!" bellowed York. "It's a bear!"

Seaman roared and swiped at him with a massive paw.

On the wall, a shadow-puppet bear attacked a shadow-puppet man in a shadow-puppet tree.

"Help!" cried York once more.

I barked and ran at Seaman, pulling him away by his long, shaggy tail.

"It's Hero to the rescue!" York cried.

All the men cheered as they watched our shadows acting out the grizzly bear attack. Some of them picked up the guns they'd been fighting with and used their shadows to pretend to shoot the bear. Every time they shouted, "Bang!" Seaman pretended to be hit. He staggered about until, at last, he rolled over, playing dead.

The men shouted for more. We must have performed that play a hundred times! But the distraction had finally worked. They'd forgotten all about the fight.

"Good job today, Maia," I said, as we curled up by the embers of the fire. "Your dance routine kept the humans out of trouble."

"How about *your* routine, Captain Hero?" said Titch. "That bear act was a stroke of genius. Totally nuts, but genius all the same!"

"It was fun," said Maia. Then she sighed. "I miss my dance classes with Ayesha . . . Let's go home tomorrow, Trevor."

I glanced at Seaman, who was already snoring. He'd been telling me all day that his back leg was still weak. I had suspected he was faking it a little, because he wanted us to stay longer. After his showstopping performance as the Ferocious Bear, I was now certain; there was nothing wrong with his legs!

First thing next morning, I called the pack together to leave.

Newton, Baxter, and Titch gathered around.

But Maia was nowhere to be seen.

16

VANISHED

We searched every corner of the camp.

Maia wasn't in any of the tents. She wasn't in any of the boats.

She hadn't gone with Sacagawea to collect firewood.

She wasn't under the pine trees, where Larocque and his men had tied up their horses. They had left before first light. All that remained were clumps of soft green horse dung.

We howled Maia's name until the men yelled at us to stop. My heart was turning inside out. Had she been taken by a wolf or a coyote? Had she fallen into the river? Maia wasn't just a member of my pack. She was my oldest friend. I'd known her since we were tiny puppies, long before we started going to Happy Paws Farm and met Baxter and Newton.

And now she had vanished.

Seaman ran out from Captain Lewis's tent. "I know what happened. I just heard the men talking. From what I can make out, Captain Clark has given Maia to Larocque as a gift to make up for all the trouble last night."

"He can't do that!" I gulped. "Maia's not a bunch of flowers! She's not his to give!"

Seaman sighed. "I know. But I guess Clark thought she was a wild dog. Like Fang and her pack. He didn't know you pups belong with the *Fly-Ing-Van* nation."

"Maia? *Wild?*" Titch snorted so hard she almost choked. "Since when do wild dogs wear silly little collars with pink sequins?"

"Maybe Captain Clark didn't notice her collar," Newton pointed out. "It kind of blends in with all those beads and feathers in her fur."

"But why would Larocque *want* Maia anyway?" whimpered Baxter. "I know she's smart, but she hates hunting and she's not much of a tracker . . ."

"Larocque doesn't want her for himself," said Seaman. "He's taking her back to the city. He has a lady friend who trains a troupe of dogs to dance and do tricks. He thinks Maia could be famous . . . the star of the show."

"Being made to prance about onstage like a circus poodle!" I spluttered.

"Ladies and gentlemen, boys and girls! It's Princess Fluffybutt, the Perfect Performing Papillon!" barked Titch in a dramatic voice.

"What's the problem? Maia loves showing off. She'll have a ball."

"All *alone*?" I shouted. "In a city far away? Without her human? Without *us*?" I didn't wait to hear any more. I was already racing back to the pine trees where Larocque's horses had been tied up. I had to find Maia and bring her back.

I was in such a hurry I forgot to give the command for the pack to follow.

Luckily, I didn't need to.

Newton, Baxter, Seaman—and even Titch—were right behind me.

17

BRAINSTORM

Larocque's group had not been gone long. Their scent was fresh and strong: the grass, sweat, and dust of the horses; the gunpowder, whiskey, and smoke of the men; and the half-digested-fish-gut stink of the wild dogs tagging along behind them. Even a human could have followed that trail!

"This way!" I shouted.

We ran and ran; through long, swaying

grass and rustling pine woods and patches where wildfires had burned the land to thick black dust. The sun beat down on our backs. Prickly pear spines stabbed our paws. Mosquitoes buzzed in our ears. Half swimming, half wading, we crossed a stream and came at last to the end of the trail.

At the top of the steep bank were the remains of a campfire. The horses stood nearby, heads down, munching at the grass.

But there was no sign of the men or the dogs.

There was no sign of Maia.

I heard a bark. At least, I thought I did. It was so soft it could have been a mouse squeak. My ears quivered as I strained to hear over the chirping of crickets and warbling of birds. Yes! There it was again.

Faint, feeble, but definitely a bark! My heart leaping, I spun around and homed in on the sound. There, under a cottonwood tree, hidden by the long grass, I found her. A metal chain had been knotted around her collar. The other end was looped over a branch, high up in the tree.

"Maia!" I cried. "Are you hurt?"

"Trevor!" she croaked, struggling to her

paws. "I'm not hurt. But I've been shouting for help so long I almost lost my voice."

The others raced to my side. "Maia! Thank goodness you're safe," gasped Newton. Baxter leaped on her and gave her a big slobbery lick to the ear.

Even Titch looked happy to see Maia. Not for long! "What happened to Fearsome Fang and her gang?" she grumbled. "Why didn't they help you?"

"They disappeared before we crossed the stream," said Maia. "I guess they got bored of following the humans and went off hunting."

Suddenly Newton's ears pricked up. "*Shhh!* What's that?"

Everyone listened. Sounds of human voices and splashing water were drifting on the breeze from somewhere near the stream.

Seaman sniffed the air. "I reckon they've found themselves a hot spring."

We all looked at one another. We knew we had to rescue Maia before the men came back. Then we looked at the metal chain. We also knew it wouldn't be easy.

Maia peered up through the leaves. "If only I could reach that branch, I could unhook the chain."

Newton frowned, head tipped to one side. "We could build a tower for you to climb," he said. "If we stack up some rocks . . ."

I know Newton is the brains of the pack, but it seemed like a crazy idea to me. But Baxter was already tearing around, looking for rocks. He always listens to Newton. If Newton's next brainstorm was to build a tower of flowers to reach the moon, Baxter would run off in search of daisies. Suddenly all my worrying about Maia turned to anger. "How did you let yourself be *given away as a gift*?" I snapped. "What kind of nincompoop does that?"

Maia hung her head. "Captain Clark and Larocque were being so nice about my dancing. I thought they were going to give me a prize or something. Next thing I knew, Larocque had bundled me into a basket and slung me onto the back of his horse. I'm sorry . . ."

I felt bad for being so mean. "No, I'm sorry. It wasn't your fault . . ."

Thud, thud, thud!

Titch had started butting her head against the cottonwood tree.

"What the blazes are you *doing*?" asked Seaman, who was helping Baxter and Newton stack up the rocks.

"Knocking down the tree, of course," Titch said between thuds. "Brainbox Newton is overthinking the problem as usual. That tower plan is way too slow."

Titch was right. The men could return at any moment. The tower of rocks was still nowhere near the branch. But the knock-the-tree-down plan was no better. The trunk was even more solid than Titch's head. I ran in frantic circles, trying to figure it out. *Stay calm*, I told myself. *Assess the situation. There has to be a way!* If Maia was tied with a rope, I could bite through it. But even terrier teeth are no match for a metal chain. And the chain was tied so tightly to Maia's collar. No dog could untie that knot . . .

Maia's collar! That was it.

Suddenly I knew what to do.

18

TEAMWORK

I couldn't bite through the metal chain, but I *could* bite through a little pink collar.

I grabbed it in my teeth and tried to rip it apart. But sequins are surprisingly tough.

"I'll help!" cried Baxter. "I can chew through anything."

Together we gnawed at the collar like starving coyotes. Suddenly it gave way. We fell back, knocking over the tower of rocks.

Maia sprang free, shaking the torn collar from her neck.

I spat out a sequin.

Seaman and Titch cheered.

Newton looked at the half-made tower and smiled. "Just this once, I reckon that's a win for teeth over brains."

Maia laughed and nudged my nose with hers. "Thank you . . ."

Suddenly she fell silent. We all heard it at the same time. *Voices, footsteps* . . .

"Doggone it!" muttered Seaman. We'd been working so hard to free Maia that we hadn't heard the humans until they were almost upon us.

"Retreat!" I yelled.

Larocque and his men chased after us. Newton and Baxter were fast enough to get away. Seaman and Maia and I could prob-ably have made it, too. But Titch was slower. She has a leg missing, after all, and she was still dizzy from head-butting the tree. I glanced back over my shoulder. The men were throwing stones. One hit Titch's tail. Another missed her head by a whisker. *Never Leave a Dog Behind*. I had to go back for her.

But as I turned, Titch stopped running. She swung around, lowered her head, and charged at the humans.

"Titch!" yelled Seaman. "Come back! You'll get yourself killed."

I could hardly bear to watch. But at the last moment, Titch swerved.

It wasn't the men she was charging at.

It was the horses!

The terrified animals reared up, squealing and pawing at the sky, and pulling the bush they were tied to straight out of the ground. Then they bolted, mud flying from their hooves. The men raced after them. All but one. He turned back, raising his gun.

"Look out, Titch!" I cried. But she was whooping in victory so loud she didn't hear me.

I closed my eyes, braced for the crack of the gun. But when the noise came, it wasn't a gunshot. It was an explosion of yipping and snarling. The wild dogs flew out from the bushes and knocked the man off his feet. The gun fell from his hands into the long grass. "Run for it!" howled Fang. "I told you humans were trouble!"

I took a last look back. The man was sitting up, trying to figure out what just hit him. The wild dogs had already slipped away into the undergrowth. "Thank you!" I shouted. And then, "Hurry up, Titch!"

We didn't stop running until we were on the bank of the Missouri. We waded into the water to drink and cool down. Titch nudged my side. "So, Captain Hero. How was *that* for a distraction? Horses love a drama. You can always rely on them to overreact."

"You were awesome," said Baxter.

"And so was Fang," said Maia, her voice still croaky.

Titch shrugged. "I guess she helped a little. But I had it covered."

"Of course you did!" said Newton, laughing.

I nudged Titch back. "Good job, Titch. Great teamwork."

I laughed, too. I never thought I would say the words *Titch* and *teamwork* in the same breath.

19

THE PARTING OF WAYS

It was time to say goodbye. Seaman was heading back upriver to the Lewis and Clark camp. We were continuing downriver to the van—and home.

I was sad to leave. York was a good man. Hunting with him had been fun. But I was happy, too. I belong with Old Jim. I knew that Newton and Maia and Baxter felt the same way. They longed to be home, but they would miss Sacagawea and the baby and Captains Lewis and Clark.

I thought Titch might decide to stick around with Seaman. She had no human family to miss. "Fearsome Fang was right about one thing," she said. "Humans are trouble." But Titch *was* missing tacos and hot sauce and tuna cat food. "Even buffalo meat gets boring after a while," she said. "So long, Duckzilla," she called after Seaman. "It's been a blast."

"Goodbye, Titch. I hope we meet again soon to swap more stories." Seaman smiled

and shook his head. "Although I can't fig-ure out how you've had so many doggone adventures when you're still just a pup."

Titch grinned. "That, my woolly friend, really *is* magic!"

Two days' walk brought us back to the van. It still looked like a willow tree. A pair of crows were bickering in its branches. But there was no mistaking that scent. *Metal. Rubber. Gasoline. Roads.*

Baxter spotted his tennis ball floating among the reeds and jumped in to fetch it.

I pressed my nose against the tree. *Pop!* It turned into the van again.

I took a last look across the Missouri River. The sun was setting behind the mountains. The plains glowed in the fiery

light. A flock of geese flew low over the water. I was going to miss this place.

Inside the van, Newton hopped up into the driver's seat and stared down at the control panel. The lights still made the pattern:

1805

Maia closed the back doors and settled down on the bed to nibble the beads and shells out of her fur.

I gave the command. "Take us home, Newton!"

Newton poked at the control panel. Nothing happened.

Baxter peered over Newton's shoulder, dripping muddy water from the tennis ball.

The lights flashed.

The van rumbled and shook and rose into the air.

20

ALL CLEAR

C latter, thud, scrape. It was another bumpy landing.

We jumped out of the van. We were back in the barn at Happy Paws Farm. It was just as we left it. Inventions hanging on the racks. Pigeons roosting on the rafters.

I peeped out the barn door. The yard was empty. Rain splashed into puddles. I gave the all-clear signal and we ran to the house. Rather slowly. We were old again, and the spring had gone out of our legs.

Titch shambled off down the road in search of garbage cans and bowls of cat food. "So long, old-timers," she called. "Until the next road trip!"

"What's that she said?" Newton rubbed his ear with his paw. "Doggone hearing's gone again," he grumbled. He sounded just like Seaman!

We followed Baxter through the dog flap and curled up by the fire.

I woke to a familiar smell. *Newspapers. Hard candies. Soap.*

There was a familiar sound, too; the *tap, tap, tap* of a walking stick. My ears pricked up. A man's voice was calling, "Trevor!" At first, I didn't answer. I'd gotten so used to being Hero, I almost forgot that meant me!

Old Jim! I ran to meet him. I leaped at his legs, wagging my tail like crazy. "Don't worry, Jim!" I barked. "I'm back on duty now. Anything to report while I was away?"

Old Jim laughed and rubbed my ears, just the way he always does. He said something to Baxter's human, Lucy, who was with him. "I've only been gone a couple of hours! You'd think Trevor hadn't seen me for days!" He picked a prickly pear spine out of my fur and gave me a puzzled look.

Lucy looked up from hugging Baxter. Her hands were streaked with mud from his fur. Then she petted Maia and frowned. She'd clearly noticed that the pink sequined collar was missing. She picked a stray bead from Maia's fur. "I don't understand. They've just been snoozing by the fire all afternoon."

Old Jim nodded slowly. He bent down and patted Newton. Grass seeds scattered from his fur. Old Jim looked back at me and then at Lucy. "Do you ever wonder what these old dogs get up to when we're not looking?"

The only one of their words I understood was *dogs*.

But I could tell Old Jim was happy, so I jumped up and licked his nose to tell him I was happy, too.

AUTHOR'S NOTE

Trevor, Baxter, Maia, Newton, and Titch are fictional characters. But the dogs they meet on their travels through time really existed. Their adventures together are inspired by actual events; events in which the real dogs played a crucial part.

Seaman, a large Newfoundland, accompanied Meriwether Lewis and William Clark and the Corps of Discovery on their expedition along the Missouri River and across the Rocky Mountains to the Pacific Ocean. This would be an important trading route for President Jefferson and the United States. They set out in May 1804 and reached the coast in November 1805.

We know a lot about this epic journey because Lewis, Clark, and several other members of the expedition kept detailed journals—journals that we can still read today. The other human characters in this story were real people, too. York was a slave who belonged to Captain Clark's family. Sacagawea was a young Shoshone woman who joined the expedition as their interpreter (and she did have a baby!). The "troublemakers" Moses Reed and John Newman were both members of the expedition who really were punished for bad behavior, including desertion and mutiny. François-Antoine Larocque was a trader for the North West Company (a Canadian fur-trading business)—and an explorer in his own right—who met Lewis and Clark on their journey.

The dangers that Seaman and the time dogs face in my story are based on real events. Lewis and Clark's men had several encounters with grizzly bears. Antelope swam across the river to escape from wolves, and Seaman really was bitten very badly on the leg by a beaver. A rogue buffalo charged through the camp in the middle of the night. One of the boats was caught up in a gust of wind and almost sank. Lewis describes how Sacagawea saved supplies from being washed away. An important compass was lost (and found again!)—although in real life, this did not happen in the boat accident. It happened when several of the group were on foot and they were caught in a rainstorm on the river. They had a narrow escape and some of their possessions were damaged or washed away (including the baby's carrier). Coyotes, wildcats, rattlesnakes, hailstones, grass fires, and mudslides were all real hazards. The journals often mention the irritations of mosquitoes and prickly pear spines. Similarly, there are several reports of the men having rather too much whiskey and getting into fights.

The real events that inspired this book happened over many months. For the purposes of the story, I have squashed the time dogs' adventures into a few days in the summer of 1805. At this time, the expedition was traveling along the Missouri River in what is now Montana. However, the locations in the book do not correspond to specific places, and I have imported some events that happened earlier in the journey. Reed and Newman had both been dismissed and sent back to St. Louis by the spring of 1805. The meeting with Larocque and his party took place earlier in the expedition, at Fort Mandan, where the men spent the winter of 1804–05. Although the two groups spent some time together, and there were some misunderstandings, I invented the incident in which the fight broke out between them. Similarly, as far as I know, Larocque didn't have a lady friend who trained dogs for the stage!

Working Together in Children's Services

Damien Fitzgerald and Janet Kay

Routledge
Taylor & Francis Group

LONDON AND NEW YORK

First published 2008
by Routledge
2 Park Square, Milton Park, Abingdon, Oxon, OX14 4RN

Simultaneously published in the USA and Canada
by Routledge
270 Madison Ave, New York, NY 10016

Reprinted 2008, 2009

Routledge is an imprint of the Taylor & Francis Group, an informa business

Note: The right of Damien Fitzgerald and Janet Kay to be identified as the
authors of this work has been asserted by them in accordance with the
Copyright, Designs and Patents Act 1988.

Typeset in Bembo and Frutiger by
RefineCatch Limited, Bungay, Suffolk
Printed and bound in Great Britain by
TJ International Ltd, Padstow, Cornwall

British Library Cataloguing in Publication Data
A catalogue record for this book is available from the British Library

Library of Congress Cataloging in Publication Data
Fitzgerald, Damien.
Working together in children's services / Damien Fitzgerald and Janet Kay.
p. cm.
Includes bibliographical references.
1. Children–Services for–Great Britain. 2. Child welfare–Great Britain.
3. Social work with children–Great Britain. I. Kay, Janet. II. Title.
HV751.A6F58 2008
362.7–dc22
2007023602

ISBN10: 1–84312–467–X
ISBN13: 978–1–84312–467–2

Contents

Introduction

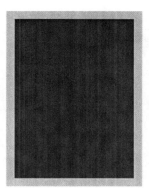

Child and family policy and practice are currently in the most actively developmental phase experienced for many years. Recent policy initiatives are driving changes in the structures, concepts and operations of children's services and within these changes the development of 'joined-up' services is a central theme. Developments in children's services in the last decade have increasingly focused on inter-agency co-operation and multi-disciplinary teams as key features of quality and effective service delivery.

Since 1997, New Labour policy has aimed to reform services to children and families as part of a wider strategy to tackle poverty and social exclusion in the UK. The concept of 'joined-up' services has developed from perceived failures in the structures and work practices of separate agency approaches to children's health, welfare and education. These failures are perceived to be rooted in the historical development of care, education and welfare services for children, which has led to largely separate planning and service provision in each of these areas.

One of the main drivers for these changes has come from the field of child protection, which has 'a long history of thinking about and operationalising what is usually thought about as "working together" compared to other agencies involved in children's services planning and delivery' (Frost *et al.*, 2005: 188). However, despite this longer term commitment to multi-agency approaches, it is from the field of child protection that the significant failures in 'working together' have highlighted the need for better service integration. As such, the integration of services for children has been accelerated after the Laming Report (2003) highlighted the failure of inter-agency co-operation as a key factor in the death of Victoria Climbié. The well-documented case of Victoria, who died at the hands of her carers despite the involvement of a number of children's services, acted as a catalyst for change and triggered a spate of reforms in the structure, focus and working practices in children's services. The resulting raft of policy and legislative change stemming from the Every Child

Matters Green Paper (ECM) (HM Treasury, 2003) has resulted in more integrated service provision and the requirement for much closer working relationships between agencies involved with children and families.

However, as past issues and failures have highlighted, 'working together' is a complex issue and there are significant professional, structural and procedural barriers to successful partnership. In addition, there are few conceptual frameworks or theoretical structures for exploring effective multi-agency work and often services and practitioners have 'been exhorted to initiate multi-agency work with little training or guidance' (Frost et al., 2005: 188).

This book explores the development of interdisciplinary agencies, services and teams for children over time and the policy developments that have both underpinned and reflected these developments. The benefits of 'working together' are discussed as are the challenges faced at agency, team and individual levels. Different approaches to multi-agency work are explored and the workforce development initiatives underpinning service development are analysed in the final chapter. The book is aimed at students and their tutors on foundation degrees, full degrees and other higher education courses focusing on young children, including Early Childhood Studies, teacher training courses, and Higher Level Teaching Assistant courses. It may also be of interest to social work students on children and families pathways, and health students on health visitor and school nurse courses and children's nursing pathways. However, the book is also aimed at practitioners in children's services, their managers and training colleagues. It may be of particular interest to staff involved in multi-agency or interdisciplinary training.

The book has a range of features to support the reader's involvement with the text, including practice examples and studies, reflection points and activities. There is a list of recommended reading at the end of Chapter 4 and at the end of the book including website addresses so readers can pursue areas of interest or relevance to their own role or course of study.

Working in an integrated way

Introduction

Since the election of New Labour in 1997 there has been a sustained output of policies, legislation and guidance to highlight the benefits of working in an integrated way (HM Government, 2004; Lloyd *et al.*, 2003). Alongside this, service guidance documents and exemplars of good practice are produced that highlight the benefits that are achieved for service users, namely parents, children and young people, by adopting this style of service delivery. There is no doubt that integrated working can often bring benefits for service users but should this always be an unquestioned assumption? This chapter will outline the different ways that services and practitioners can work together and discuss the notion of the previously outlined question. To achieve the best outcomes for service providers and users requires consideration of a range of factors. These will be discussed and strategies, which can be utilised by services and practitioners to achieve effective working practices, discussed in the context of different services.

At the end of this chapter, the reader should have achieved the following outcomes:

- have explored a range of definitions used to signal integrated working and what these can mean in practice;
- understand the benefits that can come from integrated working;
- be able to describe the factors that contribute to affective integrated working.

Why work together?

As the introduction to the book outlined, much of the emphasis for increased integration of services and for practitioners to work together has come from past failures that have had a range of consequences for service providers and users. And at worst these failures have resulted in the death of children. This point was clearly illustrated in the Laming report (2003), which ... that joint agency working and more effective exchange of ... could have prevented the death of Victoria Climbié. ... failures, it is also important to see the potential ben... address social exclusion.

Warmington *et al.* (2004) define social ... access to opportunities that connect ind... tion. Policy and service developmen... number of initiatives for childre... implement a more holistic a... focus on addressing healt... Action Zones). At a ... joined-up service... parents and ch... been set u... for chi... loc...

...
resp...
there ...
many res...
by Every C...

- be healthy;
- stay safe;
- enjoy and achieve;
- make a positive contrib...
- achieve economic well-be...

Although there are clear differenc... vision they all have one thing in co... together. The idea of providing joine... seems both sensible and desirable. Effecti... ficial to both families and practitioners as ... the family culture, deepen awareness of each si... for families, which is vital to enhancing parent... ongoing development for children (Sure Start, 2000)

- the opportunity for practitioners from different professional backgrounds to work together and learn from each other;
- additional opportunities for practitioners to develop skills to offer holistic support to families.

As this list shows the benefits of effective partnership between services and service providers is clear. However, to achieve effective partnership requires, time, effort, clear organisational structures that support partnership, a desire among practitioners to move towards integrated working and above all trust (Warmington *et al.*, 2004). This is supported by a range of evidence that shows achieving collaboration is difficult. Though if the benefits of collaboration are evident it is far more likely that significant efforts will be made by practitioners to achieve it.

What is meant by working together?

It is likely you will have identified a range of services and different... working together from the activity. When the range of service deliv...

Activity Evaluating integrated provision

Think about practitioners and services you have observed and the... have of how different services are organised. It will also be helpful t... cies you are familiar with in child and family services.

- Make a note of how different services were organised.
- If you are aware of any services or aspects of practice that... factors that you feel contributed to successful working.
- If you are aware of any services or aspects of practice th... the factors that you feel were responsible for these diff...

Services are organised in different ways. Some work... integrated way, others work in a more separate way. Se... separately but practitioners may consult each other an... basis. What are the potential advantages for services... integrated way?
Are there potential advantages for some services... stand alone services? If yes, list some examples... benefits of this style of working.

Working in an integrated way

Introduction

Since the election of New Labour in 1997 there has been a sustained output of policies, legislation and guidance to highlight the benefits of working in an integrated way (HM Government, 2004; Lloyd *et al.*, 2003). Alongside this, service guidance documents and exemplars of good practice are produced that highlight the benefits that are achieved for service users, namely parents, children and young people, by adopting this style of service delivery. There is no doubt that integrated working can often bring benefits for service users but should this always be an unquestioned assumption? This chapter will outline the different ways that services and practitioners can work together and discuss the notion of the previously outlined question. To achieve the best outcomes for service providers and users requires consideration of a range of factors. These will be discussed and strategies, which can be utilised by services and practitioners to achieve effective working practices, discussed in the context of different services.

At the end of this chapter, the reader should have achieved the following outcomes:

- have explored a range of definitions used to signal integrated working and what these can mean in practice;
- understand the benefits that can come from integrated working;
- be able to describe the factors that contribute to affective integrated working.

Why work together?

As the introduction to the book outlined, much of the emphasis for increased integration of services and for practitioners to work together has come from past failures that have had a range of consequences for service providers and users. And at worst these failures have resulted in the death of children. This point was clearly illustrated in the Laming report (2003), which made clear that joint agency working and more effective exchange of information sharing could have prevented the death of Victoria Climbié. In addition to addressing failures, it is also important to see the potential benefits of working together to address social exclusion.

Warmington *et al.* (2004) define social exclusion as having reduced or no access to opportunities that connect individuals to mainstream social participation. Policy and service developments have attempted to tackle this through a number of initiatives for children and families. These have included attempts to implement a more holistic approach to promoting health and well-being with a focus on addressing health inequalities for those living in deprived areas (Health Action Zones). At a national and local level, Sure Start has aimed to develop joined-up services to meet the education, social, emotional and health needs of parents and children (Baldock *et al.*, 2005). More recently Children's Trusts have been set up. These have a remit of developing responsive and effective services for children across health, social care and education at a senior level across the local authority, through the commissioning and development of current and new service provision. Thirty-five were set up in 2003 as pathfinder trusts and the intention is to have one in each area by 2008. The emphasis on developing responsive and effective services is clearly an important and admirable aim as there are over 11 million children in the United Kingdom (Shribman, 2007). In many respects the expectation on services to work together can be summarised by Every Child Matters outcomes, which aim for all children to:

- be healthy;
- stay safe;
- enjoy and achieve;
- make a positive contribution;
- achieve economic well-being.

Although there are clear differences between the different forms of service provision they all have one thing in common: an increased emphasis on working together. The idea of providing joined-up services to meet joined-up needs seems both sensible and desirable. Effective partnership working can be beneficial to both families and practitioners as it can enhance understanding of the family culture, deepen awareness of each situation and enhance the respect for families, which is vital to enhancing parent self-efficacy and promoting ongoing development for children (Sure Start, 2000).

Reflection point **Supporting families**

Think about a family that you have had recent contact with. This may be a family that you are very familiar with and, as far as you are aware, it has little contact with services. Or it may be a family that you know has contact with practitioners from a range of disciplines. Think about the parents and children and what services they may have involvement with over the next year. Think about what information the family may need to share with each of the service providers.

It is likely that you have identified a range of services and practitioners. Your list may include education, health (such as health visitors), family support and social care practitioners. What is certain is that the more children a family has or if one or more members of the family has a specialist or more complex need the more services and practitioners they are likely to have contact with. If families have contact with a range of practitioners, each delivering a specific aspect of support, this is likely to mean at least one specific contact with each practitioner and having to provide some information more than once (and possibly several times). The family may also have to make several visits to service providers and need to complete a number of different forms, with some of the information being required for each being the same. Based simply on this, it is already clear why working together is likely to be beneficial for parents and children, particularly for those who have a particular need or are socially excluded (Sloper, 2004). There may also be significant benefits for practitioners. In addition there may also be benefits that may not at first be apparent, including:

- a streamlined process to record family details;
- a reduction in the number of practitioners that work with each family;
- opportunities for practitioners to work in partnership to ensure an efficient response to the individual needs of each family;
- a more efficient approach to meeting with the family to support initial assessment and provide ongoing support;
- the potential to share information in a more coherent and efficient way;
- a co-ordinated response from practitioners that ensures that the information and support given to each family is consistent and supportive;
- the opportunity to share workload and avoid duplicating assessments, visits and support;

- the opportunity for practitioners from different professional backgrounds to work together and learn from each other;
- additional opportunities for practitioners to develop skills to offer holistic support to families.

As this list shows the benefits of effective partnership between services and service providers is clear. However, to achieve effective partnership requires, time, effort, clear organisational structures that support partnership, a desire among practitioners to move towards integrated working and above all trust (Warmington *et al.*, 2004). This is supported by a range of evidence that shows achieving collaboration is difficult. Though if the benefits of collaboration are evident, it is far more likely that significant efforts will be made by practitioners to achieve it.

What is meant by working together?

It is likely you will have identified a range of services and different levels of working together from the activity. When the range of service delivery models

---

Activity | **Evaluating integrated provision**

Think about practitioners and services you have observed and the knowledge you have of how different services are organised. It will also be helpful to think about policies you are familiar with in child and family services.

- Make a note of how different services were organised.
- If you are aware of any services or aspects of practice that worked well note the factors that you feel contributed to successful working.
- If you are aware of any services or aspects of practice that did not work well note the factors that you feel were responsible for these difficulties.

Services are organised in different ways. Some work with each other in a very integrated way, others work in a more separate way. Services may also be organised separately but practitioners may consult each other and work together on a regular basis. What are the potential advantages for services and practitioners working in an integrated way?

Are there potential advantages for some services to be organised and delivered as stand alone services? If yes, list some examples and make a note of the potential benefits of this style of working.

that have developed over the past years are considered it becomes clear that this is complex and utilises a range of approaches. The level at which service integration is organised also impacts on those practitioners who are part of the service. This can range from multi-agency working where although there may be a number of services involved with a family they may not work together in an organised way. This can be confusing as when the term multi-agency is used it is often assumed that this means that services have intentionally organised to work together. This is often not the case. At the other extreme, services may be organised in a way where there is one overall identity and set of outcome aims and objectives and services are delivered by a range of practitioners from a variety of professional backgrounds. Service users are likely to be heavily involved in assessment and decision-making processes and may not actually be aware of the specific professional background of each practitioner as services are delivered in an integrated and holistic manner. This style of service organisation and delivery can be defined as interdisciplinary working. Between these two models are a number of other organisational and delivery styles, each involving a different level of integration, as outlined in Table 1.1.

As stated earlier, the issue of agencies working together is complex and similar terms can be used in very different ways (Editorial to Long *et al.*, 2006). The following definitions set out the broad ways of working within each style of organisation and the likely way that practitioners will work within each.

Multi-agency working

This involves more than one agency working with a child and/or parents. Each agency may be unaware of others that are involved with the family. There is not likely to be a co-ordinated approach to the way work is undertaken, which may lead to unintentional replication. Work with each family may take place sequentially or concurrently (Warmington *et al.*, 2004).

Table 1.1 Different approaches to working together

Level of service integration					
Low level of integration and working together			High level of integration and working together		
Multi-agency working	Intra-professional working within a professional group	Inter-professional working	Joined-up working	Inter-agency working	Transdisciplinary working

Intra-professional working within a professional group

This involves practitioners within the same professional group working together. For example, teachers in support or advisory roles, working with practitioners in nurseries or children's centres or specialist paediatric nurses working with health visitors. This provides opportunities for a professional with specialist skills, such as expertise of child protection or special educational needs, sharing expertise, educating and supporting colleagues who work with families in their local community on a day-to-day basis (While *et al.*, 2006).

Inter-professional working

This involves individual professionals working with other individual professionals. This can include working with colleagues from other professions within a broad discipline area. For example, specialist nurses advising general practitioners on changes in treatment regimes for a child with a long-term health condition. In addition, it can include different professional groups working together. For example, nurses offering support and training to early years practitioners in the administration of medicines.

Joined-up working

This can be at a policy, strategic, operational or planning level. It may be prompted by government policy or directives and is reflected in many of the current polices aimed at tackling social exclusion. This approach may also be applied when thinking about how new services can be implemented and delivered.

Inter-agency working

This involves two or more agencies working together in a formal and planned way. The level of formality and planning involved will vary but it will be more than informal networking, which is seen in inter-professional working. The planning for agencies to work together can be at a strategic or operational level (Warmington *et al.*, 2004) but each agency will maintain its own identity as it works alongside other agencies.

Interdisciplinary working

As the name suggests this involves working across disciplines. It will utilise shared assessment processes and families are fully involved in service delivery when there is more than one agency working with a child and/or parents (e.g. parent-held records). Practitioners may act as advocates for individuals or groups. While *et al.* (2006) define this approach as transdisciplinary working. Practitioners from varied professional backgrounds work in an integrated way with shared goals.

Even though these definitions are set out separately, they may not be able to be applied in a uniform way. For example local Sure Start schemes often include aspects of intra-professional, inter-professional and inter-agency working and this helps to achieve a high quality service. The level of integrated working that is associated with a particular service will also be partly determined by how it is funded and the management arrangements. If there are a number of funding streams, such as Primary Care Trusts (PCT), education and social care, a service may work in a fully integrated way (e.g. using shared assessment procedures and family visiting with practitioners from different professional backgrounds) at the service delivery level but maintain separate identities at a strategic level due to funding arrangements (While, 2006). Based on the definitions above this would be described as inter-agency working but it would also contain many of the elements of interdisciplinary working. Therefore, these definitions offer one way to look at services, but it is important to remember that the whole issue of integrated working is complex and it is neither possible nor desirable to make simple evaluations of service organisation. However, the definitions do provide a structure on which to evaluate what is currently happening within services, identify where barriers may exist that are hampering further integration and what steps could be taken to develop more integrated working where it is appropriate and likely to achieve better outcomes. Clearly, for many services a blended approach – multi-agency where relevant; single agency where relevant – is the basis for achieving the most appropriate styles of working (Editorial to Long *et al.*, 2006).

Although Table 1.1 shows the different approaches that can be taken to integrated working as a continuum, it is not intended to suggest that the more integrated working practices are the better the service for children and families. If an evaluation of service organisation and delivery is made it is important to consider a range of factors. It may be entirely appropriate that they are delivered as stand-alone services. For instance, a child may need short-term support from an occupational therapist to help them with a temporary disability. In this situation there would not be a need for an in-depth assessment involving an interdisciplinary team. The required care and advice could be well provided by the therapist and when the disability had resolved no further input would be required. In contrast, if a family were referred to an agency for support a fuller assessment of social, emotional, health and educational needs is likely to be beneficial. If it were found from the assessment that a range of support across traditional service boundaries was necessary, it is likely to lead to a more efficient, responsive and consistent input if this is delivered as part of an interdisciplinary team. In addition, this model of service delivery may better enable, through a nominated lead practitioner, for support to be co-ordinated, delivered and evaluated in a way that enabled progress to be readily identified and ensure ongoing input in decision-making from the family.

Practitioners working in partnership

Within early years there has been an emphasis on working in partnership with parents for a long period as it is widely recognised that this collaboration has significant benefits for all parties (QCA, 2000). This point was aptly made several decades ago by the Plowden report, which stated:

> One of the essentials for educational advance is a closer partnership between the two parties (i.e. schools and parents) to every child's education.

> (DES, 1967: 37)

Although this report focused on education, the findings in relation to the importance of effective partnership working still hold significance today. In addition, many of the strategies that help to establish effective partnership working with parents can be equally effective for forming partnership between practitioners and between services.

For a service to work competently it needs to have competent practitioners. Part of this competence is linked to the qualities of individual practitioners. To be competent, practitioners needs to have a range of technical skills that relate specifically to the role they are trained for (e.g. a registered sick children's nurse will need to meet professional requirements as expected of them by the Nursing and Midwifery Council) and personal qualities that will help to foster partnership working.

Activity **Strategies to achieve partnership working**

In almost every aspect of service delivery there is an expectation that services will be delivered in partnership. Think about the term partnership. Make a list of all the actions that you feel would contribute to establishing an effective working partnership.

Bryson *et al.* (2006) argue that as achieving effective working partnerships is difficult, organisations will only collaborate if they cannot get what they want without collaborating. This can be complicated though if the expectation to collaborate comes form outside sources, such as a new government policy. If this is the case it could be argued that effective collaboration may be easier to achieve in newly formed organisations compared to bringing existing services together. In contrast, the existence of prior relationships and networks, which may have previously contributed to establishing trustworthiness, can have a positive impact on newly formed collaborative organisations. These factors are important to consider when setting outcomes and targets for a new service. Nonetheless, a realistic approach in any new partnership will acknowledge that to develop collaborative working an initial focus on small steps forward to help create trust is likely to help create internal and external legitimacy in the future.

The importance of trust in partnership working

Trust has been identified as a vital element that is necessary for establishing effective working partnerships (Bachmann *et al.*, 2006; Bruce and Meggitt, 2002; Dali, 2002). Trust is derived from the word integrity and signals that when trust you integrate (Schaub and Altimier, 2005). Adams and Christenson (2000) define trust as:

> *Confidence that another person will act in a way to benefit or sustain the relationship, or the implicit or explicit goals of the relationship, to achieve positive outcomes.*

(p. 480)

Activity   Trusting relationships

Imagine that you are establishing a new service that is made up of practitioners from health, social care and education backgrounds. Your leadership role in the newly formed organisation will be a key factor in the successfulness of the new service. Your behaviour and the degree to which it shows others that you can be trusted, are prepared to trust others and support the development of trusting relationships between practitioners is one of, if not the most, important part of your role. To gain and establish this trust, what behaviour characteristics would you want to exhibit to ensure you offered support and encouragement to help the rest of the team develop?

(See page 14.)

From this quote it is clear that trust carries with it a degree of reliance that other people will accept their share of responsibility and carry out the expectations on them accordingly. Within integrated service roles and tasks, which may have previously been done be a number of practitioners within traditional role boundaries, may start to be undertaken by one person. This change can occur for a number of reasons, including a desire to provide a more efficient, responsive and integrated service. As a consequence of this type of change, there will immediately be a need to rely on the ability, integrity and character of the other practitioners who share responsibility for providing the service. This is discussed again later in the chapter.

In any service a lack of trust will lead to a lack of commitment, communication and confidence. If there is a diminishing lack of trust in any organisation this is also likely to reduce the level of innovation (Schaub and Altimier, 2005). This will be problematic for all services, but could have a particularly negative impact on a newly integrated service. Take a children's centre based within a primary school as an example. In addition to the core services for children and families it provides a one-stop shop for social and health support. As it is based within school grounds it may also work in conjunction with the school management team to supply the following core services as part of the extended school roll-out programme:

- various activities;
- high-quality childcare provision around the school day from 8am until 6pm;
- parenting support and opportunities for family learning;
- wider community access to school facilities.

(Department of Health, 2006)

Reflection point **Innovative services**

Based on the description of the new Children's Centre, think about the following questions:

Why is innovation important to a new service?

How could an innovative approach to service delivery provide a better response for families?

What benefits could promoting an innovative approach to service organisation and delivery have for practitioners?

A trusting environment can encourage practitioners to work with each other in innovative ways when new approaches to working together are being considered. If an appropriate level of risk-taking is fostered, it is far more likely that practitioners will experiment with new ways of organising working practices to best respond to the needs of service users. If practitioners within a service feel over-managed and under-trusted then they are very unlikely to be innovative as this will run the risk of failure. And in an over-managed environment that is uninspiring and unsupportive the idea of failure is likely to be perceived as having negative consequences for individuals.

To foster innovation and new approaches to practice it is important that those in leadership roles have the ability and vision to inspire and trust all practitioners to develop and deliver services of the highest quality. The link between trust and leadership is clearly articulated by Schaub and Altimier (2006) who state that, 'trust makes leadership possible . . . [and] is also the foundation of leadership' (p. 20). This link is also evidenced in a number of Ofsted reports that highlight that high-quality services go hand-in-hand with high standards of leadership and management (Ofsted, 2006a). To be an effective leader, it is important to demonstrate qualities that are seen as demonstrating trust in terms of character, credibility (establishing effective communication), connection (building relationships with other people) and consistency/fairness (Schaub and Altimier, 2006).

Leadership qualities need to be seen broadly as they are an important aspect of many practitioners' positions, not only those who are in defined leadership roles. Professionally qualified practitioners, such as social workers, nurses and teachers will have responsibilities to show leadership qualities when delivering services. In addition, there are a number of roles within child and family services where practitioners are taking on aspects of leadership. An example of this is the development of the Early Years Professional Status, through which graduates, after appropriate experience and validation, will take on roles providing leadership to colleagues within Early Years settings (CWDC, 2006a). In addition, as the number of graduates within child and family services increases and diverse services are established outside the traditional boundaries of education, the need for appropriately qualified and experienced practitioners, with a range of leadership skills, will increase (Boddy et al., 2005). Therefore, it is desirable for leaders and practitioners (with appropriate support) to demonstrate trust-building behaviours. The earlier activity (see page 13) encouraged you to consider what these forms of behaviour would mean in practice. Schaub and Altimier (2006), identify four groups of trust-building behaviours for leaders and practitioners that you can contrast your own response with:

Individual characteristics of leadership

- being prepared to make decisions and act with integrity;
- provide honest feedback and being open to feedback from others;
- seeing mistakes as the opportunity to learn and develop;
- being willing to make changes when necessary.

Establishing effective communication and having credibility

- being an open and honest communicator;
- keep information confidential when necessary;
- provide accurate and balanced information;
- share difficult and/or unpleasant news;
- avoid making assumptions;
- ensuring that agreed actions are followed up and completed.

Building relationships and making connections with colleagues

- show concern and empathy to colleagues as individuals first and workers second;
- manage conflict in a way that encourages openness and brings about solutions;
- take time to learn about and understand the roles of colleagues.

Being consistent and ensuring fairness

- give feedback and input to all colleagues on an equal basis;
- hold all equally accountable for their performance;
- address performance issues as they arise in an open and supportive way;
- treat colleagues as individuals;
- ensure that there are equal opportunities for progression and development for all;
- ensure that rewards are given fairly, based on performance.

Leadership issues in relation to building interdisciplinary teams are discussed further in Chapter 4.

The importance of communication in partnership working

The issue of confidence is a key factor in the degree to which different partners will integrate. Interlinked with this is communication as it is by communicating with other people that we actively demonstrate how much trust we have in them and their desire to integrate different aspects of their role to create a joined-up service. Individual practitioners can have a significant impact on the successfulness of integrated working by demonstrating effective communication. To achieve the best from integrated working it is vital that practitioners have the ability to communicate well with others within their professional group and with those from a range of other professional groups.

Hunter (2006) explored different styles that health professionals demonstrated in their role when interacting with mothers. She grouped the different styles on a continuum that ranged from 'cold professional' to 'warm professional' to 'disorganised carer'. Although this research focused on communication between service providers and service users, it identified four types of exchange that could also have relevance to interactions between practitioners:

Activity   Cross-discipline communication

Think about an example of multi-agency or interdisciplinary working (working in a fully integrated way across disciplines) that you are familiar with and consider your response to the following questions:

- What challenges may be presented between colleagues from different professional barriers communicating together?
- What could be the potential problems, for practitioners and service users, if communication between practitioners was not effective?
- What steps could be taken to ensure that verbal and written communication was effective and of a high quality? It may be helpful to think about this from the point of individual practitioners, service managers and written policies.

If you work within an integrated service or have access to practitioners from varied professional groups you may choose to discuss these points with them.

Balanced exchange

Occurs when there is give and take on both sides. It is emotionally rewarding and provides confirmation of a job well done.

Reflected exchange

There is no give and take in the interactions that take place. Advice and support may be given (from one or both parties), but this is rejected.

Reversal exchange

Service users attempt to support service providers but this is perceived as over-familiar.

Unsustainable exchange

The service user wants more than the service provider is able to give and this challenges professional boundaries. This can lead to unrealistic expectations and over-involvement. At first these expectations may be met but this is not sustainable and can result in more negative outcomes as one or both parties feels let down and unsupported.

Although the last two refer specifically to service users, it is perfectly likely that the over-familiarity, challenge to boundaries or unrealistic expectations described could occur between practitioners. This may be particularly likely when it involves practitioners from different professional groups or when there has been a change in role boundaries. Hunter (2006) acknowledges that this model is reductionist and over-simplifies the complexities involved in communication. None the less, it does enable an exploration of the diversity of such relationships to be explored and conceptualised. This does not offer a solution, but can be beneficial in evaluating where communication has worked, where problems exist and then explorates how these can be overcome. It does highlight though that reciprocity is key to establishing and maintaining effective communication and to achieve this all parties need to be involved and able to contribute to decision-making processes. To achieve reciprocity in communication it is vital that information is given and shared between all practitioners who are involved in supporting a child and/or family (Adams and Christenson, 2000). This emphasises the need to put strategies in place to establish and maintain two-way communication where there are opportunities for all involved practitioners to contribute (Keyser, 2001; Fitzgerald, 2004).

In addition to the responsibility on practitioners, it is necessary to evaluate how service organisation facilitates opportunities for exchange and sharing of information. In the case of a new service, additional time should be allocated for this to help establish working relationships where trust can be built between colleagues. At an operational level, newly formed integrated services need to devote time to establishing an effective communication strategy that includes all partners and uses a variety of avenues for communicating with staff on an on-going basis. This is clearly articulated by Bachmann *et al.* (2006) who state that:

> *Clear, positive communication to staff is particularly essential when they are busy with the 'day job' and when change has not impacted on them yet. Two-way communication, through, for instance, regular learning labs, is crucial to gain staff trust and create and maintain motivation.*
>
> (p. 9)

It is easy to overlook the impact that policies and procedures can have on facilitating effective communication. There are a number of approaches and strategies that service managers can take to help establish good relationships including:

- establishing a shared language that is agreed and understood by all practitioners;
- producing policy documents that are free from disciplinary jargon and can be understood by all;
- if service targets are required, establishing these with input from all professional groups;
- providing time for practitioners to meet together for formal and informal discussions;
- taking time to agree and establish uniform assessment procedures that meet the needs of all professional groups and service users and avoid duplication;
- establishing effective systems for storing and sharing information/records, whilst ensuring that confidential information is appropriately kept;
- organising training sessions that provide opportunities for practitioners to learn from each other, which will contribute to ongoing development.

On a one-to-one basis an opportunity for each party to express their view and to be listened to is just as important. It could actually be argued that it is more important as in a collective situation if an individual does not feel that they have

Reflection point   A positive approach to working together

Think about a recent meeting or interaction with another person that you felt was positive. What factors do you feel led to this being a positive experience? If the scenario that you choose included a commitment from one or both people to carry out agreed actions, were these completed?

the opportunity to contribute this can lead to a negative social identity as a member of the group (Sherif, 1966). Another important factor in interactions is how it is rated by participants. If there is conflict and this remains unresolved, Wexler (1996) would see this as an insecure interaction and if there were just two people involved it is difficult to foresee an alternative outcome. As a result the two participants are likely to approach the next interaction with trepidation and low levels of trust, which in turn is more likely to lead to a negative outcome. This is a clear example of one negative cycle of interactions leading to another. Overall, this all leads to one central goal: finding ways to ensure that communication is open as this is valued by both service providers and users (Beaumont, 2005). To help achieve this, Stuart (2003) identifies a number of strategies that practitioners can use to ensure effective communication, some of which you may have identified in the previous reflection:

- avoid the use of technical jargon that other people may not understand;

- if something is said that is not understood, ask for clarification at the time;

- work with the person, not on the person;

- encourage each person to be frank and open;

- use positive non-verbal communication;

- if there are any problems, take time to clarify what they are and explore the whole range of possible solutions (the simple act of joined-up working can present solutions that may not have been possible when services work in isolation);

- be aware that people may come to issues with different value-bases. Accept this and try not to focus on it as it is usually unimportant;

- ensure that each person is clear about what they have agreed to do and what the first steps are. It could be useful to record this in a written action plan;

- acknowledge disagreements when they occur and provide time and support to enable practitioners to explore what the differences are, how they can be resolved and if any action needs to be taken to avoid similar situations in the future.

The importance of supportive working practices for partnership working

The move towards enhanced partnership working often brings with it blurring of traditional practice roles (Edwards and Knight, 1997). This can be both rewarding and challenging. Change can bring new opportunities for staff to work in different ways, with new colleagues and to expand their skills and knowledge. For staff who previously worked in services that they saw as being restrictive, new opportunities can bring a sense of autonomy that is extremely welcomed. In services that have not undergone change or have had consistent management structures over long periods it may be that top–down management processes have become accepted, which has led staff to feel disempowered and reluctant to suggest change or try new and innovative ways of working. Alternatively new ways of working can bring challenges in the form of day-to-day working or concern over professional identity and/or changes to working boundaries. New services can bring pressures and lead to staff feeling stress about new expectations placed upon them and an actual or perceived need to achieve increased outcomes. For example, if staff move to a new location and start to provide outreach support the need to visit families in their own home may place pressures on staff who have transport problems or feel less secure working without the support of their colleagues in the immediate surroundings. At a broader level there may also be anxieties about whether service reorganisation will impact on job continuity (Bachmann *et al.*, 2006). A change in working practices, such as hours, start or finish times, location or the need to work a different rota pattern may seem like small changes to service managers, but for some staff, such as those with caring responsibilities, this can cause significant problems and stress. It is vital that a move towards integrated working considers the challenges that may be created for staff and how these can be overcome alongside the potential benefits for service users.

In an effort to provide more appropriate and high-quality health care to children there has been a shift to providing a greater proportion of in-patient care in larger paediatric units. Alongside this there is acknowledgment that more care for children with long-term conditions, such as asthma, diabetes or cystic fibrosis, is being provided in the community. This is being achieved through community teams of children's trained nurses working with families and other services. To achieve this there is a clear need for practitioners with specialist skills to work in new ways with other service providers to ensure that a high level of support can be provided in the community to meet the ongoing health needs of children and promote their well-being (Shribman, 2007). But this change has significant implications for the professional identity of staff. For those who move to work in larger units that are geared to providing acute health care, they may need to work in new areas and develop additional skills and competencies. For those who work in community teams this may mean working with less direct supervision, working in families' homes and having increased contact with families, liaising and delivering care with other practitioners from varied professional backgrounds and having to provide care and support to children with a wide range of health conditions.

Professionals, who will be competent in a range of skills and competencies, often construct knowledge and meaning in the professional context they are used to working within. In this sense knowledge is likely to be at least partially determined by professional working boundaries (Tillema and Orland-Barak, 2006). Alongside this the current approach to service delivery, which is often dominated by centrally imposed policies and targets (Baldock *et al.*, 2005), can lead to practitioners feeling compelled to achieve set outcomes within traditional professional boundaries. Among practitioners, externally set targets can lead to practitioners from different professional groups, even within newly integrated services, working towards different priorities. For example, in a family support service, social workers may initially find it difficult to prioritise educational issues (Warmington, 2004). If this is not acknowledged and resolved this can lead to a blame culture between traditional agency boundaries, which will reduce trust and, if unresolved, could lead to an eventual breakdown in communication. Working across professional boundaries will take workers into new realms of organisation, which may also require new skills. This could create feelings of insecurity and personal concerns about levels of competency. To avoid this it is important for practitioners to be fully involved in service reorganisation and decisions about who will take responsibility for what roles. This should be done in a way that offers individual practitioners the opportunity to express any concerns they have before being expected to accept and perform new working practices. If, through consultations, the need for additional training and support is identified, this should be planned into working patterns and regular review points built in. When planning a new service, understandably the main emphasis is likely to be focused on establishing the new working practices, but this should not be done at the expense of taking time to provide appropriate support for all practitioners as in the long term if this is not provided it is likely to have an impact on the quality of the service and any initial gains may be short-lived.

When plans are been made for joint working or to combine services these need to give clear consideration to how practitioners within the service can be supported. Part of this, if it involves practitioners working in ways that may be different to the traditional role boundaries they are used to, should directly address the steps that will be taken to enable staff to become competent and confident in the aspects of their role that may be new to them. There will need to be a multi-layered approach to this, which addresses issues;

- at a service organisation level;
- concerning working policies and practices;
- concerning staff support and team building.

One method to address staff support is to introduce a form of supervision. This is an approach that has been widely implemented and utilised in health professions and involves formally agreed times where a practitioner is able to meet with another practitioner and have time to talk about and reflect on the different aspects of their role. To achieve the most from these sessions it is desirable that the supervisee and supervisor are agreed jointly and the supervisor does not necessarily have to be a person who is more senior in the organisation.

The main focus of the supervision relationship is about each practitioner having a trusted and critical friend, with whom they can discuss and reflect on work-related issues. As the aim is to offer support and reflect on past issues, to try and help each practitioner identify how they would approach similar situations in the future or respond to them differently in the future, it is not usually appropriate for a supervisor to have line-management responsibility for the practitioner they are supervising. Reflection on practice offers the opportunity for experience-based learning. For this to be successful the practitioner has to recognise situations in the working environment, be able to extract the key points from them and gain an awareness of how reflecting on them has the potential to enhance future practice. An important part of the supervisor role is facilitating this reflection for the supervisee. Stuart (2003) outlines three stages that can support the cognitive processes required for this:

- description of the experience;
- processing through critical analysis;
- synthesising and evaluating.

The stages may not take place sequentially, but the aim is to draw out the key facts from the experience and look for any connections between the events. The supervisor can support this process by asking questions, making links with relevant theory and supportively challenging any misconceptions or assumptions (Stuart, 2003). If the participants in the process are from different disciplinary backgrounds, the opportunity to discuss and contrast the different approaches they may use can offer valuable learning experiences.

Another form of support, particularly for practitioners who are new to a service, is mentoring. A mentor can provide invaluable help to orientate a practitioner to a service and the different approaches that are taken to working practices. The purpose of a mentor is to offer support and advice to enable the new person to integrate into the working team. The role will differ from organisation to organisation, but it is likely to offer a range of support, including:

- making them familiar with workplace practices;
- orientating them to the working environment;

- ensuring they are familiar with all the regularly used documentation;
- providing an overview of the service organisation, including management roles and responsibilities;
- providing an outline of the working week and helping the practitioner to structure their first working days;
- identifying who the practitioner will work with and arranging opportunities for them to meet with these colleagues during the first week;
- identifying their initial need for support and continuing professional development;
- ensuring that the necessary level of support is in place for the first weeks of working;
- meeting on a regular basis (this is likely to involve at least weekly meetings in the first instance) to respond to ongoing issues and address any concerns that arise.

The importance of continuing professional development for partnership working

To achieve the most from employees it is vital that they feel valued and supported by the employer. A central aspect of this support will be ensuring there is an ongoing commitment to continuing professional development. In addition to formal training and development sessions this should also include activities that help to build strong teams and develop cohesiveness. Wenger (1998) refers to the importance of developing 'communities of practice'. A community is defined by having tight connections and a compact work setting where identities are mutually defined. The importance of a shared approach that believes in the value of joint working is supported by Johnson *et al.* (2003: 70) who states the

> *necessity for group members to believe that the combined efforts of the group are not only necessary to obtain the desired shared goal but also that each member is capable and willing to do [their] share of the work.*

An important aspect of continuing professional development is opportunities for on-the-job training. This can take a variety of formats, from formally organised sessions where practitioners from all disciplines represented in a service come together, to utilising opportunities for in–depth exploration, discussion and reflection in team meetings. Anning *et al.* (2006) conducted a research project to find our how multi-professional teams work towards achieving a common purpose and develop new ways of integrated working. One data collection technique used was observation of team meetings. They stated the significance of these meetings in any new team:

> *Team meetings offer the ideal opportunity to observe interactions between members and to gain insight into how decisions are reached and disagreements resolved . . . They are furthermore, likely to be the major forum for interaction and decision-making.*
>
> (p. 15)

Although this statement clearly justifies observation of team meetings as a valuable data collection method in researching trans-disciplinary teams, it also highlights the potential of team meetings as an opportunity for continuing development. It is not necessary to explicitly define meetings as part of training but they do provide opportunities for practitioners, from varied professional groups, to share information and discuss the approaches that have been taken to support children and families. As well as information sharing, this offers opportunities for review and reflection. In some areas of healthcare, regular team meetings are held for this purpose. In these sessions, which may be referred to audit or case conferences, practitioners from various disciplines come together to review approaches that have been taken to manage patients and identify what approaches have been effective. In addition to informing current work with service users this is an ideal forum to identify what has worked well, why it has worked and take steps to integrate these working practices into day-to-day working. The informal opportunities offered by team meetings, for meeting, discussion, exchange of stories, dissemination of service information are also valuable in helping to build and develop a newly integrated team. To facilitate this, it is important to consider the location of team meetings. An ideal location will ensure there is enough room for attendees, in a clean and warm space where there are opportunities, if required, for groups of practitioners to work together. In terms of location, if a service is delivered from different locations attempts, wherever possible, should be made to rotate the location of meetings so that they take place on an equal basis across all locations. The time meetings are held at should also be carefully considered. If there are part-time staff, it is important to plan meetings so that they can attend at least some of them.

Another element of professional development is through planned educational activities. These can take place in the workplace or through outside training providers. Both of these approaches offer opportunities to provide training sessions that cross traditional professional boundaries and encourage collaborative learning between professional groups. This approach to learning acknowledges that bringing practitioners from varied professional backgrounds together can in itself promote collaboration and foster development. Another potential outcome from this type of learning is that it can expose areas where practitioners may feel less knowledgeable and this can be challenging. A partnership approach to learning can challenge this and encourage practitioners to see knowledge as shared and something that is actively constructed through continuing professional discourse. Based on this constructionist view of knowledge, the emphasis is placed on learning and communicating with each other to understand problems from different perspectives by engaging in learning opportunities (Tillema and Orland-Barak, 2006).

Over the past years there has been ongoing discussion about the approaches taken to train practitioners. Within child and family services there has been a sustained effort to increase the qualification base of the children's workforce (HM Government, 2006a). Generally though, practitioners are still trained within their own professional group. There are clearly benefits to this approach, such as helping to ensure that adequate professional knowledge is covered and that training providers are able to meet expectations that may be placed on them by professional regulatory bodies, such as the Nursing and Midwifery Council, British Psychological Society and General Social Care Council. However, with an increasing emphasis on service delivery in an integrated way, this raises questions about the approaches taken to train practitioners. If initial training places too heavy a focus on knowledge acquisition alone and does not give adequate attention to raising awareness of the benefits of joint working and include examples and opportunities to experience this it is likely that newly trained practitioners will not give significant emphasis to this style of working. To raise the profile of integrated working and ensure that newly trained practitioners have a commitment to work in that way is likely to require a fundamental rethink on how training is organised and delivered for those who intend to work in the child and family workforce.

Conclusion

This chapter has outlined the benefits that can come from integrated working, alongside the challenges that this way of working can bring for practitioners. One of the issues around integrated working is the terms that are used to describe it. They include multi-disciplinary, joined-up and interdisciplinary working. From the chapter it is clear that the terms used to describe integrated working are of less significance than the effort that is needed to work effectively in integrated services. There are steps though that service providers and practitioners can take to help achieve integrated working. The importance of communication, trust and continuing professional development is discussed to highlight how these are important components in establishing good-quality services.

The development of multi-disciplinary work in children's services

Introduction

This chapter will focus on 'setting the scene' through discussion of the historical and current development of 'working together' in children's services in relation to health, children's social care services, education and voluntary sector services. As part of this discussion, key legislative and policy developments that have been milestones in that development will be evaluated in terms of their impact on practice and future policy. Progress towards effective multi-agency working will be critically evaluated as will the impact of specific initiatives designed to promote partnership.

At the end of this chapter, the reader should have achieved the following outcomes:

- understand the diverse development of children's services;
- critically understand the development of interdisciplinary approaches to service delivery for children;
- identify the key milestones in policy and practice development in this area and a critical evaluation of the impact of these on service delivery.

The historical development of 'working together'

The past and the present

Widespread publication of recent policy developments promoting multi-agency approaches to children's services delivery could give the impression that 'working together' is a recent policy concept and a new way of working. In reality, multi-agency approaches, partnership and 'working together' have been around in children's services for quite some time, appearing in both policy and practice for decades.

Patch-based work in the 1980s

'Patch-based' social services for children and families were promoted in the 1980s to deliver services directly to 'clients' in their own communities. Part of the 'patch-based' approach was to provide a range of diverse services from a single community-based location. The author worked in such a service between 1984 and 1986, sharing 'patch-based' premises with Housing, Welfare Rights and Tenancy Association representatives, and eventually including Adult Education in the service provision.

The findings of the Victoria Climbié inquiry (Laming Report) in 2003 triggered the most major re-conceptualisation and re-structuring of policy and practice in children's services for decades (Laming, 2003). The media reporting and detailed analysis of the case gave the impression at times that this tragic death had created new understandings and clearer visions of the ineffectiveness of service delivery to children at risk of abuse. Yet the Laming Report findings were uncannily similar to the findings in a string of child death inquiry reports over a period of 30 years, starting with that of 7-year-old Maria Colwell who died at the hands of her stepfather in 1973. The 1974 Colwell Inquiry report cited poor communication and ineffective liaison between involved agencies as a key factor contributing to the failure to save Maria (DHSS, 1974). It went on to state that poor co-ordination of services and lack of information-sharing also contributed to this failure. These statements are echoed in the report into the death of Jasmine Beckford in 1984 and other child death inquiry reports that have consistently identified the failure of different involved agencies to work effectively together as a key flaw in systems to protect children from harm and promote their welfare (DoH, 1991). The *Observer* newspaper reported at the time of the Laming Report on the way that the recommendations of the Colwell Inquiry have been repeated over the years through subsequent inquiries:

These recommendations have established a pattern that has been wearily repeated, with the need for better training of staff, increased co-operation and co-ordination between statutory services and the demand for yet more resources.

(Hanvey, 2003)

Practice example

The same old song?

A Scottish Executive review of major health and social care inquiries found in relation to child death inquiries that

> Key recommendations of child abuse inquiries in the 1970s were: better understanding between professions and agencies, agreed arrangements for exchange of information between workers, effective record keeping, enhanced communication and better training and supervision.
>
> (DHSS 1982: 8)

> Child abuse inquiries in the 1980s identified problems with staff management, duplication of professional functions, lack of understanding of agencies' roles, supervision and training, implementation of inter-agency working, selective sharing of information between agencies, and poor record keeping (DoH 1991).
>
> (Galilee, 2005)

Yet a number of these reports made recommendations that contributed to changes in policy and practice designed to strengthen child welfare systems and improve working together. For example, the findings of reports such as that on Jasmine Beckford's death were influential in the development of the Children Act 1989, which was considered to have significantly improved child welfare services and systems (Brent Borough Council, 1985). The Colwell Inquiry Report led to the setting up of Area Child Protection Committees to co-ordinate child protection services locally. So, why have these measures ultimately failed to provide an effective child protection system and why over 30 years of investigation into the flaws in that system have poor communication, lack of information sharing and lack of co-ordination and co-operation between agencies and professionals continued to be cited as the major determinants of failure?

Much of the answer to these questions lies in the differential development of children's services and the structural dislocation between different types of service. The main strands of children's services – education, health and social services – have in the past developed separately within differently established services. This separate development ultimately led to a fragmented pattern of services for children, with gaps and overlap in service provision and a workforce divided by different professional cultures, different remits and goals, and ultimately different views of children and childhood. Professionals working with children were additionally divided by employment in services with different structures, boundaries, funding and governance. The main statutory services also work alongside the independent and voluntary sector services for children, equally different in their goals, funding, ethos and understandings of children's needs. Clearly one of the major factors in this diverse development of services has been the lack, for many years, of a central policy strategy to co-ordinate and direct development across the range of children's services. The outcome, however, is a set of major obstacles to overcome in order to establish effective interdisciplinary working now that this has become a key policy objective in children's services development.

In 2004 Margaret Hodge (Children's Minister) described the relationships between different children's agencies as follows:

That sort of lack of mutual trust and respect for the different professional backgrounds – not sharing the same vocabulary and language; certainly not sharing the same sort of understanding of child development and child protection – is an enormous problem. Changing that culture so that people value each other's professional competence and recognise each other's work is a hugely difficult and complex thing to achieve. I think I know the levers we need, but we are only going to achieve that over time.

(quoted in Brindle, 2004)

In the next sections, the development of children's services will be charted to try and make sense of this fragmentation and the long-term impact it has had on the quality and effectiveness of children's services.

The development of welfare services for children

The development of separate services to meet children's education, health and welfare needs is rooted in historical reasons linked to concepts of children and childhood in society at different times. Welfare services for children originally developed from changes in these concepts as Victorian philanthropists started to challenge the view of children as property and to acknowledge the need for child welfare measures. Exploring the development of welfare services is significant in that safeguarding children has become the key central issue in working together and the focus of more recent policy developments.

From Victorian philanthropy to state intervention

One of the first significant pieces of legislation which involved the state in children's welfare and care was the Infant Life Protection Act 1872, which legislated to regulate 'baby farming' i.e. leaving babies in the care of women for pay and for a variety of reasons, including allowing mothers to work or because the child was illegitimate. These arrangements had led to high numbers of infant deaths and concerns developed about the threat to infant life posed by 'baby farms'. The legislation set up a registration system, which focused on the fitness of the carer and the premises, but which was only limited in its success because of many loopholes in the law, including lack of inspection arrangements (Cameron, 2003). However, this law introduced the concept of inspection of daycare services for children and the state's involvement in preventing neglect.

In 1889 the Prevention of Cruelty to Children Act was passed and was known as the 'Children's Charter'. Prior to this, there was no legal recourse to protect children from physical abuse, as children were largely seen as the property of their families and therefore state intervention was considered both unnecessary and intrusive on the privacy of the family. However, the Victorian era was a period of great hardship for many poorer families and children suffered significantly from abuse and neglect. While neglect, hardship and exploitation were seen as norms of the times for many children, extremes of physical cruelty were starting to become less acceptable despite the commonly held belief that parents, teachers and other adults had a right, if not a duty, to physically punish children. The lack of legal support for abused children was highlighted by a well-reported case in New York where animal cruelty laws were used to prosecute the parents of a girl suffering from abuse and neglect at their hands. This case was significant in the development of the NSPCC in England and Scotland and these organisations lobbied for legal protection for children during the five years before the Children's Charter was passed.

Practice example

A human animal?

Eight-year-old New Yorker, Mary Ellen, suffered terrible violence and abuse from her adoptive parents. She was discovered by a church worker, who tried to persuade the police and other authorities to do something to protect her. An absence of laws to allow intervention left the agencies powerless to help.

In desperation the church worker turned to the New York Society for Prevention of Cruelty to Animals. Their officers went to Mary Ellen's house, removed her, and successfully prosecuted the adoptive parents, citing cruelty to 'an animal of the human species'.

(Children 1st, 2006)

The Children's Charter made cruelty to children illegal for the first time. It gave powers of arrest to the police in situations where a child was suspected of being abused and it also authorised police to enter premises where abuse was suspected of taking place. The Children's Charter triggered a spate of legislation that firmly established the place of the state in child welfare and which signalled a change in how children were viewed. Although children continued to be considered as their parent's property to a great degree, it was acknowledged that where parents failed in their task the state could step in to protect the child. In 1894 the provisions within the Prevention of Cruelty Act were extended to allow children to give evidence in court and to make it illegal to not seek medical help for a sick child. Mental cruelty to children was also acknowledged through this legislation.

In 1908 the Children's Act legislation led to the establishment of juvenile courts and a requirement for foster parents to be registered. It also extended the scope of infant life protection in care situations and child protection in general. In the same year the Punishment of Incest Act made incest illegal. Prior to this incest had been considered the business of families and the church and not the state. The Children and Young Person's Act 1932 gave additional powers to juvenile courts and introduced the concept of supervision for children considered to be at risk of abuse. Local authorities were given this responsibility and this established the principle of local authority involvement in child protection. The 1948 Children Act introduced children's committees and children's officers into each local authority, and was directly influenced by the Monkton Report into the death of 13-year-old Dennis O'Neill at the hands of his foster parent. Monkton identified the lack of communication between staff and agencies involved, which led to a failure in local authority staff in either supervising Dennis or responding to concerns about his welfare, as a contributor to his death (Batty, 2003).

Practice example

Dennis O'Neill

On 28 June 1944, Dennis O'Neill, who had been in the care of Newport Borough Council for nearly six years, was placed into foster care at the 70-acre Bank Farm in Minsterly, Shropshire. His younger brother Terence joined him at 'the very bare, comfortless and isolated' farmhouse the following week. Seven months later and two months shy of his 13th birthday, Dennis was dead . . . The issues that contributed to his death – poor record-keeping and filing, unsuitable appointments, lack of partnership working, resource concerns, failing to act on warning signs, weak supervision and 'a lamentable failure of communication'.

(Hopkins, 2007)

Up until this time the only organisation working directly with abused children was the NSPCC, which had been established in 1884. Under the 1948 Children Act, it became the duty of a local authority to 'receive the child into care' in cases of abuse or neglect. However, child cruelty still dominated legal provisions and it was not until 1952 that local authorities were empowered to investigate neglect. Although local authority involvement was firmly established through the 1948 legislation, the NSPCC continued to have a significant role in responding to abuse and neglect. However, in the same year as the Children Act 1948, the Nurseries and Child-Minders Regulation Act 1948 was passed, giving local health authorities the responsibility of registering nurseries and childminders and the power to cancel or refuse registration if the person or the premises were not fit. This Act was significant in consolidating the fragmentation of services to children as it gave the inspection of care services role to health authorities in the same year that children's services were established within local authorities to support children's welfare (Baldock, 2001).

In 1970, social services departments were created, bringing together existing social welfare provision for adults and children. This structural change consolidated the division of welfare, care and education services for children by locating children's social services firmly within a wider social services agency. The emphasis on the development of social work as a credible profession and on generic service delivery meant a more inward-looking service with a limited remit to work with other agencies. It also meant that there were few social workers for a time who had a specialist role in child and family work, although generic social work had been eroded long before children's services were re-established in social services departments.

As such, the establishment of social services departments in this way firmly placed the responsibility for child welfare with these agencies and not in other children's services. Children's social services were subsumed into wider social services, maintaining an intradepartmental focus for service delivery rather than collaboration with other children's services. In 1974 Area Child Protection Committees (ACPCs) were established to co-ordinate child protection services and to review child deaths, in direct response to the findings of the Colwell Inquiry. These committees had a multi-agency membership at senior management level and were responsible for developing child protection across all agencies, but in practice were dominated and led by social services.

The Children Act 1989

The 1989 Children Act was one of the most significant pieces of legislation for developing and establishing a particular approach to children's services delivery. The Act established principles of intervention based on children's rights codes and conventions enshrined in the United Nations Convention on the Rights of the Child (UNCRC), 1989. It also established the right of parents to be informed and involved in decision-making about their child and the principle that children were best cared for in their families, if this was safe and if their welfare was sufficiently provided for. The Children Act 1989 was considered to both strengthen the rights of children and families in child protection proceedings and also to improve child protection and child and family support services. However, significantly, the Act also clearly established the principle that social services' role in child protection and children's welfare was to be supported by health and education services. The principles underpinning the Children Act 1989 were not only influenced by the UNCRC, but were also responsive to the outcomes of child death inquiry reports in the 1980s, such as Jasmine Beckford's, which highlighted the failure of agencies to work together effectively (Brent Borough Council, 1985).

Case example

Jasmine Beckford

Jasmine Beckford died at the age of 4 years on 5th July 1984, from injuries sustained as a direct result of severe manual blows. At the time of her death Jasmine was an emaciated girl suffering chronic undernourishment. Post-mortem investigations indicated that Jasmine had suffered repeated episodes of physical abuse. The neglect and abuse which lead to her death occurred whilst she was in the statutory care of the Local Authority.

The Inquiry Panel made a number of recommendations . . . fall into three broad categories which are related to the following areas of work:

1. *The tightening of monitoring procedures.*

2. *The improvement of inter-agency collaboration.*

3. *The need for more specialised training.*

(Hampshire County Council Information Network, 2007)

The other major event influencing the provisions and principles of the Act was the Cleveland child sexual abuse case of 1986 in which 121 children were removed from their parents' care on the basis of a single medical test. The 1988 Cleveland Inquiry report highlighted the lack of co-operation and co-ordination between agencies involved in child protection including the police, health and social services (Cleveland Inquiry, 1988).

Case example

Cleveland Child Sexual Abuse Inquiry

In the early part of 1987 the number of referrals to Cleveland Social Services for child abuse rapidly increased. Allegations of child sexual abuse were being made by two consultant paediatricians at a Middlesborough hospital based on an unproven medical diagnosis termed the anal dilatation test. Once these allegations had been made, social workers removed children from their families on Place of Safety Orders, often in midnight and dawn raids. The Butler-Sloss Inquiry examined the cases involving 121 children where sexual abuse was alleged to have been identified using the test, and the actions of the paediatricians and social workers involved.

(Galilee, 2005)

Although these two cases represent the poles of under- and over-intervention in child protection situations, the identified causes for the failure to effectively protect children remain similar in that both focused on lack of effective inter-disciplinary working.

The Children Act 1989 was supported by the publication of inter-agency guidelines *Working Together Under the Children Act* (DoH, 1991) updated to *Working Together to Safeguard Children* in 1999 and again in 2006, which set out procedures for supporting and protecting children's welfare and for inter-agency co-operation and co-ordination processes to achieve effective safeguarding (HM Government, 2006c). These guidelines constituted a very clear message that the way forward to effective child protection and promotion of children's welfare was through agencies and professionals working together, in close co-operation and communication. However, they also confirmed local authority social services as the key agency in protecting children with other children's services in subordinate roles. This was underlined by the introduction of the *Framework for Assessment of Children in Need and their Families* (DoH, 2000), which placed the responsibility for assessment directly on social services.

However, despite the flaws, which have been identified since the implementation of the Children Act 1989, the Act clearly confirmed that multi-agency approaches were seen as the most effective way of protecting children from abuse. One of the key difficulties in establishing multi-agency approaches was the fact that for most involved services delivering universal services, child protection is a very minor part of their responsibility. The effective involvement of education, early years and health services in child protection was limited by this fact, and by the resulting low levels of expertise, exacerbated by the limited training and development opportunities available in this field for most staff.

Fragmentation between welfare and daycare

In addition to child protection, the Children Act 1989 provided for regulation of daycare services by local authorities and updated the 1948 legislation around inspection and standards. Local authority social services departments had become the regulators and supporters of the majority of daycare, rather than providers. Although local authority day nurseries had existed since the Second World War, when they were established to care for the children of women involved in the 'war effort' those that did not close after the war had rapidly became a resource to support 'failing families' rather than working parents, as post-war policy discouraged women from working outside the home (Baldock *et al.*, 2005). As such, local authorities provided daycare as a welfare solution to children and families in need, and working families paid, mainly for day nursery places in the independent sector when this was financially possible. However, as Cameron (2003) points out, there is little to link the care of children in welfare terms and daycare (childcare) within the Act. Whereas childcare was seen as a service provided mainly by independent and voluntary sector organisations (day nurseries and playgroups) for working parents, 'care' was a service provided for children at risk and related to the legal removal of children from their families of origin and children 'looked after' by the local authority. As such, Cameron points out that

> the local authority duty to safeguard and promote the welfare of the child was not a general duty applicable to all children, but only to specific groups of children such as those 'in need' and not those attending childcare services.

(Cameron, 2003: 89)

This dislocation between welfare services for children (provided by local authorities) and childcare services (provided mainly by non-statutory agencies and individuals) is echoed in the relationship between welfare services and education and health. It has meant that, until recently, child protection services have always stood outside other more mainstream children's services, a fact that has undermined ongoing efforts to build a multi-agency approach to protecting children.

The development of health services for children

Health services for children have developed partly alongside health services for adults and partly in their own right. Two of the key factors driving early health service development in the UK were hygiene and public health issues, which have been major factors in the progress of improving children's health (Hill and Tisdall, 1997).

Health service development was initially rooted in the Poor Laws, which progressively established collective responsibility for the poor and sick and orphaned children in the sixteenth and seventeenth centuries. Care of orphaned children and sick children in a society where early death was common led to the establishment of hospitals and orphanages in the eighteenth century, such as the Foundling Hospital in Coram Fields. However, the most significant changes took place in the field of public health in the nineteenth century, when public health legislation was introduced to tackle major health hazards such as sewage disposal, unclean water, and epidemics of illnesses. In the nineteenth century there was also a growth of hospitals for children and in paediatrics as a specialism. Despite this, mothers or relatives often had the care of sick children, particularly among the poor, as services were not free. Health insurance arrangements established at the beginning of the twentieth century initially only covered workers and not families. However, free medical care was provided for the poor to some extent through hospitals such as the Royal Free Hospital established in 1828.

Children's health and welfare

The focus on care of the child's physical needs meant that children were often seen as 'passive recipients of a routinized care process' with little acknowledgement or response to their social and emotional needs (Chalmers and Aggleton, 2003). During the nineteenth and early twentieth centuries for many sick children hospitalisation meant long periods of institutionalisation in order to receive treatment. The Hospital for Sick Children Great Ormond Street established in 1852 pioneered parent involvement with sick children in opposition to the isolation from parents and family normally experienced by children.

However, it was not until Robertson's film *A Two year old Goes to Hospital* in 1952 that there was recognition of the impact of separation and disruption to attachment for hospitalised children. This theme of parental involvement was confirmed with the Platt Report 1959 and the Court Report, 1976, which recommended a holistic approach to the sick child and family involvement in care. In 1984 the National Association for the Welfare of Children in Hospital (now Action for Sick Children) drew up a Charter for Children setting standards in health care for children.

Children's welfare in hospitals also started to become recognised in terms of their developmental needs with the introduction of the first hospital play workers in two London hospitals in 1957 and the recommendation that all children's wards should have play staff in a Department of Health and Social Security Report in the 1970s. However, implementation was slow, with only one-third of children's wards having playworkers by 1980 (NAHPS, 2007).

Despite the very different development patterns of children's health and education services in the UK, the principle of delivering health services through schools has been established for over a century. School-based health services have traditionally focused on 'deficit-spotting', which involves checks which are intended to identify children where health care is inadequate. However, increasingly schools are bases for health promotion, health screening, education and advice. Sex education is taught through schools and involves sexual health and welfare aspects.

More recent health policy

Health provision for children in more recent years includes community-based services for sick children, many of whom would have been in hospital in the past, and on hospital services for acute, short-term care, based on a policy of reducing hospital admissions and length of hospital stays. Other strands of services focus on prevention, rather than treatment of illness. These include screening and immunisation services and health promotion strategies, designed to educate and advise parents and children about healthy choices and lifestyles.

More recently health service policy has focused more on social aspects of health acknowledging that healthier childhoods cannot be achieved just through treating or preventing specific illnesses. A key factor since the Black Report was published in 1980 has been the need to address the complex factors contributing to inequalities in health chances for children according to social class and ethnicity. In 1998, the Acheson report highlighted areas where health inequalities could be improved (Acheson, 1998). In 2003, in line with this approach, the *Tackling Health Inequalities Programme for Action* (DH, 2003) pledged to reduce inequalities in health outcomes by 10 per cent as measured by infant mortality and life expectancy by 2010. The Treasury *Child Poverty Review* in 2004 set out key measures to reduce child poverty including a range of targets for health services (HM Treasury, 2004).

The National Framework for Children, Young People and Maternity Services (NFCYPMS) was introduced in 2004 to establish standards for service delivery in health services to children, young people and pregnant women (DH, 2004a). Like the ECM agenda, the development of the framework was partly driven by the Laming Report (2003), but it was also influenced by the inquiry into children's heart surgery at Bristol Royal Infirmary resulting in the Kennedy Report (Kennedy, 2002). Both of these reports confirmed the need to develop health policy and service implementation strategies that placed the child's needs at the heart of planning and delivery. The NFCYPMS is the key delivery mechanism for the 'healthy' outcome of the ECM agenda over the ten years from its introduction, with a clear remit to promote working together between PCTs and local authorities to develop local delivery plans. This strategy is in line with the *NHS Improvement Plan* (DH, 2004b), which promotes putting patients first, holistic approaches to health and well-being, and devolved decision-making.

Joint working is at the centre of this drive for structural and cultural change within NHS services for children. The framework emphasises the need for multi-agency approaches to healthy development, in line with other health policy themes and the ECM agenda, which includes 'being healthy' as one of the outcomes for children. While *et al.* (2006: 87) suggest that while the Laming Report (2003) highlighted the need for multi-agency collaboration in order to effectively safeguard children, in fact, 'children with mental health needs, children with disabilities or chronic illnesses, excluded pupils and looked after children' also needed to be supported through effective collaboration. The Health Act 1999 paved the way for health funds to be released to contribute to shared funding arrangements between services within Children's Trusts, but there remain many barriers to successful joint commissioning across the range of children's services. However, the implementation of health policy through schools continues with the Healthy Living Blueprint, which promotes the health and well-being of children in schools as part of the National Healthy Living Standard. Concerns about obesity, diet, exercise and avoidance of illness through life choices have reinforced the value of schools as a focus for delivering health services and realising health policy.

Health policy in recent years has aligned more closely with other children's services policy, particularly the ECM agenda, and has focused more on health and well-being, rather than treating sickness, the theme which has dominated policy for decades previously. While *et al.* (2006: 96) found examples of 'maturing' multi-professional work in his study of nurses, midwives and health visitors, and evidence of inter-agency work in 'all areas of practice'. However, despite an increased emphasis on delivering health services through schools and children's centres, the process of joining up services between health and other agencies is still faced with some major challenges in terms of agency culture, funding and structural change.

The development of education services

The early development of education in Britain was mainly through the development of church-run schools, which were established on a voluntary basis. The establishment of a national system of education run by the state did not happen until late in the nineteenth century. Early efforts to achieve this were not successful for a range of reasons. In 1807 Samuel Whitbread introduced a Bill advocating two years of compulsory education for children aged 7–14 years, which failed. However, the Bill demonstrated that there was already a movement for national compulsory schooling. The need for children's labour to supplement working class families' incomes and the reluctance on the part of the middle classes to 'rock the boat' in terms of social order meant that there were powerful resistors to the idea of widespread education of all children. Cost was a factor in the failure of Whitbread's Bill.

The Factory Acts of 1833, 1844 and 1867 contributed to a climate in which education for all became possible by reducing the hours children could work and making them available for education. However, there were also changes in political thinking moving towards a more collective responsibility for welfare and away from the individualistic thinking of the earlier part of the century. The need for a more skilled workforce and the increase in social unrest among the poor paved the way for the Education Act 1870 which established a national system of schooling. This was based on two separate types of schools: the voluntary denominational schools and non-denominational state schools. School boards were established where there were insufficient schools and elementary schooling for all children aged 5–13 years became obligatory, although parents were expected to pay. The board schools established were in addition to, not instead of, existing church and voluntary schools. However, the voluntary schools declined because of the better funding available to the board schools. In 1891 elementary schooling became free. Social reforms at the beginning of the twentieth century saw the limited use of schools as a site for the delivery of health and welfare services, which has existed to this day. Children began to receive health and dental checks through school and also free milk and school meals to support more healthy growth and development.

The 1944 Education Act was a major piece of legislation, establishing the system of schooling for many years to come. The Act enforced the notion of children's holistic development (physical, spiritual and mental) and reinforced the role of Christianity in the UK education system. The idea of developing the individual in order to benefit the community was a key aspect of educational philosophy. The Act established a tripartite system of secondary schooling with the provision of grammar schools, secondary modern schools and technical schools.

These were intended to cater for children with different abilities, creating a hierarchy of academic achievement between those who entered grammar school after passing their 11+ exam and those who accessed a more work-orientated curriculum and who were not expected to pass exams or show academic ability. However, the tripartite system was replaced in the late 1970s by comprehensive schools, which provided for all children over the age of 11, in response to the perceived inequalities embedded in the tripartite system.

Since 1988, the education system in the UK has been dominated by the development of the National Curriculum which standardised the curriculum in all maintained primary and secondary schools, paving the way for increased levels of performance monitoring and 'league tables'. The introduction of the National Curriculum re-focused schools on academic achievement particularly in English, maths and science in response to concerns that there was a mismatch between the requirements of industry and school-leavers' abilities.

Early education and the care of children has always been linked to the fluctuating need for women in the workplace. Nursery classes and nursery schools offered daycare and education in the Second World War, but reduced these to part-time places after the war ended. This was partly due to pressure on places but also to underline that they were not providing daycare in order for women to work, but instead were providing nursery education to support children's development. This difference was underpinned by the belief that children under school age were best cared for by their mothers, supported by the newly emerging attachment theories, and also by the more pragmatic view that jobs should revert to men returning from duty in the armed services.

The Plowden Report (1967) has been much quoted as being responsible for the development of nursery places, but underpinning this expansion remained the principle that part-time places only should be offered so as not to encourage women to return to work. Only small numbers of full-time places were offered where financial need was extreme. In general, the belief that children were best off at home with their mothers was highly significant for the separate development of education services for young children as opposed to daycare services.

The development of the independent and voluntary daycare sector

Independent nurseries run as businesses for profit have become a major part of the mixed market of children's services since numbers started to grow significantly in the 1970s in response to working parents' needs for childcare. The lack of state provision of full daycare created a gap in the market, which was gradually filled by independent nurseries in some areas. However, these nurseries developed according to their ability to make profit and therefore offered no universal geographical coverage or coherent service to all. For many areas, there was simply nothing. Furthermore, independent day nurseries have long been the prerogative of the better-off who earn enough to pay for childcare for one or more children. In more recent years, numbers of places have continued to grow as many independent nurseries now offer free nursery grant-funded places to 3- and 4-year-olds. However, as private businesses, day nurseries locate in areas where profit can be made and are still out of the financial reach of some families.

In 1962 the Playgroups Association (now the Pre-School Learning Alliance) was formed to lobby for pre-school education and support the development of community-based playgroups (Baldock *et al.*, 2005). Playgroups had developed in response to the fact that many parents could not access a nursery place for their child, which led to the development of parent-led, community-based provision to offer children social and learning experiences. However, many of these groups were run by parent volunteers for only part of the day, providing no solution to the needs of those requiring daycare in order to work. Currently the Pre-School Learning Alliance supports the development of pre-school playgroups, which now often offer nursery grant funded places to 3- and 4-year-olds as well as places to younger children. However, numbers have been affected by competition from schools and independent day nurseries offering places to 3- and 4-year-olds, including full-time FS2 places, and day nurseries offering full-day care and free part-time places to 3- and 4-year-olds. Most pre-school playgroups only offer part-time places. Between 1991 and 1999 there was a 17 per cent drop in pre-school playgroup numbers, and between 2000 and 2001 there was a 2 per cent decrease in numbers of groups and 6 per cent decrease in places.

Childminders have traditionally offered not only daycare to the youngest children but a chance for working parents to bridge the childcare gap, by offering before and after nursery and school care. Childminders in some form or other have been caring for children for the span of history, and in modern times have had a significant role in caring for young children in the mixed economy of care. In the nineteenth century, childminders cared for the children of working women, often on a semi-fostering basis. Standards, however, were often poor, with children dying or being very poorly treated in the 'baby farms' that grew up to meet the expanding need for childcare (Baldock, 2001). Childminding was registered and regulated by local authorities but standards were very variable throughout the twentieth century. The National Childminding Association was established in 1977 to promote childminding as a positive form of care, partly in response to the transfer of registration from health to social services, and partly in response to Jackson's research, which found poor standards of care in illegal childminding (NCMA, 2007).

Moss's (1987) review of research into childminding, which included Jackson's study, found that about 15 to 25 per cent of childminders were unregistered (as a conservative estimate); a third had poor quality of toys and equipment; and nearly half had overcrowded, unsafe play spaces. In addition, one study at least emphasised distant relationships between children and carer, with three-quarters of children having no specific occupation as the minder conducted her daily business around them (Bryant et al., 1984). Moss (1987) concluded that childminding provided a very variable quality of care to children at the time.

The more recent professionalisation of childminding came about largely through the National Childcare Strategy launched in 1998. Through the Early Years Childcare and Development Partnerships, local authorities sought to improve the quality of childminding by promoting training and qualifications and encouraging childminders to join local networks. Childminders who join networks can offer free nursery grant-funded places and the Foundation Stage Curriculum to 3- and 4-year-olds. This process of professionalisation has been criticised for reducing the numbers of childminders and changing their traditional role of 'mother substitute.' However, a study by Mooney et al. (2001) found that although there was a steady decline of childminder numbers between 1996 and 2000 this was attributable to the minders finding employment with better pay and conditions. Childminders who gained qualifications in early years work were likely to use this to move to better paid jobs in other areas of daycare. Currently, childminder numbers vary considerably geographically with significant issues for recruitment and retention in some areas. However, childminder networks are now encouraging childminders to work together with Sure Start Children's Centres as part of the process of joining up services for the youngest children.

Beginning to tackle fragmentation

By the beginning of the 1990s the clear demarcation between health, social and education services for children had already become a cause for concern among practitioners, academics and others involved in planning and delivering children's services (Baldock *et al.*, 2005). A snapshot of services at this time would have shown that 'care' was the responsibility of social services and focused on children in need and 'at risk', providing welfare services to these specific groups of children only. 'Childcare' services were mainly provided by the independent and voluntary sector in the shape of childminders, day nurseries and pre-school playgroups. The local authority had involvement in these services in terms of inspection and support for quality development, but did not provide daycare services to the general population of children. Such limited daycare that was provided by local authorities was targeted on children in need or 'at risk'. Education services for young children included nursery places for some 3- and 4-year-olds in nursery schools or nursery classes in primary schools, but these were limited and not available to all children by any means. In addition, the majority of nursery places, although free, were available for half days only, providing little support to working parents, unless they could afford and access childminder services to supplement the place.

Health services for children continued to be provided alongside adult health provision, although some health and welfare services continued to be provided in schools through the school nurse, dental checks and free school meals systems.

Integrated service provision existed in centres such as Pen Green and other combined centres and small-scale projects, but these were not widespread and the funding and strategic backing for such answers to fragmentation was simply not available.

However, in the 1990s there were a number of developments that laid the basis for future policy developments. The development of 'desirable outcomes' for young children aged 3–5 were the precursor for a separate curriculum for the Foundation Stage, established in 2000 (QCA, 2000). The introduction of the voucher system to provide 4-year-olds with free nursery places was a significant development because it was associated with the extension of free places in non-maintained sector daycare, eventually including some childminders as well as playgroups and independent day nurseries. Prior to this, nursery grant-funded places (free to children and parents) had only been provided by nursery schools and classes in the maintained education sector. Settings had to demonstrate that they were providing nursery education in line with the 'desirable outcomes' (later the Early Learning Goals) in order to access the grant.

More recent policy development in multi-disciplinary work

The most prolific policy development in services for children and families, since the welfare state was established after the Second World War, started in

1997 when after 18 years of Conservative rule, New Labour came to power in the national elections. Despite an initially slow start, children's services eventually became a main target for New Labour reform, and this reform became central to the government policy targets of reducing poverty and social exclusion (Baldock *et al.*, 2005). Policies in children's services have tended to be multi-layered with a range of purposes including: creating better conditions for parents to become employed; more access to early learning for children; health and welfare benefits and early response to deficits in children's development.

One of the key strategies for change within New Labour was the idea of 'joined-up thinking', which referred to the 'interrelatedness of children and family needs in the fields of health, education, social services, law enforcement, housing, employment and family support' (Anning *et al.*, 2006: 4). In practice, this basically meant that policy-making became significantly more focused on multi-agency and integrated service delivery (Frost *et al.*: 2005). One of the purposes of the policy drive was to tackle the difficulties and problems inherent in services to children and families, which were partly rooted in the separate development of key strands of service delivery as discussed above. The National Audit Office (2007) identified a number of benefits of 'joining up' which justified the introduction of multi-agency and integrated services:

- tackling intractable social problems;
- improving services delivery;
- promoting innovation;
- improving cost effectiveness.

The National Childcare Strategy and Early Years Development and Childcare Partnerships (EYDCPs)

One of the earliest policy initiatives in children's services after 1997 was the launching of the National Childcare Strategy (NCS) in 1998. The Green Paper, *Meeting the Childcare Challenge*, was published that year introducing the Strategy and setting out the remit to improve the availability and quality of childcare places for all families (DfEE, 1998).

The NCS 'was more ambitious in scope than anything produced by the previous government, but still addressed only part of the overall picture of early years provision' (Baldock *et al.*, 2005: 22). Despite this, the strategy was welcomed as a step forward in resolving some of the long-term issues in early years services which had led to seriously flawed and inadequate services and unfavourable comparisons to early years services in Europe and beyond.

The NCS was designed to increase the number of early years places and improve standards of care and education for young children. The links to broader policy were based on the view that early education was significant for poverty reduction and better social inclusion in the long term, and that increased numbers of places for children would both offer this possibility and also give parents more opportunity to work and to study.

Another key factor of the NCS was the emphasis on linking care and education of young children and eradicating the long-term split between the two in terms of agency responsibility, planning and delivery.

The main tool of delivery of the strategy at local level was the introduction of EYDCPs, which were multi-agency partnerships drawn from local authority social services and education departments, health services, independent and voluntary sector organisations and training bodies.

The role of the EYDP was to represent all the relevant early years interests in the area and to draw up an Early Years Development Plan based on joined-up working.

(Library Association, 2007)

EYDCPs were responsible for implementing the NCS in local authorities by developing early years services, primarily by supporting the increase in numbers of places for children aged 3 and 4 and also by improving quality and developing the children's workforce. The Early Years Development Plan was a key tool in this process. EYDCPs existed from about 1998/9 until new structures in children's services eradicated most of them in 2004/5.

EYDCPs were found to be flawed in many ways, partly because most of them were dominated by local authorities and other partners had weaker roles, and partly because some of them suffered a lack of clear strategic direction. Partnership co-ordinators did not always have the skills or vision to plan effectively, or the time to develop these skills. For example, in the early days, failure to spend training budgets was a concern in some partnerships and related to lack of knowledge and experience of all aspects of the training market or yearly changes to training targets. However, the establishment of EYDCPs firmly placed responsibility for service development in local authority areas and triggered the focus on expanding services across the range of providing sectors, which greatly increased the number and range of early years places available to children. In addition EYDCPs also established the principle of multi-agency working in early years service planning and delivery.

Early Excellence Centres

Early Excellence Centres (EECs) were first established in 1997. They were designed to provide 'one stop shop' service provision for young children and families and to be models of good practice in service integration. EECs provided integrated early education, daycare, parenting and adult learning services to the communities they were developed in. Some provided other services including daycare for under-3s and out of school care or crèche places so parents could access learning opportunities. By 2003 there were 107 EECs and many of these were already being rebranded as Sure Start Children's Centres. EECs were the forerunners of the current children's centres and were seen as innovative and ground-breaking in terms of the range and type of services provided and the development of joint working with other agencies. Although rooted in early education, staff teams were essentially multi-disciplinary and work with other agencies necessary to meet the needs of parents and children. The evaluation of EECs between 1999 and 2002 found that the challenges in integrating early years services may have been underestimated:

> *The three year evaluation of the EEC pilot programme has shown that deep, transformational change to integrate multi-agency services into a cohesive, comprehensive web of support for children and families, which has the potential to impact on cycles of deprivation over time, is an enormously challenging and ambitious agenda.*

> (Bertram *et al.*, 2002)

The evaluation highlighted some of the emerging problems in achieving integrated children's services, focusing on the need for strong and visionary leadership; good communication; clear roles and responsibilities; and the development of a shared philosophy through joint training and the development of understanding and respect for professional differences. The authors found that poor communication; poor morale among staff and recruitment issues relating to funding and pay issues were the main inhibitors of developing effective integrated services.

Sure Start Local Programmes

Sure Start Local Programmes (SSLPs) were established first in 1999 to support children in the earliest years of life and their families through integrated service provision based in centres developed in the poorest areas of the country. The target group was under-4s and their families, and the projects incorporated a multi-agency approach and partnership with parents as key principles.

Services provided by SSLPs include:

- advice on parenting;
- health promotion and referral to specialist services;

- support for families with special needs children;
- family support for ethnic minorities;
- childcare;
- drop-in centres;
- language and literacy projects;
- volunteers befriending projects.

Partners are:

- community groups;
- voluntary organisations such as NEWPIN and NSPCC;
- local authorities;
- health services;
- parents.

(Sure Start, 2007b)

The development of SSLPs was a critical step on the road to integration. Not only did the programmes develop with a multi-agency approach from the start, but they came out of a multi-departmental process in central government. The 1997 Comprehensive Spending Review, which reviews central government spending priorities, established a cross-cutting review for early years to involve all the government departments involved in early years services. The number of departments was so great that Tessa Jowell was appointed to chair the group in her own right, not as a departmental representative, and she had a specific impact on refocusing the development on under-4s. In addition, many other agencies such as the Pre-School Learning Alliance were involved from the start in the planning process (Glass, 1999). The process also involved a review by Marjorie Smith of the Thomas Coram Research Unit into evidence-based research on 'what worked' for children and families (Smith *et al.*, 1998).

The development of SSLPs was innovative in terms of establishing a multi-agency approach from government level downwards and the focus on evidence-based service provision and parent partnerships at the heart of the projects. SSLP development drew heavily on the US Head Start programmes which had been established for over 30 years at the time.

Sure Start local programmes represented a new way of doing things, both in the development of the policy and in its delivery. It is an attempt to put into practice 'joined-up thinking', but it is also an outstanding example of evidence-based policy and open, consultative government.

(Glass, 1999)

SSLPs have been progressively evaluated through the National Evaluation of Sure Start (NESS, 2007) which has reported on the value of SSLPs to children and families, and the effectiveness of partnership working with parents and with other agencies. In terms of multi-agency work some of the general findings have shown that SSLPs have worked better in terms of developing partnership with parents than they have with other agencies, and that in some areas there is limited involvement of key agencies working with children and families. Benefits to children and families have been identified but there is evidence that SSLPs may have failed to improve the lives of children and families from the most disadvantaged backgrounds. One of the lessons from the SSLPs is that it takes time to embed projects such as this into communities and into new ways of working. The majority of SSLPs are currently converting into Sure Start Children's Centres which are the newest wave of integrated support centres for young children and families.

Every Child Matters (2003) and the Children Act 2004

The Green Paper was published in 2003 in response to the Laming Report (2003) and constitutes one of the most radical changes to children's services planning and delivery ever. The ECM agenda encompasses a wide range of initiatives, which support new ways of working and thinking about children and families. The Children Act 2004 was the legislation required to implement some aspects of the ECM agenda. The main principles of the agenda are joined-up planning and service delivery to support vulnerable children within a framework of services for all children. Key shifts in approach are the acceleration of joining up services and a cultural change to place children and their families at the centre of service planning and provision. The key features of the agenda are discussed in detail elsewhere in this book in relation to the five outcomes for children listed in Chapter 1.

Key features include:

- Common Assessment Framework;
- lead professional;
- information-sharing;
- workforce reform;
- common core of skills;
- integrated working;
- Children's Trusts;
- Children and Young People's Plans;
- Children's Centres.

Activity   Keeping up to date

Readers are recommended to keep up to date with their knowledge and understanding of current policy agendas in children's services by accessing the ECM website at *http://www.everychildmatters.gov.uk* on a regular basis. The site contains information about all aspects of the ECM agenda and new information is posted regularly. It is important to read other documents as well, which provide a critique or evaluation of policy and practice.

Conclusions

In this chapter, some of the historical reasons for separate development of children's services have been briefly explored and some of the more recent initiatives to resolve the ensuing fragmentation of service planning and delivery have been discussed. The background to current policy agendas and service developments has been outlined to give a context to the discussion in other chapters about current aspects of working together.

3

Challenges to developing joined-up working

Introduction

In Chapter 1, some of the reasons for 'working together' have been discussed including some of the theories and concepts underpinning the purposes of joint or integrated service provision. Chapter 2 explores the development of both strategies and services to combat the fragmentation of children's service planning and delivery that has arisen through separate service development and lack of central planning historically. In this chapter, the discussion will focus on issues and problems facing integrated services and 'joined-up' services, and will explore the reasons why working together is a challenge. The chapter will focus mainly on examples at strategic and service delivery levels, as the challenges for individuals and managers working in multi-disciplinary teams will be explored in Chapter 4.

It is clear from the discussion in Chapter 2 that one of the key issues for multi-disciplinary working is that a long history of separate service development has left a legacy of structures, cultures and working practices that have promoted single rather than multi-agency work in children's services. In this chapter, the impact of these factors on current strategies to integrate some services and create closer working relationships between others will be considered alongside some of the strategies to address these issues.

At the end of this chapter, the reader should have achieved the following outcomes:

- understand the main factors inhibiting 'working together';
- knowledge of why these factors have emerged;
- understand the complex issues involved in developing more 'joined-up' services;
- identify the extent to which these issues and problems have been addressed in some current examples of different areas of children's services.

Is 'working together' really the best way?

Brown and White's (2006) literature review for the Scottish executive examined the evidence for 'joining up' children's services and found a wide range of literature on the barriers to integrated working. They found a number of common points on barriers to successful integration:

- concern about funding integrated services;
- cultural differences between professionals;
- clarity about roles and responsibilities and the purpose of partnership working;
- leadership;
- organisational climate.

(Brown and White, 2006)

These issues are discussed in this chapter and Chapter 4, which looks at integrating teams in more detail.

Brown and White (2006) also explored whether integrated working is the best way of delivering services to children and families and concluded that

the complexities of integrated working are unlikely to be overcome to produce its intended benefits unless a clear and sustained focus on the long-term outcomes for clients is maintained.

They also cite a number of authors to suggest that we should not assume that integrated working will always be the most effective way of working but that evidence should be sought to confirm that this is the case. The authors cite Percy-Smith (2006) who suggests that the answers to the question 'what is the impact of partnership working?' are very difficult to find. Percy-Smith (2006) reviews the literature contributing to 'an emergent consensus about the pre-requisites for effective partnership' but also argues that this does not mean that these partnerships will produce either better services or outcomes for children and families. Given the high costs of integrating services, more needs to be known about whether the outcomes justify these.

In addition, the authors argue that the reason why evidence confirming the benefits of integrated working may be limited at present may be partly because of a focus on integrated processes, rather than outcomes, in the studies done so far. The message is clear that, although evidence on how to overcome barriers and achieve successful integration is important, this should not be focussed on at the expense of gathering data on whether integrated services actually improve outcomes for children and families.

One of the issues for consideration is that developing integrated services is both time- and resource-consuming and this expenditure needs to be offset against the potential benefits from integrating services. As such, when time and resources are limited, it may be that integrated service development is not the most effective way of delivering services, at least in the short term. One of the difficulties is that it is not always easy to get evidence that the investment in integrated services development is paying off in terms of better quality services to children and families. Even in areas where improvements can be measured it may be difficult to attribute them to changes in service delivery patterns and arrangements as there are many other variables.

Brown and White (2006) also found studies which suggested that integrating services may not be better or could even be negative in terms of outcomes for children and that improving the 'organisational climate' of single agencies could be more beneficial than developing integrated services (Glisson and Hemmelgarn, 1998; Gardener, 2003 cited in Brown and White, 2006). They

Practice example

Extending services in primary schools

Evaluating the impact of extended services delivered to pupils and parents through a set of primary schools in a socio-economically deprived area was difficult because of the following factors:

- some of the services were delivered in Foundation Stage classes, aimed at supporting early learning to improve scores at KS1 3 to 4 years later;

- measure at KS1 could be taken years later but could not necessarily be attributed to the additional services;

- other variables could include demographic change and other family support projects taking place in the area;

- some children accessed services directly (after-school and breakfast clubs, additional in-class support), while others/the same children had parents who joined training and education courses;

- determining which services made the most impact was nearly impossible in the short term, except through individual and anecdotal evidence;

- long-term monitoring of improvements could not be attributed to one service or even to integration of services.

suggested that the significant factors influencing outcomes for children is the extent to which agencies are supportive of their staff and provide a positive working environment for them.

To summarise, it is clear that we should not take for granted any assumption that integrated service structures, planning, delivery, teams and ways of working are automatically going to provide better outcomes and more effective services for children. This needs to be established through evidence gathering and measures of improvements. This process may be inhibited by the difficulties of separating the impact of integrated services on outcomes from other variables. It may also be inhibited by the focus on developing and evaluating the processes of integrating services rather than the outcomes. Finally, the costs of integration are high and this needs to be considered in terms of the real impact of this type of change on outcomes for children and families to determine whether this type of working is actually cost-effective in delivering the best services possible.

Structural change in central government

The fragmentation in service planning and delivery that many practitioners have experienced 'on the ground' has for a long time reflected fragmentation in government bodies responsible for different aspects of children's services. One of the main divides for decades was the split responsibility for children's policy, legislation and regulation between the Department of Health (DH) and the Department for Education and Skills (DfES) in their various guises. While the DH has responsibility for children's health and social services, DfES has had responsibility for schools and education services. In addition, the separate development of children's health services within the wider NHS structures has created another barrier to cross-agency policy and strategy development.

In order to facilitate initiatives to support change and new partnerships between agencies, changes have taken place in the structures and remits of central and local government bodies responsible for children's services. It was clear to many practitioners and researchers for a long time before this actually happened that fragmentation of responsibility for services for children and their families across different government bodies had to be tackled in order to promote multi-disciplinary service delivery. These changes came about slowly at first, with the transfer of responsibility of early years from health to education in 1998 signalling the direction of government plans for change. The subsequent shift of inspection of daycare services from local authorities to Ofsted in 2000 confirmed the decision to give the lead role in children's services to education in the shape of the Department of Education and Skills and not to health and social services in the shape of the Department of Health. This transfer had the eventual effect of combining inspection for care and education in daycare services which provided funded early education for 3- and 4-year-olds (Baldock *et al.*, 2005). However, persistent concerns have been expressed about the consequent marginalisation of health and social services as a result of this decision. These concerns were crystallised when it became clear that the vast majority of the new Children's Service Authorities combining children's social care services and LEAs, which have been generally established from 2005 onwards across local authorities, have appointed an ex-Director of Education as their director.

The Sure Start Unit was established in 2002 within the DfES to lead on early years developments and planning and was an important stage in both signalling a change in approach to children's services and supporting an integrated approach to policy development. The establishment of the Sure Start Unit was also significant in that it gave a clear focus for early years services within central government. Within the DfES, the Children, Young People and Families Directorate became the home of the Sure Start Unit and the lead government body in developments of children's services. New roles within government were established to support the focus on children's services as a key area for policy development. These included the new post of Minister for Children in 2003 in the newly founded Children, Young People and Family Directorate within the DfES, and the appointment of Children's Commissioners for Wales (2001), Scotland (2004) and finally for England in 2005.

The Children's Commissioner for England was introduced through the Children Act 2004. However, this role was criticised before it ever became a reality because it only had a limited remit to review individual children's cases and because it has always been seen as a more limited role than the Welsh Children's Commissioner. This was exemplified during the passage of the Children Bill through Parliament by the opposition between children's rights groups, who supported a rights role for the Commissioner, and the Ministers for Sure Start and Children's Minister who were against this approach.

Issues in joining up local government

A key element in the process of integration has been the development of revised structural and working arrangements in local government to support more integrated service planning and delivery. In this section, some of the difficulties faced in achieving 'joined-up' local services will be discussed in terms of general issues and specific services.

Cultural issues, roles and responsibilities

One of the main issues frequently cited as a barrier to effective collaborative working is the different cultures and ways of working that have developed within the range of agencies within children's services. Brown and White (2006) explored a range of studies which concluded that health and social care agencies differed in terms of key aspects required for effective integrated working. These were 'terminology, attitudes to information sharing and professional principles'. Cultural differences do not just encompass the structural arrangements of different agencies but are more to do with the ways in which the agencies view their roles with children and their focus and goals in terms of service delivery. Differences in views on what the focus of service delivery should be can cause tensions between agencies and poor integration of service delivery.

Another factor identified by Brown and White (2006) is the problems that may be caused by lack of clear roles and responsibilities between practitioners from different backgrounds when working together. In order for joint working to be successful not only do roles and responsibilities need to be clear, but aims and objectives need to be understood and agreed between all partners. One concern is that specialist skills and understandings may be lost if practitioner boundaries are blurred and that steps need to be taken to ensure that separate expertise is maintained in order for interdisciplinary working to be effective. However, there is evidence that in some areas practitioners may be working outside their 'comfort zone' or competence, e.g. in completing assessments within the Common Assessment Framework (discussed further below). Brown and White (2006) found in their review of the literature in this area that the following negative consequences may arise from poor definition of boundaries between roles and blurring of boundaries:

> Consequences include disputes over responsibilities, feelings of inequity, stress and anxiety about what is being contributed from each party. Role ambiguity can result from such 'blurred boundaries' and may have negative effects on job satisfaction, trust between parties and ultimately may lead to unsustainable relationships.

> (Rushmer and Pallis, 2002)

The most important factor to prevent this role uncertainty and lack of boundaries is to have clear aims and objectives and clarity of responsibility. Regular reviews of services and their effectiveness is needed to ensure that appropriate adjustments are made to the principles and protocols for working together in a particular integrated service. As the discussion on the Common Assessment Framework below confirms, developing services 'on the ground' and relying on 'bottom up' development to clarify developments may be negative in terms of building effective integrated services.

In the next sections, some recent examples of 'joined-up' services will be explored to consider some of the difficulties faced in achieving effective integration.

Children's Trusts

The Children Act 2004 placed an expectation on local authorities and NHS services for children and families to develop strategies for integrating children's services or co-ordinating service delivery and planning more closely by 2008 at the latest. Despite the Children's Trust model already being established, the legislation did not specify that the Trusts should be set up as such. However, the majority of local authorities have opted for a Children's Trust as the main vehicle for joining up services.

> Children's trusts are partnerships between different services which provide, commission or are involved in delivering better outcomes for children and young people.
>
> (Valios, 2007)

The purpose of Children's Trusts is to facilitate the establishment of integrated services for children. They involve all services within a local authority area that provide or are involved in planning or commissioning services for children. They are expected to make significant improvements to services for children and families, measured by improvements in outcomes in line with the Every Child Matters agenda.

Children's Trusts are expected to include the following features:

- co-located services, such as children's centres and extended schools;
- multi-disciplinary teams;
- a Common Assessment Framework;
- information-sharing systems;
- joint training and effective arrangements for safeguarding children.

> (Valios, 2007)

Core services that are expected to be partners and/or part of integrated service planning and delivery are children's service authorities (education and children's social services) and health services for children including GPs and PCTs. Other services may be included such as Youth Offending Teams (YOTs), Connexions and a range of voluntary sector organisations.

Children's Trust pathfinders had been established in 2003 in 35 authorities and evaluated through the National Evaluation of Children's Trusts from June 2004 onwards. More recently, evaluation has focused more closely on 11 authorities. The initial report published in September 2005 found several issues that needed to be considered in the developing Children's Trusts. These included:

- the need for realistic time scales for the new trust's to 'bed down';
- establishing new cultures and approaches to planning and service delivery;
- funding inter-agency training;
- the size of the change agenda and the ability of local authorities and their partners to achieve change within national agenda.

(DfES, 2005)

The evaluation also identified user participation as an area where strategies varied between authorities and where there was a lack of coherent planning in some areas. One of the key concerns about Children's Trusts has been the role of schools within trusts. Unlike other children's services, schools were not given a legal duty to co-operate with other agencies within the Children Act 2004. Although their involvement is expected by local authorities, at the time of the first evaluation only 10 per cent of schools were considering working with local trusts. In addition, the co-location of services in schools caused disquiet amongst parents who felt this could compromise confidentiality of health information and over-burden schools. Despite positive feedback about new roles and ways of working and the development of new types of teams, recruitment and retention of staff was a clear problem at this time.

Despite joint planning through Children and Young People's Plans (CYPP), developing joint commissioning of services was challenged by agency budgetary arrangements that made aligning budgets difficult. During discussion with representatives in two authorities in 2005, similar remarks were made about the difficulties in funding multi-agency training and in both cases the phrase 'a whip round' was used to describe how funding could be accessed between health, education and social services. In many cases, the sheer numbers of partners and the pace of change proved a challenge. Children's Trust boards (e.g. Children's Trust Strategic Partnership Boards) incorporated health, education and social services, but also many included Youth Offending Teams, user representatives, and voluntary sector organisations (UEA, 2005).

This early report by the evaluation team at UEA identified the following barriers to children's trust development:

- complex geographical service interfaces;
- insufficient funds;
- ring-fenced budgets;
- lack of time;
- multiple initiatives;
- multiple targets;
- short-term initiatives;
- changes in management personnel;
- problems recruiting and retaining staff.

(UEA, 2005)

Funding can be a key difficulty both in terms of sufficiency of funds and in ability to make funds available for joint activities. Johnson *et al.* (2003) identify budgets and costs as one of the external barriers to integration. Many services will have national or local targets imposed on them by which they will be judged. If there is a move towards inter-agency working this may require pooling of budgets to fund the work of the new organisation. This transfer of funding, which often initially involves a higher level of risk as the resource is no longer under the direct control of the contributing agency, can be resisted if it is felt it will impact on the ability to achieve externally imposed targets. With a new approach to service delivery, there may be increased hesitation to pool budgets as there is no history of past success to offer reassurance. It may also be that the amount available to pool may be restricted by other necessary expenditure.

Despite these potential issues, steps have been taken to free budgets for pooling where this was previously difficult. The Health Act 1999 made it possible for health funds to be pooled with local authority funds to facilitate joint working:

> *It provides for local strategies to be developed for improving health and health care, and for new operational flexibilities to allow NHS bodies and local authorities to enter into joint arrangements for the purchase or provision of health and health-related services (e.g. social care).*

(DH, 1999)

However, pooling funds remains an area of difficulty where limited resources are called upon to provide for both single and joint service delivery. In addition, the report identified specific problems with involving the voluntary sector, which struggles with 'short-term funding and high staff turnover' due to grant funding and frequent changes of direction as a result of turnover in funding and staff (UEA, 2005). This concern is echoed by the NCVYS (2007), which suggests that there are barriers in the way Children's Trusts are established which inhibit the involvement of voluntary sector organisations.

Another problematic issue identified early on relates to what has become to be known as 'coterminosity', i.e. shared or lack of shared geographical boundaries and populations between local authorities and PCTs. This has been a major difficulty in co-ordinating services delivery in some authorities. However, the task of finding commonality between services with different governance, management structures, targets and views of their task has proved to be mammoth. The pathfinders also specifically identified issues around the ability of involved agencies to change at the same pace.

Practice example

Challenges to integration

Brighton and Hove Children's Trust, established in 2003, started with joint planning and commissioning between the local authority and PCT. Initially the plans focussed on partnership working, but with the view to structural integration as the ultimate goal. As such, their Trust is described as 'simultaneously up and running (that is, planning and implementing change) and under development (that is, gradually moving the services into their final shape' (Hawker, 2006: 25). There is a long list of things to do and areas to address, which are summed up as follows:

> What it means is that local partnerships are faced with the need to make wholesale changes to a range of key services all at once, and to manage it all as one large-scale and multi-faceted change programme.
>
> (Hawker, 2006: 26)

The challenges faced in this Trust were identified by Hawker (2006) as:

- *building a wider partnership:* between the children's centres and other early years providers from the private and voluntary sector;

- *developing new, more integrated ways of working:* the risks of fully integrated teams in terms of supporting and supervising different professionals in a single team;

- *developing a new service model:* the challenges of bringing together diverse budgets, including previously ring-fenced budgets, to support objectives based on needs that have been agreed by all partners;

- *balancing local autonomy with central specification:* finding strategies to ensure local 'clusters' can develop responsive services within the overall Children's Trust remit;

■ *sustainability:* extending the offer to 15 hours and 38 weeks to children in early years placements may threaten sustainability as centre's fail to cover the cost of free places if they maintain quality by employing relatively costly qualified staff and teachers, because the grant 'does not reflect the true cost of provision'.

(Hawker, 2006: 33)

A more recent report on Children's Trusts (DfES, 2006) emphasises the need for change to be managed and paced in order to be successful and reiterates the range and complexity of the change agenda. The report suggests that while acknowledging the need for a steady rather than rushed change of pace, there is also a need for areas of rapid success to demonstrate the successes of integration and convince others of this approach. The report also suggests that there are issues in measuring the outcomes of integrated services both in terms of time scales and the difficulty of isolating outcomes attributable to the integration of services through Children's Trusts. Engaging all partners continues to be a challenge to Children's Trusts with PCTs and GPs being the most common 'missing partners' and a need to start and sustain the process of involving private sector agencies in the Trusts. Finally, the challenge seems to be moving from initiating change to sustaining the momentum of 'the unrelenting culture of change' (UEA, 2006). The focus on supporting and maintaining those involved in change management suggests the possibility of 'burn out' or stagnation at all levels of planning and delivery as the time scale for implementing this complex strategy takes its toll.

To summarise, the development of Children's Trusts has involved a complex process of structural and cultural change and there are questions over whether the emphasis on structures has meant that the need for a massive change in ways of working, job roles, contexts for work, and perspectives on the tasks involved has been de-emphasised as a result of this. It may be that initially the government failed to recognise the enormity of the transition required in local government to successfully integrate services and that this is now the key issue for the immediate future.

Directors of Children's Services (DCS)

The Children Act 2004 required the appointment of a DCS in each authority to direct integrated education and children's social care services and to progress partnership and integrated service development. The majority of these directors were in place at the point of publication and presiding over 'joined-up' education and social care services for children. In February 2007 the new combined national organisation the Association of Directors of Children's Services (ADCS) was launched to represent the new directors. However, the process of combining these two services has not been without difficulty.

> 'Joining up is still a problem,' says Coughlan. 'Many councils have established common assessment processes and integrated teams, but there is still a whole set of cultural factors impeding co-working. These are departments that haven't worked together in decades.'
>
> (Bawden, 2007)

A key concern has been that the majority of directors come from education services rather than social services. This has prompted concern that there will be a loss of expertise in managing services for vulnerable children, including child protection services, within the Children's Services Authorities (CSAs) particularly during the transition stages. CSAs are the new local authority bodies incorporating the former local education authorities (LEAs) and children's social care services. Certainly the role of the DCS is challenging for all appointees as there is a steep learning curve for DCSs from whatever background. Some of the issues facing DCSs are ensuring that:

- a common language can be found between children's social care services staff and education staff;
- ways of working, structures and objectives can be clarified between the two sectors;
- trusting and open relationships can be developed between senior managers in the service;
- all services can be maintained and developed through the transition periods.

Local Safeguarding Children Boards (LSCB)

LSCBs were established to replace the Area Child Protection Committees (ACPC) which were previously responsible for strategic planning and management of child protection services in each local authority. ACPCs were generally considered to be ineffective, lacking a legal basis for ensuring a broadly representative membership and the power to act in response to deficits in local child protecting procedures and services. The LSCBs were established through the Children Act 2004 and are subject to guidance through the Local

Safeguarding Children Board Regulations, 2006. Their main remit is to develop policies and procedures for 'safeguarding and promoting the welfare of children in the area of the authority'. In general, LSCBs have been welcomed, with many believing that the statutory basis for membership will give the boards more power and efficacy than the ACPCs. However, there are a number of potentially problematical issues about the transition to LSCBs identified by Morrison *et al.* (2005). These include:

- whether there will be effective links between LSCBs and wider children's planning bodies;
- what the operational definition of safeguarding is;
- whether there can be true collective accountability among the agencies involved;
- whether the boards will be able to effectively manage performance;
- what sort of service user consultations will be included.

One of the key issues is how 'safeguarding' is defined and how the transition from the ACPCs' narrower focus on child protection to the broader focus on safeguarding is achieved. The concept of safeguarding children includes bullying, discrimination, accidents and ensuring access to preventative services that support children's health and development, with accidents as the main cause of children's deaths in the UK (Ryan, 2006). However, there are concerns that supporting children across the range of safeguarding needs may be hampered by the focus on child protection cases and poor information gathering on what children's needs are. Another factor that needs to be addressed is the relationship between child and adult services, as for many children, safeguarding may best be achieved through services to adults in terms of parenting support, drug and alcohol services, domestic violence support and adult mental health services. Finally, many services to children have high thresholds for access and this may prevent support for all aspects of safeguarding (Ryan, 2006).

Common Assessment Framework and lead professional

The evaluation of the 12 areas where the Common Assessment Framework (CAF) and lead professional (LP) were piloted determined that, despite a slow start, progress with implementing common assessment and a lead professional role was perceived as generally positive. The evaluation also indicated that this approach may produce more effective results for children with additional needs and their families (Brandon *et al.*, 2006). However, there are a number of areas that the report suggested were problematical. These included:

- extra workload caused by the CAF and LP roles;
- not all of the agencies involved were able to adapt easily to implementing holistic assessment and direct work with parents;
- the responsibility for CAF and LP was not always spread across all sectors;
- in some areas there was a lack of clarity on how to implement CAF and lack of support to do this;
- the range of skills needed to do the assessment well were not always apparent in all frontline workers;
- some of these problems lead to 'anxiety and frustration' among workers;
- lack of clear guidance could lead to conflict between workers from different agencies and a loss of professional confidence;
- in some cases CAF was being as used a referral mechanism leading to further single-agency assessments taking place.

There was also evidence that 'bottom up' implementation strategies which relied on 'learning on the ground' were often negative and that implementation worked better when there was a clear implementation plan and guidance (Brandon *et al.*, 2006). This is echoed in the report by Brown and White (2006), which suggested that integration works better when there are clear guidelines and directives, goals and responsibilities within the service implementation plan. Other factors that were causing problems implementing CAF in these early stages were the use of DfES generated training materials that had not been adapted to local needs; failure to learn from other areas; and confusion caused by too much individual discretion. It may be that a belief that 'growing' expertise in using the CAF, rather than providing a clear strategic basis for implementing it, has been an error in planning as this has not ensured the best transition to this way of working.

One of the key issues seems to be that not all the workforce have yet got the relevant skills to implement the CAF and take on the LP role. This means that the principles underpinning common assessment and a multi-agency approach could be compromised if relevant training is not made available to all staff from all agencies. There is also a wide division between the different agencies experiences of and expertise in holistic assessment and working with parents which impact on how well staff adapt to CAF. This has resulted in a 'patchy' approach to eliciting informed consent from parents and in some cases no consent being given. Finally, in some cases CAF has been used as a referral system rather than as an holistic assessment and this has resulted in more limited child and family involvement and additional assessments taking place. This latter point highlights the possible lack of commitment or misunderstanding of the purposes of CAF in some sectors of the workforce.

To summarise, the implementation of CAF has been challenging for some sectors as there are different levels of skills and understanding about holistic assessment and direct work with parents. In addition, a 'bottom up' approach may not have been the best way to develop CAF and clearer strategic guidance and implementation planning is needed. The additional workload that CAF and the LP role brings needed to be acknowledged and the responsibilities for these shared more evenly across the sectors.

Information-sharing

One of the key outcomes in child death inquiry reports from Dennis O'Neill onwards has been the failure of professionals and agencies to share information effectively. This was highlighted in the death of Victoria Climbié. Hudson (2005a: 538) notes that 'serious communication difficulties between agencies' were identified during the inquiry into Victoria's death. The reasons given by workers for inter-agency communication difficulties were several according to Hudson, with 'staff feeling unable to share information across agencies unless there was a definite protection issue' (2005a: 538). Concerns included:

- breaching confidentiality;
- the need for parental permission to share information;
- limitations on sharing imposed by legislation (Human Rights and Data Protection legislation).

The Children Act 2004 legislated for the introduction of information sharing and assessment (ISAs) databases in each local authority on which every child's basic details are recorded and through which practitioners can register concerns about a child for other practitioners to be aware of. From the start, however, the concept of electronic data sharing has caused disquiet. The initial main areas of concern were cost, the impact on privacy, and the technological issues the electronic systems would raise. Concerns about child and family rights and privacy were raised when it was clear that government would have to revise human rights and data protection legislation for the system to be legal.

The original plans were amended during the turbulent passage of the Children Bill 2004, through Parliament, restricting the amount and type of data that can be held electronically. 'Trailblazer' pilots were set up in a number of local authorities to develop the systems and implement their use. The local databases are now linking nationally through the introduction of Contact Point, previously known as the Information Sharing Index. However, the introduction of ISA systems has been one of the most controversial aspects of the ECM agenda. Hudson (2005a: 539) identifies 'three dimensions of contention' about the introduction of ISA systems:

- technological dimension;
- socio-legal dimension;
- professional-cultural dimension.

Technological issues include concerns that the creation of a national database will be prohibitively expensive and technologically challenging. Matching databases between services at local level is also proving to be a technological challenge. Security issues are also a concern. Essentially, the databases have a wide range of users from a number of agencies. Although they are all Criminal Records Bureau (CRB) checked and have had training, there is obviously some potential for access by inappropriate individuals. A study by the Foundation for Information Policy Research (FIPR) (Anderson *et al.*, 2006) concluded that there was risk that the database could be hacked into and vulnerable children targeted. This report also concluded that the expense of the proposed national system will 'divert scarce resources' from children's services and that by extending concerns to a wider group of children, put those children who are at risk of abuse in more danger.

Hudson (2005a) argues that the 'critical socio-legal' problem with electronic information sharing is that it can influence the tension between the child and family's rights to privacy and confidentiality and the necessity of overruling these rights to protect children form abuse. The authors of the FIPR report criticised what they called the surveillance approach to children, which they said was unnecessary and an intrusion into family life. They concluded that this approach could shift responsibility for children away from families and onto children's services. They suggested that children could also suffer 'e-discrimination' through the number of concerns indicated by professionals about them on the database and that this may influence the attitudes of professionals towards them (Ward, 2006). The central message of this report is that while child protection concerns should be a basis for intrusion into family privacy, this should not extend to families where there are no such concerns. The themes raised in the report are broadly echoed in the concerns expressed by rights organisations, such as Liberty. The final area of contention, the 'professional-cultural dimension' refers to the challenge that information-sharing brings to the processes of integration. Hudson (2005a) argues that professionals struggle with information-sharing as an aspect of inter-professional working and that issues of developing trust and cultural change are significant to the extent to which professionals feel able to share information comfortably with those outside their own agency. As such, there is disquiet among some practitioners about the amount and content of information to be shared.

To summarise, lack information-sharing has been a key area of concern in children's services in relation to child protection and the need to identify and track children vulnerable to abuse. However, the introduction of local and national databases on the majority of children has lead to concerns about children's rights and family privacy, the difficulties of keeping such information confidential, and the possibility of it being misused.

Extended schools

Extended schools are those which offer services to children and families beyond the basic educational remit. As part of the ECM agenda, extended schools are currently being established in every authority although many schools were already involved in offering some of the core services before the Green Paper. It is planned that by 2010, every school will offer a core of extended services. This includes:

- childcare from 8am to 6pm all year round;
- a range of additional activities to support study and enrich the curriculum, e.g. through after-school clubs;
- support for parents, including parenting classes and family learning;
- referral to other child and family services, e.g. speech therapy, child and adolescent mental health services;
- community access to facilities for ICT, sports and arts.

At the time of writing, 3,000 schools are making the core offer available. The idea of offering health and welfare services through schools is not new as many such services have existed for over a century (e.g. school meals, health and dental checks). However, the most recent initiatives draw on US models and have been developed first as community schools in Scotland (Smith, 2004, 2005).

The NFER audit of 160 schools offering additional services found five types of service provision:

- additional schooling provision offering curriculum and leisure opportunities to pupils beyond the traditional school timetable;

- community provision offering learning and leisure opportunities or general community facilities (e.g. drop-in or advice centres);

- early years provision, such as crèches or pre-school facilities;

- family and parent provision involving support relating to their child's learning or to a more general parenting or family role;

- other agency provision (e.g. from health, youth or social services);

- specialist provision, offering high-calibre facilities in areas such as sports, arts, information technology or business.

(Wilkin *et al.*, 2003)

However, there were considerable variations between schools in the range and type of services offered.

The evaluation of the pathfinder extended schools found that they focused on activities that supported pupil learning but that they had been less successful in locating community services in schools or making genuine partnerships with communities (Cummings *et al.*, 2004). This may be due to a number of factors, including the development of schools as contained bodies with some degree of separation from the communities they are based in (Smith, 2004, 2005). However, schools are also focused very much on individual learning and achievement rather than informal learning and community development, which means that while curriculum enrichment activities may be successful, genuine partnership with the community takes more time. The NFER study found that in the UK extended schools tended to focus on education rather than welfare enhancement (Wilkin *et al.*, 2003). A key factor in developing a more community-orientated approach would be developing opportunities for consultation with communities about their needs.

Practice example

Wychall Primary

Tracy Wearn, community co-ordinator at Wychall primary in Birmingham soon found that you can't just invent projects and services that you think the community needs and then publish them in a menu. 'We know there are lots of teenage mums in the area, for example,' she says. 'So we decided that it would be a good idea to set up something for them. Unfortunately, we don't know many teenage mums personally so trying to set up a group for them without making contacts first wasn't successful.'

(Haigh, 2006)

Time is also a factor in building relationships with other agencies, as meeting the core service offer is dependent on this, including the private and voluntary sector. For many schools these will be new types of relationships and there are issues about the role of heads in managing this type of change and the need for effective co-ordination of the services provided. This may be a steep learning curve for both managers and staff in schools and has implications for how managers spend their time. Ofsted (2006a) found in their study that extending schools services resulted in overload for some heads, and there were training needs in terms of developing and managing multi-agency services.

Smith (2004, 2005) suggests that while schools focus on achievement, other services may focus more on children's welfare, which may constitute a challenge in managing collaborative working, changes to the role of school staff, and reliance on staff from outside school to help deliver targets. This may extend the role of teachers and other staff or may curtail it depending on how the workforce planning and development takes place. Funding is also an issue, especially as there is an expectation that parents will pay for some activities, which may impact on access in socio-economically deprived areas. Ofsted (2006b) in their report on 17 extended schools comment on the uncertainties schools face in terms of long-term funding for additional services. The problem in developing community access has continued since the earlier evaluation reports. A more recent study by the TDA found that 'only 23 per cent of all schools are providing parenting support and community use' (Rowntree, 2006). There are concerns that schools are not making sufficient efforts to attract parents and reduce the barriers to their involvement. Although most of the evaluations have suggested that schools are developing good relationships with parents, in fact these are mainly mothers and fathers who are much less well involved in extended schools.

Practice example

Ms Allen, Deputy Head

Ms Allen reviewed the time she spent on social care, housing queries, advice on parenting, finance, health – all the issues with which many a primary head, particularly in disadvantaged areas, will identify. She discovered that she was spending more than half her time as a social care adviser.

(Haigh, 2006)

To summarise, extended schools are seen as positive, and in the main, successful, developments to support learning and achievement. However, their development may be based on short-term or uncertain funding and this may leave them at risk. In addition, while educational outcomes may be positive, schools have struggled more to engage communities on a wider basis, possibly because of the need for different ways of working and cultural barriers to this type of relationship. Finally, the demands on heads and other managers are considerable and need to be considered in order to sustain success.

Integrated inspection of children's services

The Children Act 2004 established a requirement for an integrated inspection framework for children's services to reflect the shift to integrated service planning and delivery. Although Ofsted was the lead body in developing this framework, a number of other inspectorates have also had to develop new ways of working together to inspect children's services in terms of the extent to which they are achieving the five outcomes for children outlined in the ECM agenda. The main development has been a Joint Area Review (JAR) within the Framework for Inspection of Children's Services in each CSA, the first round to be completed by 2008. The reviews are completed by multi-disciplinary inspection teams, drawing on a range of existing evidence, some from other inspections, and fieldwork which may involve individual children's experiences. As well as reporting on outcomes for children, JARs also report on the success or otherwise of integration and co-operation between services in 'working together'. The arrangements for the new inspection process were established rapidly and with a limited consultation period. Hudson (2005b: 519) comments: 'Notwithstanding the period of consultation, these changes constitute a rapidly formulated top-down approach to policy-making, and questions have to be raised about the prospects for implementation.' Hudson (2005b) goes on to point out that the inspection regime has a remit to enforce the development of effective inter-agency working through the inspection process, but questions the extent to which this is actually possible. One of the issues is the extent to which the five outcomes can be measured successfully through existing targets and indicators. Hudson suggests that these are too narrow in scope and too often drawn from education measures to reflect the breadth of the ECM outcomes, and, as such, their use has reduced the scope of the outcomes.

> *'Enjoying and achieving' seems to be reduced to school attendance and achievement, while 'Making a positive contribution' has been largely cast as the avoidance of antisocial behaviour.*
>
> (Hudson, 2005b: 521)

One of the other concerns is that while contributions to achieving the outcomes lie with a wide range of services and individuals working together, many of these are outside the remit of CSAs and therefore beyond the scope of the JAR. How can the inspection pinpoint accountability for particular services or outcomes in this complex situation? An example given is that schools have been left with a high degree of autonomy despite the Children Act 2004, as they were not given a duty to co-operate within the legislation. Hudson (2005b) notes that there is a tension between the schools' legal autonomy and the need for them to be involved in joint working in order for targets to be met.

As with any interdisciplinary body, the diverse inspectorates have to negotiate their different working practices, standards and cultures in order to work together successfully. Cultural difference between Ofsted inspection and the more developmental role of social care inspections led to concerns about the compatibility of the two approaches. CSAs may also struggle under the burden of joint inspections designed to simplify the inspection process. An evaluation of the way that the JAR works with the Audit Commission's corporate assessment inspection process found that while the inspection process was seen as generally at least as good as previous processes, the joint process did not reduce the burden of inspection or 'add value'. CSAs found the joint inspection process difficult because of the different focus of the two inspections, scheduling difficulties and duplicate information requests (KPMG LLP (UK), 2007).

To summarise, joint inspection processes may reflect some of the difficulties experienced in 'joining up' other services for children and families. In addition, the inspection process faces the challenge of determining accountability for services which may be partially or wholly planned and delivered outside of the CSAs. The remit to promote integration through inspection processes may be hampered by the limitations of performance indicators and measures which do not fully reflect the broad scope of the ECM outcomes for children.

Conclusions

In this chapter, some of the barriers to establishing 'joined-up' services have been explored through discussion of current services and strategies for developing multi-agency co-operation. While many of the evaluations of these services reflect considerable progress towards integrated services and effective co-operation between services for children, there are a number of areas where difficulties are encountered. Clearly the need for cultural change and embedding of new ways of working takes time and requires a clear strategic lead to ensure progress. Common aims and objectives and clarification of roles and responsibilities are important for achieving better working together. Other issues are funding, training and leadership to ensure that the complexities of working together are recognised through a sufficient resource base. Finally, the sheer volume and complexity of the current change agenda is a challenge in itself to all children's service providers.

4 Interdisciplinary teamwork

Introduction

As discussed, in Chapter 2, interdisciplinary teams are not a new phenomenon, but recent policy developments have encouraged and/or stipulated integrated service delivery, stimulating the development of more interdisciplinary teams and a much clearer focus on expectations of those teams. However, it is acknowledged that developing effective interdisciplinary teams is complex and involves consideration of changing cultures, work practices, principles and goals for practitioners involved. The benefits of interdisciplinary working were discussed in detail in Chapter 1 and will be assumed for the purposes of this chapter.

This chapter focuses on the development of effective interdisciplinary work in multi-disciplinary teams. The discussion will include aspects of teamwork and leadership issues relevant to interdisciplinary teams. Motivations and barriers to successful interdisciplinary teamwork will be discussed and a range of case studies and examples used to illustrate a variety of approaches. The chapter will focus on how practitioners and leaders can support effective integration and co-operation between staff from different disciplinary backgrounds through a range of developmental strategies.

At the end of this chapter, the reader should have achieved the following outcomes:

- know about different types of interdisciplinary teams;
- identify a range of strategies for interdisciplinary team development;
- know about success factors for interdisciplinary teamworking;
- understand the complex and embedded issues that may make interdisciplinary team development a challenge;
- know about leadership issues in team development;

- understand the key motivations for interdisciplinary team development within the policy context.

Types of interdisciplinary teams

What is a team?

Before examining types of interdisciplinary teams it may be helpful to think about what teams are in general. A team can be defined in simple terms as two or more individuals with a recognisable goal, requiring co-ordinated activity between team members in order to achieve that goal.

Teamwork is considered to be an appropriate approach to work in 'organisations that deal in ideas, concepts and services' (Neugebauer, 1984b in Rodd, 1994: 99) such as children's services. Rodd (2006: 146) suggests that teams in early years services are 'a key resource for the provision of quality childcare and education for young children'.

For many practitioners, teamwork may be more complex now than in previous times. Changing delivery structures, patterns and approaches mean that many staff are working in more than one team or in teams with different layers of involvement in which they could be a core member or more peripheral member. Recognising the types of teams we are working in and our different roles in them is one of the factors in successful teamwork. Another key factor is the available time scale for team development. Teams are not made overnight, but are developed over time through team-building processes. Teams are also developed through appropriate leadership, which supports both individual and team development.

What are interdisciplinary teams?

Interdisciplinary teams are those that are made up of members who are from a range of disciplinary backgrounds, with different professional qualifications, practice experience and 'home' agencies. The majority of practitioners in children's services will be working in interdisciplinary teams at some stage of their careers or for some part of their time. Interdisciplinary teams involve the pooling of different knowledge, skills, backgrounds, training, qualifications and expertise in working with children. Potentially, they may offer the most effective way of working with children and their families because of this range, but interdisciplinary teams are complex and their development often requires a great deal of skill from team members and leaders. However, it may be important to note that this range of practitioner expertise and understanding can be both the source of creative energy in interdisciplinary teams and the source of team conflict or fragmentation.

Range of types of interdisciplinary teams

Interdisciplinary teams in children's services have often in the past been discussed as a single type with little recognition of the variety of such teams operating within those services. However, as changes in service delivery modes towards increased integration have become the norm, many types of interdisciplinary team have emerged. Interdisciplinary teams can be permanent or they can be temporary. They may involve practitioners from a range of disciplinary backgrounds who are employed by a single agency or they may include teams which have some members who are still employed by their 'home' agency. They may be teams which have a single focus and which only operate as a team in respect of that focus, for example, the 'team around the child' for child protection case conferences and procedures or for SEN support.

Some interdisciplinary teams may have a limited life as a project team with a clear and time-limited remit. Others may be mixed, having permanent and temporary members, or core and peripheral members or some seconded members.

Activity **The 'team around the child'**

Read the case study below and note the advantages of having this range of practitioners involved in the conference. What factors need to be considered to ensure good communication between the practitioners during the life of the team?

The child protection case conference for Rose, 7, and Damien, 3, included the child protection liaison teacher from Rose's school and the child protection co-ordinator from the Children's Centre that Damien attends. The social worker from the Children's Social Care Services team who has been allocated to Rose and Damien attended as does the clinical psychologist from Child and Adolescent Mental Health Services (CAMHS) who has been assessing Rose's behavioural issues. Damien's health visitor was included and her manager also attended. These practitioners and professionals all have involvement with Rose and Damien and their family and have a remit to support their development and welfare.

Individual practitioners may be members of more than one such team at any time or they may be members of both interdisciplinary teams and single disciplinary teams.

Activity

Read the extract below about establishing a new service. What approaches can be used to establish the new team and ensure that all practitioners feel included?

The Children's Centre

The Children's Centre staff are from a variety of disciplinary backgrounds, including social work, teaching, health and early years. Within the centre, many of the staff are permanent employees but the deputy is seconded from the health service and the daycare centre has been established and staffed by a nursery chain from the independent sector. The social worker is permanently attached but receives supervision and support from her 'home' agency.

In addition, teams may be permanently or temporarily co-located. On the other hand, they may only meet at fixed intervals or they may be 'virtual' and not meet at all. The members of some teams may be partially co-located with an interdisciplinary team and partly located with their 'home' agency team. Rodd (2006) suggests that interdisciplinary teams are likely to grow larger as multi-disciplinary children's services develop and become more complex. However, larger teams are considered to be more effective in achieving goals in terms of the range of skills, knowledge and expertise of the team members.

Reflection point **Are multi-disciplinary teams growing?**

In a recent session with post-graduate students who were all practitioners in children's services, we did an exercise that involved each practitioner drawing a spider diagram of the other agencies/professionals they worked regularly with. We were all (tutors and practitioners alike) quite taken aback at the sheer number and complexity of relationships practitioners needed to have with other agencies/professionals now, and with the diversity of types and composition of multi-disciplinary teams each practitioner was involved in.

Every Child Matters: Change for Children (2007) identifies three models of multi-agency working:

1. Multi-agency panel

In this type, members are not permanently part of the panel, but identify with and remain employed by their home agencies. The panel has a chair or manager who is also employed by her home agency. The panel meets regularly. This model includes panels, networks and the 'team around the child'.

2. Multi-agency teams

These times are more permanent and have more of a team identity with recruited or seconded members, a team leader and a team identity. They are more likely to be co-located although this is not always the case. This model includes teams such as Sure Start and behaviour support teams.

3. Integrated services

In this model, the team is co-located, usually as part of a community-based service hub, providing interdisciplinary services to children and families. The team has a common identity, philosophy and goals and is managed as an interdisciplinary team. Service level agreements outline the basis of practitioners' involvement and there is a clear funding structure. Examples of integrated services include family support services and children's centre teams. Obviously these are models and many actual interdisciplinary teams are hybrids of these types rather than identical to them. However, the models exemplify the range of interdisciplinary teams that now populate children's services and which are continuing to develop.

The significance of the existence of a range of types of interdisciplinary team has several elements. Clearly, different types of interdisciplinary team are more suited to different service delivery patterns and type of service. In addition, different types of interdisciplinary team will have different advantages in terms of service delivery and effectiveness. Finally, barriers and problems in establishing interdisciplinary teams will vary between types. It is important also to remember that team type may not have developed as the 'best option' in terms of achieving goals. There may be many factors contributing to the way an interdisciplinary team is configured, and not all of these may be related to the team objectives. Team members may continue to be employed by 'home' agencies for pragmatic reasons such as continuity of pay and conditions, even if this does not enhance team solidarity. Team members may not be co-located if there is no funding to achieve this, even if co-location would support their work together. Team members who have part of their work with a 'home' agency may have to prioritise this even though this may detract from their ability to commit to the team.

Team members and multiple teams

For many practitioners in children's services, membership of teams has become more complex and they are more likely to be members of more than one team and these may be of different types with different remits and membership. This can be both stimulating and stressful for individuals who may gain a great deal from the variety and range of teams they belong to or be challenged by this. Practitioners need to develop skills in being able to change team roles and behaviour according to the team they are in, and to adapt to new ways of working in teams. Some practitioners are not only members of more than one team, but can be leaders in some teams and not in others.

Activity **Janice's Teams**

Janice is a FS2 teacher in a small urban primary school, a role that she shares with Karen. Janice is also the SENCO for the school. Janice belongs to the following teams:

Classroom team – working with a teaching assistant, a support worker for a disabled child and on occasion the EAL support teacher. Janice is the leader for this team during her 'part' of the week and she plans and co-ordinates the day-to-day teaching and assessment in the class with them.

Classroom teacher – team-working with Karen to plan and co-ordinate the overall teaching and assessment strategy in the class over the year.

Whole school team (SENCO) – working with all the other teachers and staff in the school to develop SEN strategies and training and development. Janice is the leader of this team which operates intermittently.

Individual child teams (SENCO) – working in different 'teams around the child' for each child with SEN in the school. These teams are often 'virtual' in that they only meet occasionally, but they have a clear set of goal and objectives to support the child. Janice co-ordinates these teams, which include speech therapists, physiotherapists, social workers, behaviour support staff and parents.

SENCO – team-working with other SENCOs to develop good practice around children with SEN within the authority. This team meets regularly but not frequently.

Consider the range of Janice's roles and responsibilities in teams.

1 What sort of skills does she need to perform her roles effectively?
2 What sort of challenges may this range of roles raise for Janice?

Challenges to interdisciplinary team development

It is unlikely in the current policy climate that many readers have not already worked in or are working in an interdisciplinary team, either on a permanent or temporary basis. As such, many of you may be aware of some of the difficulties in working in teams drawn from a range of professional and practice backgrounds, training and qualification bases and approaches to service delivery. These may be rooted in the different perspectives and identities discussed above and in different approaches to the team tasks based on these. Tensions may arise between team members if they do not have a common basis for communication, a common professional 'language' or understanding of each other's views. Johnson *et al.* (2005) found internal organisational barriers to developing multi-agency work include differences in professional cultures, the approach to service delivery and differences in management style.

In some teams insufficient time and attention is given to supporting the team's development or there is a lack of effective leadership to support team-building processes. There may not be opportunities for teams to develop because of time constraints on the 'life' of the team. Other factors may be due to the way the team is structured and organised, in terms of line management responsibilities, allocation of roles and responsibilities and support for staff members. Location of teams and team members may be a problem especially for teams which may not be able to meet regularly.

Current experience in children's services is, therefore, that there are organisational, interpersonal and development factors which can hinder effective interdisciplinary teamwork (Day *et al.*, 1998). In addition, there may be traditional deeply rooted hostilities between different disciplines that may strongly influence their views of each other as individuals in the same team. In this section some of the challenges to interdisciplinary team working will be discussed.

Practitioner/professional identity

Every practitioner's approach to their work and philosophy underpinning that approach will have developed uniquely over time and will have been subject to a range of influences during that development. Single discipline teamwork may be perceived as less challenging than interdisciplinary teamwork because some of those influences are likely to be more common to those from similar professional or practice backgrounds. This commonality gives team members a shared basis on which to build the team, which is usually shared with the team leader. It is normally based within a shared concept of the purposes of the role; how the role should be performed; what constitutes effective service delivery and the underpinning principles shaping these aspects.

Chandler (2006) identifies three aspects that will influence a particular practitioner's approach to their role:

1   Personal history and motivations underpinning choice of profession.

2   Training and experience in their role (presumably also including qualifications).

3   The 'beliefs, values, aims and objectives' of the service in which the individual has usually worked.

(adapted from Chandler, 2006: 142)

This unique and personal trajectory will have taken place for every member of an interdisciplinary team, developing their views, beliefs and values as well as their goals, working practices and focus. Clearly, it is likely that members of

---

Activity   Identity development

Raised in a family of professionals in public service, the author worked as a trainee social worker for 2 years under the supervision of a range of peers from whom she gained a strong view of the purposes and practices within child and family social work. This view was refined and extended to include the values and ethics of social work during her qualification course. The first qualified role she worked in was very demanding and as the most inexperienced member of a very experienced team, she developed a strong sense of the need for team solidarity and support and faith in her peers to provide this. Working in child protection, in which social services were the dominant agency, this early experience supported the view that social workers had the primary and most significant role in safeguarding children.

Using the three aspects identified by Chandler above, write down the key periods of time, experiences and events that have influenced your development as a practitioner.

1 Think about which teams, training, people and posts have most contributed to your view of yourself as a practitioner and what that view comprises.

2 Draw a timeline showing the major influences and events which have shaped your view of yourself as a practitioner and your view of your role in children's services.

interdisciplinary teams will less often have developed similarly than those in single discipline teams. One of the tasks within interdisciplinary teams is to explore identities and how these can be reconsidered within the interdisciplinary context. However, individual practitioner identity can be challenged by becoming part of an interdisciplinary team. Staff may face threats to their identity through 'homogenisation' of roles and tasks, or they may be concerned about their own disciplinary background being less valued or seen as less useful than others. Staff may have been uprooted into new physical contexts or may be working away from supportive colleagues from their own discipline as discussed in Chapter 1. They may also be experiencing different pay and conditions, working practices and perspectives. There is further discussion of this issue in Chapter 6.

One concern that practitioners and professionals do express about interdisciplinary work is the fear that they will lose their professional identity and become more of a 'Jack of all trades' if they work closely with others from other disciplines. There is no doubt that blurring of professional boundaries may take place in interdisciplinary teams and maintaining individual professional identities while developing more holistic approaches is a balancing act. One of the key challenges to individuals in interdisciplinary teams is to both maintain their unique identity based on their own professional or agency background and also to become an effective part of an interdisciplinary team, which essentially means learning new ways of perceiving children and childhood, new approaches to team goals, and new working practices and philosophies.

Professional viewpoints or perspectives

One of the main challenges to interdisciplinary work is the variety of views and approaches held by different practitioners within the team, in terms of working with children and families. Viewpoints or perspectives are developed as part of practitioner identity, and encompass the way in which the practitioner views children and childhood, families, services and service provision and society more generally. These perspectives are not static within professions but may change over time. However, they are likely to differ between professionals from different disciplines and this may lead to failure to communicate well, see each others' point or even basically understand the underpinning principles guiding each others' approach to work.

Practice example

Social workers and police

In a case of suspected child sexual abuse a social worker and police officer have different remits that affect their view on what should be done next. A police officer's core role is to identify crime, apprehend suspected criminals and collect evidence to aid prosecution of these individuals. This may mean investigating and arresting adults close to the child. A social worker's core task is to safeguard children from abuse and ensure the child's welfare is secured in the future. According to the Children Act 1989, this should involve working with adults close to the child to support them, as well as the child, in the proceedings taking place.

Some of the reasons for different perspectives lie rooted in the practitioner's views of children and childhood and their role with children. Educationalists may see children from the viewpoint of their cognitive development; social workers will prioritise their welfare; health workers will be most concerned with the child's physical health and development. At first glance, these viewpoints may not seem incompatible but they may lead to different views on priorities in assessment and service delivery.

Activity Quality protects

Read the extract below and think about how it differed from more recent developments. How would continuity of health and education provision for children in public care be maintained now?

A classic example of the significance of viewpoint underpins the introduction of the Quality Protects initiative in social services in 1998 (DfES, 2007a). The Utting Report (1997) identified some truly appalling outcomes for children in the public care system, in respect of education, qualifications, employment chances and mental health amongst other things. One factor that emerged was that when children came into care their educational and health records were often 'lost' as they moved between placements or from home and they often experienced severe dislocation in continuity of health and education services. The result was poorer quality health and educational outcomes for these children.

The social workers who made the decisions about children's placements and/or removal from home were simply less focused on the child's education and health needs than they were on the child's immediate and pressing welfare needs. Quality Protects was introduced as a programme to improve outcomes for 'looked after' children and part of this initiative was to introduce systems to track and monitor their education and health needs and records.

Anning *et al.* (2006: 52) frame their discussion on differing perspectives on children and childhood within an 'overarching' theory that these are socially constructed. They argue that practitioners come to understand the needs of and responses to children and families in terms of different socially constructed discourses shaped by their training and practice. As such, they found that the different multi-professional teams studied each held a 'dominant model of explanation' which underpinned their practice with children and families. However, they also concluded that teams could be effective while incorporating different perspectives on childhood, children and families and that these differing perspectives could actually enhance the work of the team.

Professional hierarchies

The difference in professional identities suggested in the section above may have implications for interdisciplinary teams being able to make decisions based on all perspectives. Practitioners in such teams may develop a sense of the status of their own viewpoint in relation to others and these may not be equal. Powell (2005: 79) argues that in any interdisciplinary context there will be 'multiple perspectives' and that these are based on a 'sense of competence or expertness' associated with being a professional. However, this concept has implications for interdisciplinary interactions, in that, there may be 'a developing hierarchy with some views being held in greater esteem than others.' This hierarchy of 'expert views' may militate against reaching any consensus within an interdisciplinary team and may result in any team view being shaped by the most dominant 'expert view.' Powell (2005: 80) goes on to argue that this hierarchy of value placed on expert views may result in some views remaining unheard and a failure to reach a 'convergent perspective'.

Practice example

Cleveland child sexual abuse

The Cleveland child sexual abuse case highlighted the dangers of hierarchies of expert opinion. The case came to light when it was identified that in a period of 5 months 121 children had been taken into care because they were believed to be sexually abused based on a single, controversial medical test. The social workers involved placed a higher level of credence on the view of the two doctors involved, and the medical 'evidence', than they did on their own assessments of the child and family, as was the norm at the time. Most of the children were returned to their parents after the case became popularised through the media and the medical test was brought under criticism. The case highlighted poor communication and relationships between some of the services involved.

Each practitioner's place in the hierarchy may depend on a number of factors including length of training, level of qualifications, public status of profession and the extent to which the profession or role they are in is seen as having specific forms of 'expertise'.

Structures and practices

All agencies have structures and organisational features that are peculiar to that particular type of organisation. These features could include:

- the goals and aims of the service;
- working conditions and contractual arrangements for staff;
- written policy and guidelines;
- unwritten policy and expectations;
- values, beliefs and ethical issues;
- statutory responsibilities;
- thresholds/conditions for involvement;
- jargon and communication systems;
- quality of the relationships between leaders and other staff.

Differences in these may result in communication, status and hierarchical difficulties between practitioners from different types of professional or practice backgrounds. Team members may feel disorientated or disempowered if taken out of familiar structures and placed in teams which are part of another agency. They may have expectations about how work will be organised and about work practices that are not met in the new team. They may also be unprepared for new expectations around these issues that are part of the new agency organisation, but not evident in their agency of origin.

Work cultures

The concept of professional culture is quite difficult to pin down but encompasses the context, practices, written and unwritten policies, perspectives and priorities of the profession. One definition of culture is:

> *A pattern of basic assumptions invented, discovered or developed by a given group over time . . . that has worked well enough to be considered valid to be taught to new members as the correct way to perceive, think and feel in relation to these problems.*

(Schein, 1985)

External manifestations of a culture may be how professionals present themselves, their language and use of jargon, their priorities and practices, leadership and management and accountability arrangements. Internal factors may include the beliefs on which their approach to work rests, the ethical and theoretical bases for their approach to work. Differences in culture may be more apparent to practitioners who move to work in services they have not previously been employed in.

Schein (1985) defined organisational culture at three different levels:

1   This level incorporates what is observable about the organisation such as policies and work practices, the known history of events in the organisation, including 'heroes and villains', and how the work is organised.

2   This level includes what is known about expected behaviour and relationships and modes of operating in the organisation, the unwritten rules and expectations about how to behave and communicate with each other in the team.

3   This level includes the values and beliefs, principles and assumptions underpinning levels 1 and 2. These are not always articulated and may not be consciously considered but are strong determinants of behaviour.

This model helps us acknowledge that much of a particular work culture may be 'taken for granted' and not consciously acknowledged and may not be susceptible to change unless there is a process of consideration on 'why we do the things we do'. However, stepping into an unfamiliar culture can be a major challenge to the confidence and self-esteem of practitioners who have to 'learn' the new culture over time before feeling comfortable within it.

Stereotypes of other practitioners

One of the factors that may be most insidious in preventing effective interdisciplinary team cohesion may be the views and beliefs that practitioners have about each other's professional status and practices. These can often be stereotypical, meaning that all practitioners from a particular group are viewed in the same way, often negatively, by other groups of practitioners. These stereotypes may evolve from expressed viewpoints about other services, which are part of an agency's work culture. They are often based on the cultural differences discussed above and the view that 'our' priorities and approaches, beliefs and principles are more important or significant then 'theirs'.

Factors that may work against team cohesion are often deeply embedded in the views and beliefs of different practitioners and may not be consciously held or subjected to any reflection or scrutiny. This may make some of these factors difficult to both acknowledge and to address and it is generally acknowledged

---

Activity **Stereotypes**

Consider some of the practitioners you have worked with or been on placement with. What sort of stereotypes have you come across about them and their roles? Think about practitioners from a range of children's services:

- social workers
- health visitors
- early years practitioners
- GPs
- teachers.

Do you think the people you have met conform to these stereotypes in practice?

How might these stereotypes affect your view and relationship with other practitioners?

that developing interdisciplinary teams is a challenge. So why put the effort in? In the next section, the motivations to make interdisciplinary teamwork effective are discussed.

Motivations to develop interdisciplinary teams

Clearly one of the key factors in tackling the challenges of interdisciplinary team development is that we are currently expected to do this. These expectations are discussed in more detail in Chapter 1, which explores the policy context and in Chapter 2, which discusses the benefits of interdisciplinary work. The Every Child Matters: Change for Children website (2007) has a plethora of material promoting and supporting the process of integration at organisational and team level. Current children's services policy is the main driver for the development of interdisciplinary teams, based on the belief that 'working together' is a key factor in the success of improving services to children and families. However, interdisciplinary teams are not a new phenomenon and one of the other drivers for developing these more effectively is an increased level of knowledge and understanding of the issues that may promote or inhibit their success and effectiveness. Simply put, we know more about these types of teams now and this information can be put to use to ensure improvements in interdisciplinary team-building.

On an individual level, interdisciplinary teamwork creates many challenges for the practitioners involved in them as discussed above. However, when such teams do work effectively team members often report high levels of satisfaction with their team; the opportunity to learn from others and develop new skills and understandings; the chance to be more effective; the development of more holistic approaches to meeting children's needs and new ethos and approaches to work. Abbott *et al.* (2005) reported that professionals working in six services with children with disabilities had benefited from multi-agency working particularly in the area of job satisfaction and personal development. The study found that the interviewees had been able to expand their roles and that there was some blurring of roles, although this caused some concern that there may be loss of role identity for some staff. However, the study reported that there was no negative effect on staff workloads from multi-agency working and better relationships and communication were an outcome as were improved outcomes for families in the shape of improved co-ordination of services (Abbott *et al.*, 2005 as cited in While *et al.*, 2006).

Practice example

BESTs

The evaluation of BESTs (behaviour and education support teams) which are multi-agency teams supporting behaviour policies and individual children's behaviour in schools found that staff on the BEST teams learned from each other and gained new skills and understandings. The development of the multi-agency team was a key factor in the success of the projects. This development was characterised by regular communication, the development of a multi-agency ethos, information-sharing and a more holistic approach to child and family needs (Halsey *et al.*; 2006).

Increasingly more of the children's workforce are benefiting from joint training and more holistic approaches to working with children. Increasing numbers of practitioners are entering the workforce from multi-disciplinary courses such as degree courses in Early Childhood Studies or Playwork and more practitioners are studying on foundation degrees which present a more holistic approach to children and families. As such, parts of the 'newer' workforce are less likely to have the same tight professional boundaries and delineations between roles that the 'older' workforce have experienced. Workforce development is discussed in more detail in Chapter 6.

Some views on effective interdisciplinary teamwork

In all teams, achieving effective teamwork is dependent on a number of factors. Larson and LaFasto (1989) found that team structures needed to have four features in order to be effective. These are:

1   clear roles and accountability within the team;

2   an effective communication system;

3   methods of monitoring individual performance and providing feedback;

4   an emphasis on fact-based judgements.

These features are significant in that they relate to both task and process. Clear roles are important in that role duplication or lack of accountability for aspects of the work militate against success in achieving the task. Effective communication systems are vital within teams to ensure team cohesion, accountability, clarification of roles and team-bonding. The authors also acknowledge that teams are made up of individuals and that effective team-functioning is dependent on individuals working well in their team role and in themselves. The final point is significant for completion of the tasks and challenges the belief systems that can arise in different teams and services. Fact- (or evidence)-based judgements are important in task completion as they encourage the team to reflect on and analyse their ways of working and to absorb new information and concepts. However, what constitutes a 'fact' may be contested in interdisciplinary teams as the knowledge base from which facts are drawn may vary between team members.

Marsh (1994) raises the following points on which effective teamwork in early years settings is based:

- sharing of values, ideas and aims;
- highly developed interpersonal skills;
- positive relationships between colleagues;
- multi-professional training;
- effective communication about children's needs;
- clarification of goals through discussion;
- time to plan and organise as a team;
- selecting staff with appropriate personal, leadership and interactive skills;
- shared responsibility for day-to-day effectiveness in service delivery.

Some of the significant issues that can be drawn from Marsh's points are:

- teams need to have the chance to meet and communicate regularly;
- there needs to be active team-building to promote positive relationships and a team identity;
- all team members need to 'buy into' the tasks, beliefs and ethos of the team and to take responsibility for the team's success.

With reference to a review of multi-agency service delivery by Atkinson *et al.* (2001), Anning *et al.* (2006: 9) summarise the key factors for successful interdisciplinary work as

> *commitment, clear leadership, a clear focus with common aims, and the importance of regular meetings and spending time on the groundwork of professionals learning to communicate and understand each others' working activities.*

Activity   Interdisciplinary team members – a profile

Read the list of characteristics below and determine what staff development activities could support the development of these in individual team members.

An effective interdisciplinary team member may have the following characteristics:

- a strong professional identity and secure base of knowledge and expertise in their own discipline;
- excellent interpersonal and communication skills;
- the ability to challenge their own and others' views, beliefs and attitudes;
- a desire to extend their knowledge and understanding of children and families and an openness to others' perspectives;
- a problem-solving approach;
- empathy, patience and a supportive approach to other team members;
- flexibility and openness to change.

Other significant characteristics or attributes are:

- experience of working with other agencies or professionals;
- working experience outside their 'home' agency e.g. secondment or temporary roles;
- leadership skills and experience.

Factors influencing effective interdisciplinary teamwork

There is no single way to develop effective interdisciplinary teams or to ensure that such teams work well together. The variety of types of teams and the differences in their composition means that each team will be unique and will require unique approaches to its development. However, there are some approaches that are common to all teams, which can be considered, and some that may be specifically relevant to interdisciplinary teams. In this section, skills and strategies will be discussed, along with models of team development and functioning and leadership and management issues for effective teamworking.

Dimensions of team functioning

There are a number of factors that influence how teams form and the extent of their effectiveness. One of the challenges is to think about how teams function and what their purposes are in order to conceptualise these factors. Jeffree and Fox (1998) suggest two dimensions of team functioning: *task* and *process*.

The *task* is the goals of the team, the reason for the team to be formed and the expected outcome of team functioning.

The *process* is how the people work together in the group and how they bring together their knowledge, skills and qualities to achieve the task.

These two dimensions are equally important and attention has to be given to both aspects in order for teams to work well. For example, if the process is poor and teams members do not work well together it is unlikely they will achieve their task fully or effectively. However, teams that are unclear about their goals or task may not function well either. The task obviously varies between teams but there may be similarities in the process by which teams develop and begin to function.

Bachmann *et al.* (2006) suggest a number of strategies that practitioners can apply to promote integration and sustain the process:

- look for ways to reduce the complexity of the team;
- consider the size of the team – integrated working can be more successful if the size of the partnership is reduced;
- take time to communicate positive messages, such as feedback from service users;
- ensure there is good leadership;
- establish and maintain an appropriate level of resources;
- access to appropriate continuing professional development for all practitioners in the team;
- have a shared objective so there is a clear and unified provision.

When there are plans to bring practitioners from different professional backgrounds or services together this will require preparation. For a new approach to be successful it is vital that there is a shared ethos. This should always be developed in consultation with practitioners from each of the professional backgrounds that will form the new team. Johnson *et al.* (2003) identified that when decision-making was pushed down to where care and support is given it helps to achieve successful integration. As well as valuing practitioners this can encourage the creation of a shared ethos that is directed towards the central aims of the new collaboration, such as promoting health and well-being rather than responding to need. This approach offers the opportunity to draw on the best of past practices and use them to develop new approaches to meet the new service ethos.

Reflection point **The journey to integration**

Hurst (2006) gives an account below of the move towards creating an integrated service. The account illustrates how many of the points discussed above were applied to practice.

An overview: The journey to integration

To bring different services together as one organisation requires each of them to be pliable. Often this can be challenging, but particularly so when it is bringing education, social service and health departments together as a children's centre. Many of the changes needed to achieve this may be able to made by managers and practitioners within the service but structural changes at local authority and trust level are also needed. At Atherstone, a children's centre in Warwickshire, the move towards integration is being viewed as the need to be interconnected like the veins and arteries in a heart. Integration has been achieved at senior management level and the focus is now on management and operational level integration. This will utilise all opportunities for mixed team working to help practitioners start to view themselves as children's centre workers working in an integrated way. To achieve this it has been necessary to introduce changes to working practices, relocate some workers and invest time and energy in developing new partnerships. Overall the challenge is to equip practitioners with the skills and knowledge to work in new ways that they are comfortable with – taking the best from the past to develop to create something new for the future.

Stages of group formation

All groups are subject to change and development in their functioning over time. A new group will not behave in the same way in week one as they do several weeks or months later. This change over time can be called group formation or team development and it is directly connected to the 'process' aspect of team functioning discussed above. However, unless this process of team development takes place effectively, it is unlikely that the group will be able to achieve their 'task' or meet their goals and objectives as planned.

The stages of group formation and functioning can be characterised by the familiar model of:

- forming
- storming

- norming
- performing.

(Tuckman, 1965)

This model is well known and has been adopted into the Every Child Matters: Change for Children (2007) website. The model outlines the stages that groups may go through before they are able to work successfully together.

1   The forming stage takes place when teams form or when changes in a team such as members leaving or new members joining creates a 'new' team. This is often a tentative, questioning stage with some 'false starts' at recognising the goals of the team and the individual member's roles in the team. There may be anxiety at this stage and feelings of uncertainty. Team members may not know each other or understand their relative roles. Rodd (2006) suggests that team members will look to the leader for guidance at this stage and are unlikely to challenge the leadership role because of their uncertainty. For similar reasons, they are not likely to challenge each other or to take risks during this period of 'getting to know you' in the team.

2   In the storming stage, confidence has grown and team members may challenge their own and each other's roles, the nature of the task or goals and possibly their leadership. Team members may also challenge each other's expertise or come into conflict over differences in values, principles, approach to the task or perceptions. There may be 'infighting, power struggles, disputes and destructive criticism', which need to be managed effectively so as to minimise the impact on the setting or service (Rodd, 2006: 155). The storming stage may last for a long or short time depending on a range of factors including leadership skills, clarity of the task, and the effectiveness of team-building strategies. Some teams remain in this stage throughout the team life and do not progress, resulting in unresolved conflict and an unstable, ineffective team. Other teams may progress but revert to storming at times of stress or when conditions change.

3   The norming stage is when the team starts to settle down and where processes in the team become more familiar and less turbulent. The team starts to work together better and to share significant issues about the work they are doing and key issues related to this. Team relationships start to form or improve and the team become more like a team.

4   in the performing stage teams start to work well together and to achieve their goals and perform their tasks. Team members are all 'pulling their weight' and team tasks are being achieved. Systems work well and structures are supportive.

Tuckman's model appears linear but in fact many teams may move back through the stages or revert to a previous stage when under pressure or when new members join, the leader changes or other new factors influence team-functioning. The model has a number of useful features. It helps us recognise that team processes are vital for completing the task and that teams do not come together overnight and start to function effectively immediately. There is a time dimension to effective team-functioning that has to be considered. It also helps us recognise the dynamic nature of team-functioning, in that teams do not form and then become fixed. They may have periods of stable functioning but external and internal changes and challenges can push teams back into earlier stages of the model. The model also highlights the leadership role as a key factor in successful team-formation and functioning.

Leading the interdisciplinary team

A key role in both developing and maintaining effective teams is that of the leader or manager. Leaders need to be able to develop skills that are specific to their role and which will support the team-building process. In children's services the main resource for service delivery is staff and therefore leaders need to have skills that directly relate to staff development. Leaders also need to be certain of the leadership role in interdisciplinary teams. Summarising from the discussion so far and below this will include:

- identifying the team task and ensuring team roles are clear in order to achieve the task;
- supporting the processes of team-formation and development;
- team-building;
- conflict management;
- supporting individuals within the team.

However, there are a number of challenges to leading interdisciplinary teams and a range of knowledge, skills and abilities which leaders need to develop in order to be successful.

Structural issues affecting team leadership

Anning *et al.* (2006: 45) identified several areas that constituted challenges to leading interdisciplinary teams, relating to how the team was structured. They suggest that agreement on the following needs to be reached in order to clarify some of the issues:

- Who has line management responsibilities for team members?
- Who co-ordinates the work of the team?
- Who provides professional supervision/support to team members?

The issue for many interdisciplinary teams is that one leader may not be able to carry out all the leadership roles successfully, particularly providing supervision and support to staff from different backgrounds to their own. In addition, staff who are not permanent in the team or who are still employed by their 'home' agency may be 'managed' rather than 'led' by managers outside the interdisciplinary team. In their study, Anning *et al.* (2006: 45) found that it was

> not unusual to find a team member being line managed by one person (from their host agency), coordinated by a team leader, and supervised professionally by a third person.

These structural anomalies could take up time and have a negative effect on staff morale, detracting from both this and from the team task. As such, the authors suggest that there needs to be 'absolute clarity' about 'who is doing what' in these three areas in order to enable interdisciplinary teams to function effectively.

Team-building

Team-building refers to the processes involved in developing teams and team relationships in order to achieve effective functioning. Team-building does not take place as a single event but is ongoing through the life of the team so the team is built again and again to reinvent itself in line with change. However, team-building should also develop capacity to cope with change and new developments within team members and the team as a whole. Team-building is essential to ensuring teams work together and members understand each others' roles and responsibilities in relation to their own.

There are a number of factors that need to be considered in order for effective team-building to take place:

- Effective teams can be viewed as systems, in that they involve the team members but they also involve the relationships between the different team members, the relationships between members and leaders, and the level of coherence in team-functioning.
- Effective leadership is one of the most significant factors in building groups of individuals into teams.

- Successful work groups share the leadership role.
- Giving time for team-building is crucial (e.g. meetings, away days).
- Team-building exercises need to focus on particular issues and promote the team identity and good communication.

Rodd (2006: 163) identifies two aspects of team-building:

- staff morale
- task demands.

These relate to the need to ensure that team-building and support is directed at both supporting the individual and completing the task. Ways of ensuring leaders address both these issues are discussed below.

Building effective interdisciplinary teams

Key issues in building effective interdisciplinary teams will vary to some extent between teams but there are some common features:

Group roles
In order to achieve effective team cohesion and to ensure tasks are completed successfully, it is very important that all members are confident in their understanding of their own and others' roles in the team. This is particularly significant in interdisciplinary teams, where roles may be less well understood than in single discipline teams. Members need to know what each other does and how they fit into the team as a whole. However, team-building and role-defining is not a single activity. It needs to be re-visited every time there are changes to team composition, structure or task.

Activity	**Re-building the team**

You are working as part of an integrated family support team and have made good initial progress. Two months ago another three practitioners from the Portage service joined the team. The aim of this was to integrate the support services for all families together under the work of one team. Since the new members have joined you have a sense that some momentum has been lost.

What strategies could you use to reinvigorate the momentum of the team?

Goals and objectives

Team members also need to be able to answer the question 'What are we doing?' and to understand the main goals they are trying to achieve. It is important that these are articulated as in some cases they are not and as such may be misunderstood. Leaders have a significant role in the process of clarifying goals and ensuring these are made clear to the team. However, teams must also be involved in setting, refining and evaluating their goals.

Individual member's contributions

One of the issues that may arise in interdisciplinary teams is the extent to which team members may get involved and contribute to the team. This is particularly relevant for team where membership may be part time or impermanent and where team members (or some team members) may have other team commitments in their 'home' agencies. The extent to which individual team members make a commitment to the team is a key factor in success.

Positive group interactions

This refers to the ways that team members behave towards each other, relate to each other and deal with issues that arise in the team. All teams have to work towards positive group behaviour in order to function well. However, in interdisciplinary teams this factor is crucial because the possibility of dissent can be much higher than in single discipline teams. Leadership is a key factor in developing good working relationships between all team members.

Dealing with conflict

Unresolved conflict, disagreements, lack of harmony, misunderstandings, misconceptions and personality clashes are key factors in damaging team effectiveness. In interdisciplinary teams there is much scope for negative behaviour between team members or the team as a whole. Resolving conflict is important but Whalley (2001) argues that conflict can be used to create healthy debate and to share different perspectives. As such, some conflict may be positive as long as it is not personal and not unresolved.

Activity   Pen Green

Pen Green is a community development centre for children and families which has become a model for good practice in developing multi-disciplinary teams working in partnership with parents. However, when Pen Green first opened the staff and managers faced a number of challenges that needed to be addressed in order for the centre to be successful in its aims.

■ What were the challenges in building an effective multi-disciplinary team at Pen Green?
■ How were these challenges met?

Challenges faced in building the multi-disciplinary team

■ The main supporting agencies (education and social services) had no shared language, or conceptual framework.
■ There were different pay scales between teachers, nursery nurses and social workers.
■ There was a divide in philosophy between care and education staff.
■ There was a wide range of qualifications, styles of working and experiences of supervision and support amongst staff.
■ There were issues about reconciling roles and responsibilities in the light of a range of pay.

Ways in which these challenges were met

■ developing a 'truly multi-disciplinary steering group' (LEA, Social services, Health Authority, voluntary organisations);
■ all staff were placed on the same conditions of service;
■ using the wide range of qualifications and experience as a resource;
■ all posts had the same generic title;
■ role-sharing e.g. working in the nursery, home visiting;
■ negotiating roles on the basis of strengths and experiences and pay level;
■ staff were encouraged to visit other centres;
■ establishing a comprehensive staff development programme, team-building days, management training;
■ regular supervision of individual staff based on the social work model;
■ conflict was seen as healthy and creative;
■ linked team meetings for all teams were established with a rotating chair and designated time to meet.

(Whalley, 2001)

Key strategies for success in leading interdisciplinary teams

The key points can be summarised as follows:

Individual staff

■ Choose staff with a commitment to teamworking in general and interdisciplinary work in specific.

- Make sure all staff have appropriate support in line with their professional needs and backgrounds.

- Ensure it is clear who is line managing and allocating work to each staff member.

- Ensure any relationship or formal links to the 'home' agency are clear.

- All team members need to understand their own and others' roles and responsibilities within the interdisciplinary team.

- All team members need to have the chance to build on and maintain their own practitioner/professional background, experience, training and qualifications.

Team

- Make time for teams to meet and share their different philosophies, work practices and perspectives as well as discussing the task in hand.

- Make opportunities for informal as well as formal meetings and the development of interpersonal relationships between team members.

- Make time for training and development to support cohesion, shared practice and clearer understanding of goals and objectives.

- Leaders need to role model positive relationships and respect for all disciplines in children's services.

- Leaders need to ensure that hierarchies of value are not developing between different disciplines within the team, i.e., staff from specific disciplines are not being seen or adopting a hierarchy in terms of the extent to which their disciplinary background is valued within the team.

- Roles need to be shared between the team in terms of skills and ability, not by disciplinary background.

Task

- The overall aims and more detailed objectives of the team's work needs to be clear to all members and others outside the team.

- Roles and responsibilities for different aspects of the task need to be allocated by skill and aptitude and to be clear to all.

- Leaders need to monitor and support staff in their allocated roles and to meet their own objectives.

- Differences in view or perspective on the task need to be shared openly and agreement reached on how to proceed.

Activity **Managing family support services**

You are applying for a centre manager position to manage the co-ordination of a family support service, nursery, health visiting team and portage service (portage provides support and advice to families and children who have complex learning difficulties) into a children's centre. In preparation for the interview you are asked to draw up an action plan to show your main priorities for the first three months that the centre is open. Draw up a month by month plan that outlines the actions you would take if appointed to the role in each of the following areas:

1 to establish the management team and set early priorities;
2 to start to establish an integrated team;
3 to set up and organise the premises;
4 to support and communicate with staff.

- All aspects of the task and roles need to be valued equally and supported.
- Staff training needs to be available to support the achievement of goals and objectives.

Communication and interpersonal skills for leading interdisciplinary teams

Communication is both a tool of leadership and an outcome. Leaders need to use communication as part of their leadership strategy but they also need to recognise that communication is one of the team tasks (Read and Rees, 2000). There are a number of purposes of communication in interdisciplinary teams:

- conveying the vision (the expected goals and outcomes);
- providing support, affirmation, praise and acknowledgement to team members;
- managing and disseminating information through the team and to internal and external others;
- promoting an image of the team and the work they are doing;
- linking parents, children and practitioners;
- motivating staff as individuals and as a team;
- resolving conflict within the team;
- clarifying, refining and developing the tasks.

(Read and Rees, 2000)

Leaders need to develop interpersonal and personal skills to be effective in their roles. Rodd (2006) suggests the following attributes for leaders in order to be successful in their role and to inspire their team:

- confidence
- self-knowledge
- positive attitudes to new experiences
- positive attitudes to change.

Communication and interpersonal skills may include:

- clarity of communication;
- empathy and sensitivity to others' needs and feelings;
- different levels and modes of communication to meet different needs;
- appropriate humour, warmth and sharing;
- good listening skills and making time to listen;
- self-control, self-management and restraint in responding (i.e. giving thoughtful and considered responses, putting aside or managing own feelings and dealing with others' emotional expressions);
- self-assertion.

Self-awareness

Leaders of interdisciplinary teams need to be aware of their own background and professional identity in order to ensure that this does not influence their relationships within the team in negative ways for some members. This may

---

Activity   Sharing knowledge

Interdisciplinary teams need to share their knowledge and experience in order to develop good working relationships, respect for each other and an understanding of each others' professional perspectives. Sharing knowledge and expertise can be done informally, through team meetings or shared training (Anning et al., 2006).

1. Reflect on how your team shares knowledge and how this process is supported.
2. Consider what types of knowledge interdisciplinary teams need to share.
3. Outline the role of the team leader in promoting the sharing of knowledge.

involve addressing any stereotypes of other practitioners or agencies the leader may consciously or subconsciously hold. They need to be able to assess their own strengths and weaknesses and to draw on a range of support to meet their own needs. Leaders also need to be aware of any ambivalence they may have about interdisciplinary teams and their inexperience or lack of knowledge and understanding of others' disciplinary perspectives. Self-awareness about the ability to delegate or to share work and/or the leadership role with other members of the team is also important for leaders of interdisciplinary teams.

Networking and negotiating skills

Leading interdisciplinary teams may involve making different sorts of relationships or developing new relationships with a wider range of agencies and practitioners depending on the type of team. This may be due to having non-permanent or seconded staff on the team or having an interdisciplinary team where some members are also part of multi-agency panels. However, all children's services teams need to relate to a wide range of others and these skills are increasingly needed to negotiate these complex relationships successfully.

These skills may also be needed where there are difficulties in clarifying structural issues as discussed above. Within the team, negotiation skills are important for conflict resolution and role clarification.

Conclusion

The complexities and demands of interdisciplinary teams are a significant challenge to practitioners and leaders and the barriers to achieving successful teamwork are daunting. However, for many practitioners interdisciplinary work is already a reality and for others this way of working is their future. Developing the necessary skills and attributes to work in and/or lead teams of diverse practitioners is a key element in the success of wider development of children's services. This chapter has covered some of the main issues in this area but the reference section at the end of the book contains works that further develop the themes identified (Anning *et al.*, 2006; Rodd, 2006; Smith and Langston, 1999; Whalley, 2001).

Turning policy aspirations into practical reality

Introduction

There has been an unprecedented expansion of existing services for children and families and the creation of a range of new services in recent years. Much of this expansion has been brought about by new legislation and policy expectations from the Sure Start Unit (Department for Education and Skills, 2004). Recent initiatives and service developments, to implement the government's commitment to bring services closer to families and communities, require higher levels of interdisciplinary working. Examples of this are the establishment of 3,500 Children's Centres (many on school sites) and through all schools becoming extended schools by 2010 (DH, 2006). The National Service Framework for Children, Young People and Maternity services sets out expectations that will involve health professionals working closely with other professionals to help ensure the Every Child Matters outcomes are achieved for all children. These outcomes are clearly challenging and to achieve them the expectation of services working in a more integrated way will have to become a reality. National guidance, legislation and policy initiatives will contribute partly to achieving these outcomes but a central focus in realising these ambitious aims will be the responses of individual practitioners, a point emphasised by While (2006) who stated:

> Government policies have provided the context for cross-boundary working within children's services, the implementation of changes in practice rests with the service organisation and the individual professionals within them.

> (p. 96)

When government policies and initiatives are announced they often attract headlines, but these are short lived. If they are widely reported again it is generally because a policy has not had the expected impact or a target has not been achieved. This highlights the key challenge of legislation, policies and initiatives – translating them into practice. And this is made harder because what may work in one area may not work in another. When implementing new services they are more likely to work if they take account of the context, utilise the best of past successes and empower practitioners to work in innovative ways. This chapter will explore the impact on practitioners of a range of policy developments and initiatives through three key changes:

- the Common Assessment Framework;
- the lead practitioner role;
- information–sharing.

These impacts can be both beneficial *and* challenging for practitioners and this will be explored to help you develop a critical awareness of issues related to integrated working. The activities within the chapter will promote reflection on approaches to practice that could enhance positive outcomes for children and families.

At the end of this chapter, the reader should have achieved the following outcomes:

- a clear understanding of the role of practitioners in embedding policy expectations in practice;
- an overview of recent key developments in assessment, information–sharing and the lead practitioner role;
- reflected on a range of strategies that could be used to enhance practice.

The missing link

If you read through policy and guidance documents for practitioners there is inevitably an emphasis on two issues: change, and the benefits of this change for service users. However, the missing link that is often not stated in making this a reality is the practitioners that will deliver it. This raises a number of important questions:

- How will the change impact on practitioners?
- What opportunities are there for practitioners' development?
- Are there any potential negative impacts for practitioners from the change?

As stated in previous chapters, there are often clear benefits to service users when practitioners work together but this may not always be required. To avoid unnecessary time, effort and energy, it is completely appropriate to question if a joined–up approach, involving practitioners across practice boundaries, will bring greater benefits (HM Government, 2004b). If questions are raised about the appropriateness of new developments it may be claimed that this is negative. Practitioners should not be put off through comments such as this. It should be clear at the start of any change that there is at least potential for benefit. If this does not seem to be the case, then discussion and analysis of how to proceed should be encouraged as this will increase the confidence in the change and make it more likely to succeed. If there is clear potential for benefits then this is a sound basis to proceed. This is clearly illustrated by the points below, which show the benefits of health professionals working with schools (DH, 2006):

- Allows health concerns to be addressed alongside educational, social and emotional development, which promotes adoption of healthy choices.

- Delivering health provision through schools ensures that it reaches all children, which includes those who may be hard to reach as they have limited or no contact with other services.

- Schools, particularly in rural areas, may be the only or main resource in the community that are accessed by all families.

- The approach provides the basis for effective collaboration with educational practitioners and this may better address the holistic needs of each child, particularly if they have more complex needs.

- Joint working offers the opportunity to learn from each other, offer support, share expertise and develop a more informed awareness of how the work of other practitioners contributes to Every Child Matters outcomes for children and families.

- Work to support the healthy development of children is seen as part of ongoing development and learning rather than as something separate.

- There will be increased opportunities, through partnership with parents, to promote health and well-being for families. For example, this could include increasing rates of breast feeding and promoting smoking cessation.

There is often a tendency for practitioners to immediately look to themselves for the reasons why something has not been successful and what they can do to resolve this. However, some of the factors that contribute to effective joined-up working are outside the control of individual practitioners. Eilbert and Lafronza (2005) explain that the level of organisational affiliation and adaptability impacts on the level of integration that can be achieved. Important factors that facilitate practitioners being able to work together include having a common vision, a clear development plan, good leadership, clearly defined roles and a clear understanding of funding issues (Bachmann *et al.*, 2006; Eilbert and Lafronza, 2005).

Common Assessment Framework

You have been the allocated social worker for a family for three years. Two years ago you worked with the family as both parents have a physical disability and required some support. After an assessment, adaptations were made to the home environment and support was put in place to offer assistance with household tasks and childcare. This was evaluated and found to be working well. It was agreed that no additional input was needed but the family had your contact details if they needed to contact you. There are two children, Sarah who is 4 and Louise, who is 2. Sarah has recently started in foundation one. You have been contacted by the SENCO requesting support as they are concerned about Sarah's learning. You meet with the SENCO and it seems clear that the concern is around learning and you suggest this. The SENCO agrees but is adamant that a Common Assessment is needed because of the 'family situation' and says that you are the person who needs to carry this out.

How would you respond?

The main purpose of the Common Assessment Framework (CAF) for children and young people is to assist practitioners to assess additional needs that children have so that appropriate and effective intervention can be provided early. The Framework is designed to be used with children who have additional needs and are at risk of poor outcomes, particularly in the five key areas identified by Every Child Matters. Not all children who receive support from services need to have a full assessment. The decision about when a common assessment is needed is made by individual practitioners. Many local areas may hold guidance that can support practitioners in this decision. For children with complex needs it may be that they meet the threshold for statutory assessment and support (HM Government, 2006d). Over recent years some local authorities have moved away from issuing statements of special educational needs for some groups of children with complex special needs. Rather than take significant amounts of time and money in a long and complex assessment process a more streamlined approach is being used. The child's educational setting works with support services, such as educational psychologists, to carry out an assessment and decide on interventions. To support children who may have had a statement of special needs, additional funding is then delegated to the educational institution. In addition to devolving money to schools the process is designed to free up time that educational psychologists would have spent on assessment so they are able to work more with children and families (Fitzgerald, 2007). As the amount of funding that is attached to statutory statements is often low, this approach has the potential to utilise time, expertise and resources much more efficiently. However, it may mean that children with complex needs, who would previously have had a statutory assessment, will require a Common Assessment. If this is the case, it will be necessary to evaluate if the Framework has the potential to meet the identified needs at least as effectively as a statutory assessment would.

The decision to undertake a Common Assessment should be taken in consultation with the child and family. For young children, practitioners will have to use appropriate styles of communication to promote participation and gain the views of the child (there are a number of sources that discuss strategies to include children's views, e.g. Fitzgerald, 2007). By involving the child and other family members in the assessment this will enable a full and accurate picture of the family situation to be gained. In addition, it will produce a clearer understanding of the actions that are needed to support the family. If a family do not agree to an assessment being undertaken this must be respected as consent is needed before it can be started. As discussed in previous chapters, this emphasises how working in an open, respectful and inclusive way, that promotes a genuine partnership, is more likely to gain the trust of service users and consequently their consent. In addition to information from a Common Assessment, practitioners may still carry out specialist assessments and it is important that families are clear about this. The Common Assessment is not designed to replace specialist assessments, but it could inform these and help to prevent children and parents having to repeat the same information over and over again.

The Common Assessment can be thought of in three stages:

- preparing to carry out the assessment by checking if one exists already and gaining informed consent;
- carrying out the assessment;
- identifying what support would benefit the family and, where necessary, liaising with other practitioners to put a plan together to address the outcomes.

To help decide if a full assessment is necessary, there is a pre-assessment checklist that practitioners can use. The tool focuses on broad areas of development and helps practitioners to identity if there are unmet needs.

> **Activity**   **It's not my job mate! (part b)**
>
> Based on the information from the SENCO and the guidance on the Common Assessment process, you are not convinced that a full assessment is needed. To be clearer this is the case you visited the family to review how things are. There are no new issues and things are well. The parents are aware of the concerns from school and agree to you being involved. At the next meeting with the SENCO you feed back this information and explain that you are happy to help. You confirm that the SENCO has completed the Common Assessment training and have a discussion about the options for proceeding.
>
> Based on this information what action would you take to identify any unmet needs Sarah may have?

A Common Assessment can be used in a variety of circumstances, but it is not intended for use with children where there are safeguarding concerns. The current approach, of following procedures set out be the Local Safeguarding Children's Board, will continue to be followed. If there are unmet needs and these can be met by the practitioner carrying out the assessment there is no need to complete a full assessment. If not, then a full assessment will help to clearly articulate what the current situation is and this information can be shared as necessary to involve other services that can provide the required support. A full assessment will collect information on development, parents and carers and the family environment. This will cover a broad range of areas including:

- health (general, physical and communication);
- emotional and social development;
- behavioural development;
- identity (self-esteem, self-image and social presentation);
- family and social relationships;
- self-care skills and independence;
- learning (understanding, problem-solving, participation, progress and achievement, aspirations);
- basic care, safety and protection from parents;
- emotional warmth, stability, guidance, boundaries and stimulation from parents;

- family history, functioning and well-being;
- housing, employment and financial considerations;
- social and community factors and resources.

From the information collected, overall conclusions can be drawn together to identify solutions and agree the actions to support the family. If this support is put in place early there is the potential to empower the family by ensuring that input is targeted towards the promotion of well-being and enhancing quality of life. The Common Assessment may also highlight that a family is having their needs met and there is no need for additional input. If additional services are needed the practitioner completing the assessment may have to take a brokering role. This is discussed in the next section.

Activity **It's not my job mate! (part C)**

It was agreed that a pre-assessment checklist would be completed. The SENCO explained that he was happy to carry it out but had not done one before and was concerned that he may not know enough about all areas. You suggest that you complete it together and in consultation with Sarah and her parents. You also offer reassurance that if no information can be found about a section of the assessment it often means there is no unmet need. If this is not clear though, the partnership approach that you are taking with this case is a good way to proceed. The pre-assessment shows that the only area of unmet need is around learning and developing and it is agreed that a full assessment is not needed. The information collected will be added to by additional information from the teacher and advice will be sought from the educational psychologist attached to the school.

How do the actions taken compare with your plan?

Reflect on the overall idea of the Common Assessment process. Does it offer a good basis for practitioners to work together to respond to children and families holistically?

From this assessment a common understanding of children and families will enable practitioners, from different professional backgrounds, to plan how they can work together to meet identified unmet needs. The activity above illustrates how a partnership approach can use the assessment process in a way that places the child and/or family at the forefront of decision-making by involving them throughout the process. Importantly, it also emphasises that assessment is not intended to be the automatic default option and should only be used when appropriate.

Activity **Making assessment effective**

Think about the outline given above of the purpose and process of the Common Assessment.

What would services and service providers need to do to ensure that the assessment was completed effectively and the agreed actions were put in place?

What factors would help and hinder the successful introduction of the Common Assessment Framework?

The move towards prevention, which is at the heart of the Common Assessment, will require a high level of inter-agency collaboration to identify unmet needs and provide effective support. However, there are potentially a number of underlying assumptions that this will just happen. For the Common Assessment to become recognised as a valuable and effective tool a shared language and approach to service provision will need to develop. The move towards integrated services, such as Children's Centres and extended schools, will support this but where services work in using a multi-agency approach, time and effort will be needed to develop common referral standards.

Pithouse (2006) carried out a pilot study in Wales exploring the introduction of a Common Assessment process and a number of conclusions emerged from this that can inform practice. During the implementation period there was a drop in referrals and no corresponding increase in child protection referrals. However, feedback from practitioners identified that not all aspects of the assessment were/could be completed by professionals, as illustrated in the activity above. The assessment guidance clearly states that it is not necessary to complete all sections. This was particularly evident for the emotional and relationship needs. However, this area may need careful monitoring to be sure that sections are being left uncompleted because they are not needed rather than because a practitioner does not have the knowledge to complete it, which could result in vital information being omitted. A central aim of the assessment was to promote the participation of children in the process, but there was little evidence of this on completed assessments.

Brandon *et al.* (2006a) explain that both the Common Assessment and lead professional role were designed to reduce the time and effort spent by practitioners collecting information and families providing the same information time and time again. From their evaluation of 12 pilot areas they identified that different CSAs were at different stages of implementation, which is not surprising. The study identified a number of factors that could help or hinder the implementation of the CAF:

Helps implementation	Hinders implementation
enthusiasm among services and practitioners	lack of joined-up working or conflict of interests
perceived benefits fro families	lack of trust
good past experiences of multi-agency working	mismatch between the vision and practice
a learning culture	skills/confidence gaps
existing ICT systems	anxiety about workload
clear processes to support the introduction	unclear implementation processes
good training, support and supervision	lack of support

The role of the lead professional

Activity (part A) Taking a lead

Read the following account and decide what your initial response would be in this situation.

In your role as a behaviour support worker you are asked by a local nursery to visit Carl, a 4-year-old boy who they have said is having behaviour problems. You make arrangements to go and observe Carl and meet with his key worker. You contact his mother to explain what your role is and explain that you will contact her after you have observed Carl and spoken with staff. She explains that she is concerned about his behaviour at home too and that she wonders whether it is linked to the change in his medication. It is clear that Carl and his mother are in contact with other services but the nursery has not told you about this. From the information you have it is clear that the situation is more complex than it initially seemed and you arrange a time to visit Carl and his mum to observe what he is like at home and have a chance to talk with her so you can get a clear picture of the situation so you are able to help.

From observing Carl at nursery and talking to his key worker it is clear that he is often tired at nursery and it is at these times his behaviour is poor and he finds it hard to socialise with the other children. His key worker also mentions that a woman has been a couple of times to see 'how he is doing' but he is not sure what her role is. You visit Carl later that week during the morning and notice that he is much more alert and although he is boisterous he will listen when you ask him questions and he does sit for short periods and play with his toys.

You ask Pat, his mum, about the change in medication and she explains that he has epilepsy and his medication was changed two weeks ago by the nurse specialist whom he sees at the hospital. You explain about the woman who has visited the nursery to see him and Pat thinks it may be the family therapist who visit the family monthly. Pat also tells you about the speech therapist who Carl is seeing for his 'speech problem' but she is not sure what the problem is. From your discussion it is not clear that most of the practitioners working with the family are aware of the others involved.

In addition to integration to make services more accessible there has been an emphasis on ensuring services are able to provide a joined-up and seamless response to the issues that children and families may need support with. Where there is more than one service supporting a child or the family this can be a complex issue. In response to this the government introduced the role of lead professional (HM Government, 2004b). The idea of this role is that one practitioner takes a lead to ensure that the services delivered are co-ordinated, coherent and that they achieve the intended outcomes. Based on the scenario above, it is clear that this role has a significant potential to achieve benefits for children and families who are in contact with a number of different service providers. In addition, when there is a more co-ordinated approach as well as providing a better service for children and families there is an increased likelihood that services will also be used more efficiently. The role of 'lead professional' is not new. What is different in the current approach is that it is expected that where children and families are in contact with more than one practitioner, which is more likely where there are complex issues within a family, this role will be provided by one of those practitioners. Previous to this it may have occurred but this would have been because of the efforts of one or more of the practitioners involved taking the initiative to co-ordinate the activities of practitioners working with the service users. The role of the lead practitioner covers three core functions:

- acts as a single point of contact for the child or family;
- coordinates the delivery of the actions agreed by the practitioners and child or family;
- reduces overlap and inconsistency in the services received.

(DfES, 2006)

The decision about who takes on the role of being the lead professional should be made on an individual basis. The key skills required to carry out the role include:

- the ability to communicate in a clear and concise way with the child and family and develop a positive relationship;
- the ability to organise and manage a range of information;
- the ability to identify, using the Common Assessment Framework, what support is needed and establish agreement about how best to provide this;
- working in partnership with all practitioners involved with the child and family and take account of issues raised from different professional perspectives;
- co-ordinating the delivery of agreed interventions and carrying out regular evaluation to inform future actions.

These skills and competencies will be held be a range of practitioners and are transferable across professional boundaries. The decision about who takes the role of lead professional should be made by considering a number of factors (HM Government, 2006b). Firstly, a practitioner should not feel pressured into taking on the role. Child and family services are diverse and include practitioners with a variety of qualifications and roles. This can range from practitioners with very limited experience and qualifications, such as a level two childcare qualification (equivalent to GCSE level), to practitioners qualified to doctoral level in a specific professional area. Higher qualification levels do not necessarily make a person more suitable to taking on the lead practitioner role, but it is important to consider how practitioners who hold lower levels of qualifications will feel in taking on the role. There is also the issue of pay and conditions and what it is fair to expect practitioners to take on within the boundaries of their role. These issues are discussed in more detail in Chapter 6. Secondly, practical considerations, such as which practitioner is having the most contact with the family and how long this contact is likely to be maintained are important factors. If a practitioner is working with the family to offer advice or even intense intervention over a short period, it may be decided that they are not the right person to take the lead role in this situation. In addition, the importance of developing a relationship with parents should be a prime consideration. Mcwilliam *et al.* (1998) highlight a number of qualities that contribute to the establishment and maintenance of effective partnerships. These can be summarised as having a family orientation, positiveness, sensitivity, responsiveness and friendliness. Many of these qualities are demonstrated through discussion and interaction and this emphasises the power of effective communication as a powerful factor in facilitating quality interaction (Jordan *et al.*, 1998; Keyes, 2002; Hunter, 2006). Overall, again this highlights the absolute need for trust within partnerships between the lead practitioner, other service providers and service users (Adams and Christenson, 2000; Bachmann *et al.*, 2006). Another factor that contributes towards the development of a trusting relationship is having respect for each family. This is demonstrated by showing understanding and receptiveness for each family context and culture (Dunn, 2005; Smith *et al.*, 2003).

A number of practical issues need consideration when deciding who should be the lead professional. The amount of time a practitioner has to devote to the role is important. If a practitioner is responsible for managing their own caseload there will be times when they have a range of complex cases or a heavy caseload and it would not be appropriate for them to take on additional work. Location is another consideration as it may be impractical for a practitioner located in a different geographical area to take on the role. Alternatively, if a practitioner is located away from colleagues and the child or family but is located at a place where regular review meetings, such as a case conference where all involved practitioners are present, this may be a good reason for that person to take the lead role. Finally, each case needs to be seen individually and choices made that are appropriate. For example, if a child has a specific issue, such as a speech and language difficulty, the key deciding factor of who takes the lead role may be decided by the specific skills and knowledge of practitioners. In this situation the speech and language therapist may take the lead role as they would be best placed to offer support to the child and guidance to other practitioners. These issues highlight the point made in the introduction about how careful thought and planning from practitioners is the key catalyst in turning policy into effective practice.

Activity (part B) Taking a lead

Following your initial contact with the nursery and family you find out the additional information below. How do these actions compare with what you decided in response to part A? It is clear that no practitioner is taking a lead role and this is needed. Based on the discussion above you decide that you need to take on this responsibility in order to achieve a more co-ordinated and

organised response. What actions would you take to respond to the informa-
tion you now have about the case?

From the discussion with Pat, you now have a better idea of the different practitioners working with the family. It is clear though that there does not seem to be a
co-ordinated response. Some support seems to be being duplicated by different
practitioners and other support that the family and nursery may value, such as advice
on strategies to help Carl develop more positive social skills, are not being provided.

When you asked Pat what you could do that would be of most help for her and Carl
she explains that she sees lots of people but is not really too sure what they do. You
agree to make contact with the practitioners who are working with the family and
when you have a clear understanding you will contact her again so you can decide on
the next steps. From subsequent enquiries you find out the following practitioners are
involved with the family:

- a community-based clinical nurse specialist who offers support and advice for
  Carl's epilepsy;
- a hospital-based paediatric neurologist who Carl visits yearly to manage his epilepsy;
- a family therapist who is meeting with the family to look at approaches to parenting as there is disagreement between mum and dad about how to respond to
  Carl's behaviour;
- a speech and language therapist who is involved at the request of nursery as they
  questioned whether Carl's behaviour was connected to an underlying receptive
  language difficulty;
- a nursery nurse from the local authority early years team who works with Carl
  because of his poor concentration for one session each week.

To support lead professionals there will need to be a commitment from both
services and all practitioners. For the role to work across different localities and
authorities there will have to be changes at different levels and flexibility in working practices. For example, as discussed above, there will need to be Common
Assessment procedures in place. This may have to include some pooling of budgets, which understandably, given the target culture that is synonymous with public services, may be resisted. The role clearly offers significant potential to bring a
more coherent approach to the delivery of services for children and families with
additional needs. When practitioners are being asked to take on the role they
will need to be appropriately supported. To be convinced of the benefits of
accepting this additional responsibility practitioner will need access to training
and ongoing support. For it to be accepted by all service providers, work is
needed to ensure that it is accompanied by the necessary status and authority to

act (INTEC, 2005). Managers need to ensure that practitioners who take on the role have additional time to meet the demands of the role so they are able to organise and plan, liaise with other professionals and receive support and training.

Another aspect of the lead professional can involve identifying where additional services are needed and brokering their involvement (HM Government, 2006b). This can be problematic though if additional resources are required to put this in place. If the lead professional does not have access to any funding streams, which is usually the case if they are not in a management or leadership role, this could lead to delays or in the worst scenario the service not being provided at all. Again, this highlights how structural and organisational processes can be a barrier in turning policy into practice. In response to this there have been a number of trials for budget-holding lead professionals. Consultation on these proposals has identified potential benefits for children at risk of exclusion, with emotional and behavioural problems and families who are homeless or in temporary accommodation. The perceived practical benefits are that it could lead to quicker delivery of services and more creative solutions to identified issues. Interestingly, many of the solutions that were identified as having the potential to offer support included paying for membership of clubs, providing money for babysitting and payment for play sessions. At first glance, this looks very simplistic, but it is potentially these types of activities that have significant potential to support children and families and they are often not available from other sources. In contrast, this type of approach also has the potential to be problematic. It could add to the complexity of the role, cause tensions between practitioners, be difficult to monitor the quality of services and lead to barriers between service users and the lead professional if the money is not used in a way that both parties agree with (Quill, 2006). It is positive that new solutions are being explored but these points show the need for piloting and careful evaluation.

Activity (part C) **Taking a lead**

Now that you have taken on the role of the lead professional you decide that the best way forward is to bring all the practitioners involved with the family together. How does this compare with the actions you decided to take from part B?

Read the overview below that summarises the meeting and draw up an action plan to show how you would take the case forward.

All practitioners and Pat are present at the meeting. To make everyone aware of what is happening you ask each of the practitioners to give an overview of their involvement with Carl or his parents and any feedback on their work to date.

Community clinical nurse specialist

Sees Carl and his parent(s) every 2–3 months to review his drug regime, monitor any change in his condition and when required liaises with other health professionals. There was a change in medication six weeks ago and from recent feedback this may need to be reviewed again as it may have reduced Carl's concentration and added to behavioural difficulties.

Hospital neurologist

Sees Carl yearly and liaises closely with the nurse specialist about his drug regime. Based on feedback, she decides that it would be beneficial to carry out some further neurological tests to inform the next decision about his treatment.

Family therapist

Has met with the family on three occasions over the past six months but has not identified any specific issues.

Speech and language therapist

Has visited Carl in nursery once. His functional speech is appropriate for his age but there has not been enough time to complete a more detailed assessment.

Early years community team nursery nurse

Has visited Carl for one session each week over the past six weeks. Generally works with a group of children to promote turn-taking and positive behaviour.

Pat (Carl's mum)

Reported that she found the support from the nurse specialist very helpful. She was not clear about what the speech and language therapist and nursery nurse were doing but was grateful for their help. She had recently seen her GP as she was not feeling 'herself' and she had recommended six counselling sessions.

Nursery key worker

Reported that Carl's recent behaviour and interactions with other children had been erratic.

From the meeting summary it is clear that the practitioners involved with the family are offering a good range of support. However, it also seems that there is some overlap in the support being provided and aspects of support that would be beneficial are not being provided. A clear aim in this situation would be to identify exactly what is needed, whether it is being provided and if not who could take responsibly for providing it. When making decisions about changes a key aim is to ensure that all practitioners are informed, agree with the identified actions and are clear what their responsibility is in the process. From the meeting it is clear that a more consistent approach is needed. Based on this the following actions are proposed:

- Carl and his family will have additional tests with the neurologist and with the clinical nurse specialist will review his current treatment regime.

- The clinical nurse specialist will meet with nursery staff to give them some information about epilepsy, how it can impact on children at nursery and what practitioners can do to support children. The nursery will be asked to keep a diary of Carl's level of attention and concentration for four weeks as this will help to evaluate any change in his treatment regime.

- From discussion with the family therapist and Carl's parents the issues with Carl's behaviour (in this context the word behaviour is used to indicate all observed actions) seem to have some link to his epilepsy/medication. As this is being reviewed now it is decided that no further contact is currently needed. It is agreed that the therapist will contact the family again in six months to make a decision about any further support that is needed or whether the family can be discharged. In the meantime the family have contact details for the therapist, if needed.

- It seems likely that Carl does not have a speech and language difficulty. The speech and language therapist will visit Carl on one further occasion to complete the initial assessment. She will also provide some advice and strategies that the nursery nurse and Pat, Carl's mum, can work on to help develop his concentration and social interaction.

- To promote positive interactions at home and offer support to Carl's parents, Dave, the nursery nurse, will visit Carl at home each week. This will be reviewed in eight weeks. This will coincide with Pat visiting the counsellor and it is hoped that this will contribute to creating a supportive and positive relationship between the family members.

- Over the next six weeks, when the majority of intervention is being provided, it is agreed that as lead professional, you will visit the nursery and

Pat on alternate weeks to co-ordinate the delivery of the agreed actions and maintain communication between the family and practitioners.

■ A review meeting is arranged for eight weeks. The meeting will be attended by the clinical nurse specialist, community team nursery nurse and Carl's key worker from nursery.

Activity (part D) Taking a lead

Read the extract below that provides an overview of the meeting that was held as planned after eight weeks of intervention. As you read think about how the situation has changed since you were first asked to see Carl (part A) and consider the following:

■ *How has the role of lead professional helped the family?*
■ *Identify the skills used by the lead professional that have led to more efficiency and effectiveness in this case.*

Carl had completed the additional tests organised by the neurologist. The clinical nurse specialist had met with the nursery staff and they had completed daily record sheets to details Carl's level of concentration and note any incidents that had occurred. This information, along with the results from Carl's tests, had informed the review of his medication. Over the past two weeks his nursery key worker had seen an increase in his level of concentration and there had been some very positive examples of Carl interacting with other children. The nursery practitioners had also been using behaviour intervention strategies suggested by the clinical nurse specialist and behaviour support worker (lead professional). The nursery reported that they had found the meeting where these strategies had been devised helpful as it had enabled them to ensure a consistent approach when interacting with Carl. The community team nursery nurse also used the same strategies when visiting Carl at home. Pat, his mum, reported that this had been really useful as it had given her and his dad a consistent approach to use. This had helped relationships all round at home and things were very positive. It was agreed that no further input was needed from the community nursery nurse. The speech therapist had completed the assessment and no issues were identified. It was agreed that it would be helpful to have another meeting in four weeks with the nursery key worker, Pat, the clinical nurse specialist and behaviour worker. If at the next meeting there were no new issues, it was likely that no additional support would be needed from the behaviour support service.

The final account in this activity demonstrates the impact that the policy of having a lead professional can have in practice. Clearly, these accounts present one scenario involving a lead professional but it is important to remember that the role can differ significantly depending on the additional needs the child and/or family have. Whatever the context, to be effective a lead professional will benefit from having a range if skills, including:

- strong communication skills;

- diplomacy;

- the ability to respond sensitively;

- successful at building trustful relationships with children, families and colleagues;

- able to empower children and families;

- confidence to challenge decisions where necessary;

- able to work in partnership with colleagues from different professional backgrounds;

- able to organise and initiate discussions to identify and resolve identified needs;

- knowledge of local and regional services for children and families;

- aware of own skills and working boundaries and those of other practitioners.

(HM Government, 2006b)

Some children, as is the case in these scenarios, may have a key worker. The key worker may also take on the role of lead professional but this should be considered rather than expected. Another consideration is whether at times it may be more efficient to change the lead professional, such as during a transition time. However, as with many policies, the success of the lead practitioner role is likely to depend on a number of other factors. There will need to be:

- acceptance and buy in from all practitioners in the locality;

- appropriate support and training;

- time allocated to enable the role to develop;

- a genuine desire and commitment to work in an integrated way.

The key consideration is what is likely to lead to continuity of support for the child and/or family (INTEC, 2005). The factors outlined from Brandon *et al.* (2006b) in the table above that help or hinder the implementation of the CAF can also be applied to the lead practitioner role and support the points detailed above.

Information-sharing

Whatever system is in place for gaining and holding information to enable children and families to gain effective support, the sharing of information in an appropriate way and ensuring it is accurate and up to date is a significant challenge. As discussed in Chapter 2, failings in information-sharing were often at the heart of past failings in service provision, many of which resulted in fatal outcomes for children. In response to this the government have invested time and effort to develop more effective processes for the sharing of information.

There are three key elements to this: how information will be stored; how it will be shared and the role of practitioners and what they are able to share. Again, the driving force behind this is the challenge of creating services that follow the child and/or family, rather than professionals or organisations (DfES/DH, 2006). As discussed, there is an intention to develop a national database to hold identifying information on every child, their carer and any services that are involved. There is often anxiety around information-sharing and this is usually related to confidentiality. In response to this the government have produced guidance to provide practitioners with advice on when and how information can be shared. This includes advice about the legal issues as there is a range of legislation and conventions, such as the Children and Childcare Acts, UNCRC and Data Protection, that will need to be considered.

One of the challenges that practitioners may face is finding out whether a Common Assessment has previously been completed. If the approach described above, which explains the purpose of the assessment and fully involves family members is followed, this should mean that families are clear when a Common Assessment has been completed. In the future there are plans for this information to be recorded and available through ContactPoint, which was previously known under the working title of the Information-Sharing Index (ECM, 2007).

In addition to these broad issues, Beaumont (2005) emphasises that records are an important aspect of service provision and user experience and a vital communication tool. The idea of information-sharing could also contribute to developing trust between practitioners, which is vital for integrated working. But there are a number of areas, technology and procedures aside, that will need careful consideration for this to be successful. With increased sharing this raises the issue of relationships between practitioners and service users. For effective sharing, information will have to be recorded in a way that is understood by all involved parties. This will need a commitment from practitioners to avoid the use of jargon wherever possible and to provide opportunities for others to raise questions about anything that is not understood in the recorded information.

Another potential concern is that with an increased emphasis on sharing information it could actually lead to less being shared. Two potential reasons for this are that practitioners may omit information because of concern about upsetting parents and secondly, more information could be held on records of individual services due to concern about judgements being made by other practitioners about decisions and actions. As with the other initiatives that have been discussed, a supportive, open and 'blame avoidance' culture will need to assured. It this approach is fostered within services it has the potential to lead to innovative approaches in assessment and service provision.

Reflection point **A joined-up response**

Think about what you have just read about the CAF, lead practitioner and information-sharing. Consider how each links with the other and the potential the three developments have to integrate working among different groups of practitioners.

Conclusion

Although the Common Assessment Framework, lead practitioner role and information-sharing have been discussed separately in this chapter, this is simply for manageability and clarity. In practice, there are clear links between them. The Common Assessment Framework, lead professional role and effective sharing of information together offer practitioners a shared approach to understand, plan, implement and evaluate the success of interventions to meet the identified needs of children and/or families. To have the impact that is intended though there will need to be continued confidence and enthusiasm from practitioners if turning policy aspirations into practice is to become a reality. To achieve this aim, practitioners need to be supported by good leadership, access to appropriate training and development, clear communication, a problem-solving approach to issues that arise and encouragement to try new approaches to practice. The three key issues discussed in this chapter are still at an early stage of development and it is not yet possible to know the full impact they will have in practice. This impact will also be influenced by the planned developments in these areas, particularly the work on information-sharing, which is an area that is still causing concern. If these initiatives are to bring more consistency to working practices and create integrated and seamless services, the expectations on new developments must remain high.

Developing the workforce to meet the challenge of integrated working

Introduction

From the previous chapters it will be clear that services for children and families are in the process of fundamental change. In addition to impacting on the way government, local authorities and services are organised and function this change has brought a substantial level of change to the workforce. Many of the targets set out in policies, such as the government's response to the workforce consultation exercise (HM Government, 2006a); confirm that the pace of this change will continue. Although it is not possible to be certain the exact path this will take the next decade, it can be said with a high degree of certainty that the children's workforce will look substantially different by 2015. When the idea of integrated working is discussed it may initially seem that although there will be some change for practitioners, the majority will fall to service organisation and service providers (particularly managers). Historically this was often the case, but current and proposed changes are likely to have the most significant impact on the workforce – practitioners who deliver services on a day-to-day basis. This will provide both challenges and opportunities to practitioners across the whole workforce. The main areas of change for the workforce are around capacity, modernisation and skills development. This chapter explores some of these proposed changes and critically discusses the potential benefits and challenges that will come from this change programme for practitioners. As part of the discussion, this chapter raises the question: if the aim is to develop a world-class workforce for the child and family sector, do current structures and organisation of services have the potential to achieve this ambition?

At the end of this chapter, the reader should have achieved the following outcomes:

- have an understanding of the key changes that are taking place to develop the workforce;

- considered how the current approaches and planned developments could contribute to develop a world-class workforce.

Skills development

As part of the commitment to modernise the child and family workforce it is recognised that there needs to be a more coherent approach to develop, utilise and recognise the skills of practitioners. One of the difficulties that has always existed in the early years workforce is the vast range of qualifications that practitioners can hold (Johnson *et al.*, 2006). This is particularly problematic when aiming to bring greater alignment to qualification structures between sectors. In response to this the government has signalled their intention to create an Integrated Qualifications Framework (IQF) by 2010. In addition to making qualifications more transparent to employers and raising the quality of services, it is intended that the framework will raise the profile and status of practitioners as it will recognise their skills, knowledge and experience and open opportunities for mobility and progression across a range of services. The proposed framework will have eight levels, which will include higher education awards and professional qualifications and will be designed to allow both horizontal and vertical career progression. Ultimately it will aim to give guidance to practitioners who are planning their career pathway. It will enable practitioners to move to work in others areas, whilst recognising their past experience and identifying what additional training may be needed (CWDC, 2006b).

This is clearly a welcome step forward, as in the past practitioners have faced substantial difficulties in having qualifications from one awarding body accepted by others in terms of equivalency or to enable progression onto further training. If the aim of establishing a world-class workforce is to be realised, this is a central issue that must be addressed. However, as with other developments, there are a number of challenges that will need to be overcome, and there is yet to be substantial discussion of these. Throughout the NHS all practitioners and support staff (apart from doctors and dentists) have recently had their roles evaluated to move towards an integrated pay framework, Agenda for Change. Linked with this process, there has been a matching of knowledge and skills of each employee to bring closer integration between continuing professional development and career progression. For an organisation the size of the NHS, this has been a formidable task. It is undoubtedly encouraging for the child and family workforce that through this process, albeit at a much greater cost than initially envisaged and in a much longer timescale, that the planned changes through the IQF can be achieved. However, there will need to be careful thought and considerable time put into this process as initial good intentions do not ensure the delivery of a good outcome.

To illustrate this it will be useful to reflect on two examples of past changes linked to qualifications, career development and progression. For nurses and midwives, before Agenda for Change was introduced, the vast majority had their roles determined by a grading system. The majority of practitioners were graded between A (e.g. a support worker) and G (e.g. an experienced community midwife). When grading was introduced the majority of roles started to link the amount of experience in one area to the grade attached to it. So if a school nurse wanted to move into a health promotion manager role she may not have been deemed suitable because she would not have been able to meet the criteria that asked for three years' health promotion experience. A negative result of this was that practitioners often had a broad range of skills and knowledge in one area, and even if this would have been a significant advantage in another area, they were often prevented from transferring to that area on the same grade because their experience was seen in a narrowly defined way. For many practitioners this had the unintended affect of limiting career progression.

Over the past years, there has been a large increase in the number of graduates from (Early) Childhood Studies degrees entering the workforce. There is clear evidence of the benefits of this for children and families in terms of improved standards of provision and outcomes for children (Sylva *et al.*, 2004). However, for those graduates who had entered the degree with non-vocational based qualifications (e.g. AS/A levels), many found themselves in the position of being told that they were not able to work unsupervised with children as they did not have a practitioner-based qualification at level three or above. In response to this many of the degree programmes added a 'practitioner option', which generally required students to produce a portfolio of evidence to show practical and theoretical knowledge. This evidence had to cover a range of areas, such as child development, working with parents and safeguarding children and when this is evidenced to the expected standard the student would gain practitioner recognition. On the surface this seems both desirable and sensible. To achieve this in many contexts, the undergraduates did not have to undertake any additional work or placement days – it was simply based on the work that they were already covering, but to meet the criteria they had to present it in a different format. Again this is a clear example of what in many ways is no more than a bureaucratic process that does not give adequate recognition of one form of skills and experience to meet a requirement imposed by Ofsted as the regulatory body. For the child and family workforce, as long as there continues to be a vast number of roles and qualifications, it is this type of complexity that will need to be adequately addressed if the aims of the framework are to be realised.

Common core of skills and knowledge

The common core sets out the skills and knowledge that practitioners in the children's workforce need to work effectively with children and families (HM Government, 2006c). The framework is organised around a common set of values and there are clear links with many other frameworks, policies and legislation produced around the ECM agenda:

- equality;
- respect diversity;
- challenge stereotypes;
- improve life chances;
- provide more effective and integrated services.

There are six areas of expertise for practice at a basic level that all practitioners, across disciplinary backgrounds, will be expected to have:

- effective communication and engagement;
- child and young person development;
- safeguarding and promoting the welfare of the child;
- supporting transitions;
- multi-agency working;
- sharing information.

This range of skills will support practitioners to work in partnership with children and families to achieve the outcomes outlined in ECM, develop strategies for integrated working and to promote engagement with the new roles and assessment. The aim of developing a common core of skills among the diverse children's workforce has the potential to assist practitioners to work in an integrated way and promote interdisciplinary dialogue. Across the United Kingdom this will be easier to monitor and achieve in some areas than in others. For practitioners working in professional roles, it is likely that they will possess many of the skills at the intended level. For others, such as those working in support roles and without formal qualifications, this may take longer to achieve. Another issue is linked to consistency among the workforce and the skills required to carry out roles in the different countries of the United Kingdom. For example, there is a common nursing curricular across the four countries of the United Kingdom but child protection arrangements are different. Therefore, the core skills will assist practitioners to carry out the broad aspects of a role but regional differences may mean that other skills are required in addition and it will be important that this is taken into account.

Capacity

The children's workforce covers a range of areas, including early years, social care, foster care, schools, health services, youth services and the voluntary sector. Over the past years there has been a significant increase in the number of practitioners within the child and family workforce. Many of these additional practitioners work within private sector nurseries and in support roles in schools. A key challenge for the future will be around recruiting and retaining the required number of practitioners. One of the most dominant professional groups within the workforce has been teachers. Over the past years significant challenges have been placed on teachers to raise the standard of literacy and numeracy skills for all children, based on the premise that a successful educational experience would offer all children the best chance to achieve their potential and enhance their quality of life in both the short and long term. To develop a highly skilled workforce, care will be needed to ensure that all practitioners feel valued and there is no sense of hierarchy, either actual or perceived, where one professional group is seen as more important than another.

As services are being developed there are going to be substantial changes to roles within the workforce and more team-working across disciplines. A key issue though is not just about increasing capacity, but about ensuring that the people in roles have the skills expected of them. For example, with the increased emphasis on providing effective support for children's mental and emotional well-being, practitioners, who may not have specific training in this area, will need to be addressed (BMA, 2006).

As the move to integrated working has gathered momentum a key challenge has developed around pay and conditions. This is an issue for both professional and support staff within the workforce. As new roles have emerged, such as leading co-ordinated teams for family support or a management role within children's centres, certain groups have been disadvantaged because of issues linked to pay and conditions. For example, there has been a desire among Children's Trusts, in the move to establish interdisciplinary teams, to include teachers. Often this has not been possible because to recruit teachers at their current pay scale is generally prohibitive as they are paid more than a number of other professional groups.

Another important way to increase capacity is to enhance retention. The emphasis on skills development and a co-ordinated qualification framework

Practice example

Pen Green

Whalley (2001) acknowledged that one of the difficult issues in integrating staff from different practice backgrounds in the early days of Pen Green was the different terms, conditions and pay they were used to. National pay scales, terms and conditions meant that it was difficult to offer staff the same package, as some staff e.g. teachers, were on different pay scales, working hours and leave entitlements to early years practitioners, social workers and so on.

will help to address the capacity challenge. However, in the short to medium term, as the emphasis on developing the skill base of practitioners already within the workforce is achieved, there is a clear need for a review. To achieve sustained development this will need to be wide ranging and include remuneration, leave, working arrangements and access to development to support the move towards integrated working.

Modernisation

The Children's Workforce Network and Children's Workforce Development Council (CWDC), as detailed in Figure 6.1, work with government to recruit and retain a skilled workforce, strengthen integrated working and improve leadership and management. As stated earlier, over recent years there has been a significant increase in the number of graduates working within early years and there is a desire, through the establishment of a large network of children's centres, to increase this further as there is a clear correlation between the level of qualifications that practitioners hold and outcomes for children (Sylva *et al.*, 2004). The case for having practitioners who are well qualified is emphasised with the statutory introduction of the Early Years Foundation Framework (EYFS) framework from 2008 (DfES, 2007b). The framework will combine best practice from Birth to Three Matters and the Curriculum Guidance for the Foundation Stage to have an approach that combines care and learning for children up to 5. This will mean that there will be statutory duties on early years settings, from the private, voluntary and maintained sector, to deliver the framework. This presents a significant challenge for the early years sector as it is combined with the expectation that all early years practitioners will be working

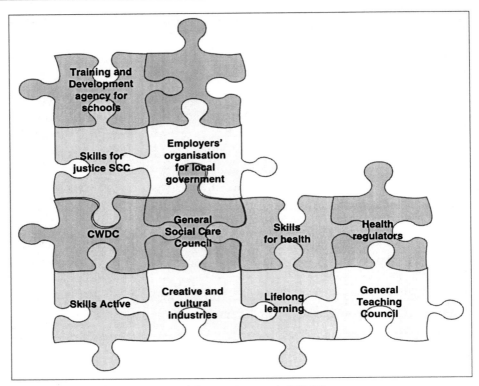

Figure 6.1 Children's Workforce Network (CWN)
(adapted from HM Government, 2006a)

to a minimum level three qualification. At present a large number of practitioners have qualifications below this level.

Recent developments have introduced new roles and qualifications to the early years sector and there is discussion about changes needed to the training and boundaries of other roles. As from 2007 practitioners with Early Years Professional status have been employed in early years settings. These professionals are deemed to have equivalency with qualified teachers (QTS). To gain the qualification, practitioners with a suitable level of experience with children from 0 to 5 years old, follow a programme of training followed by a validation process to ensure that the standards required for completion have been achieved (CWDC, 2006a). A leadership training programme and postgraduate qualification – National Professional Qualification for Integrated Children's Centre Leadership (NPQICL) – was introduced. This development was initially aimed at children's centres managers and then for roll out to management and leadership positions across the early education and care sector. These are extremely positive developments, but two significant issues need addressing at a national level to achieve the desired aim of having practitioners with these qualifications in all early years settings. As discussed in Chapter 3, there are many private and voluntary settings that provide care and education for children. Over the past years the expectations on these settings, to provide high quality education and care and meet nationally imposed standards, has increased. This is clearly a positive move but a consequence is that costs to providers have increased and in competitive markets, even with government subsidies, this has led to significant numbers of practitioners being employed, often paid at or slightly over the minimum hourly wage. Market reality dictates that independent (and often voluntary) providers have no option but to at least break even and ideally produce a surplus. Consequently, even with financial support from the government, given the uncertainty associated with numbers and how long funding will continue, it remains to be seen how practitioners holding these professional qualifications will permeate the private and voluntary sector between 2010 and 2015.

The social care workforce is integral to delivering the five ECM outcomes and through the *Options for Excellence* review outlined its aims to improve the status of the social care workforce, improve the public profile of social care and provide better training opportunities to raise the skill level of the workforce. This has increased the number of trainees on social work degree courses and saw a rise of over a fifth in the number of people registered on care sector NVQs. The long-term vision for 2020 is for practitioners to be highly skilled and working to the social model of care, which places the service user at the centre and views barriers as societal issues. There is also a commitment to look at the role of the social worker and other social care practitioners to see how changes and enhancements can be made to help achieve the long-term vision (DfES/DH, 2006) Again, these are positive and welcome developments, but even though the review has consulted many in the organisation that makes up the CWN, it has not seized the opportunity for a fundamental review with all partners that make up the CWN.

Making fundamental changes to achieve a fundamental difference

As stated in Chapter 1, there has been ongoing discussion about the approaches taken to the organisation of child and family services, and the approach to training practitioners. This has taken place hand-in-hand with investment and partial reform of the roles practitioners hold in the sector. Claims are often made that we are in the 'most radical period of reform ever seen in the provision of services for children and families'. A perusal of the myriad of government legislation, non–statutory guidance, case studies, reviews and information on the DfES, SureStart, CWDC and Every Child Matters websites would certainly support the statement above. However, is the present activity as radical as this information suggests and importantly is it going to enable the goal of creating a world–class workforce to become a reality?

Activity — **Where we are, where we want to be, how to get there**

As you read through the preceding chapters a broad range of issues have been discussed around the move towards more integrated and multi-agency working. This has included: how central government actions impact on the style and form of services; how past failings in service provision, some of which have led to enquiries, have brought about a shift; how there can be barriers, at a number of levels, that impact on the successfulness of change. And this can be seen as culminating in the key challenge – how practitioners turn the expectations of policy and legislation into practice. Think about these points and the proposed changes that have been discussed in this chapter in your response to the following questions:

1 In what way does the organisation of government central departments, CSAs and professional training (e.g. social work, nursing, physiotherapy and teaching) help or hinder the proposed changes to the workforce?

2 Think about a speech and language therapist, manger of a private nursery and a social worker. How is each of these of practitioners generally thought about? Do you think that one is seen as making a greater contribution than the other? If so, how might this impact on the potential to develop an integrated and world class workforce?

3 Do you think there are equal opportunities for continuing professional development for all practitioners within the workforce? If not, are there any groups whom you think have particularly good or particularly poor access to professional development?

4 Are the current approaches to training practitioners (e.g. nurses, social workers, teachers, nursery nurses, early years professionals) likely to help achieve the aim of developing a world-class workforce?

5 Is the level of reward (pay, leave entitlement, access to development and training, working patterns and work/life balance) an important determining factor in achieving a modern and integrated workforce? Why?

6 If you were giving the task of making five recommendations to government to achieve a world-class workforce, what would they be and why?

To help evaluate how effective the changes are that have taken place and that are continuing to happen, it can be helpful to look at practice and organisation in other European countries. Throughout Europe, many countries have a significant level of investment in early childhood education and care and it is possible to see how some of the changes in the UK are beginning to reflect aspects of organisation and practice in Europe. A permeating feature in many European countries, which does not apply in the UK, is the role of pedagogues in service provision (OECD, 2006). The pedagogical approach is based on seeing each child as a complex being with a vast potential for development. To help children achieve this, pedagogues receive theoretical and practical training to support children to achieve their full potential by promoting social, emotional, health and educational development. The role of the pedagogue first developed in Germany. Pedagogues work in a variety of early childhood settings in partnership with parents and work in a way that combines social care and education. Across Europe there are different levels of training, usually requiring from three to five years' education at vocational colleges and university (CWDC, 2007). To explore this further and help analyse the developments in the UK it is helpful to look at some specific European approaches.

In Denmark, services for children are an integral part of the social welfare system, headed through two ministries: the Ministry for Family and Ministry for Education. The pedagogue role is widespread in early education and care services and there is a requirement that all managers and deputies in childcare settings are qualified pedagogues. There are two types of pedagogue, educational and leisure. Levels of pay for pedagogues and other practitioners are good. A single curriculum framework is used by practitioners to support the development of children. In Sweden, pedagogues are widespread and interestingly the training for pedagogues and teachers is very similar, with each following a programme based around psycho–pedagogical training. In addition to pedagogues, services employ childcare assistants, who receive three years' training. All children from the age of 1 have a right to pre-school education and all centres have a director and educational pedagogues. Overall there is a significant investment in training, with 98 per cent of practitioners trained to work with children. In contrast, Austria has a lower level of uptake for daycare and this means settings have more mixed age groups. The national approach to service provision is delivered through a ministry that covers maternal, infant and youth welfare. All practitioners who work with children are expected to have a good level of education and over 60 per cent of staff have a professional diploma. The pedagogue model is used and to qualify requires five years' training. Some pedagogues work with specific groups, such as children with special educational needs, which requires additional training (OECD, 2006).

Boddy *et al.* (2005) argue that to meet the government's vision of an integrated workforce in child and family services, the UK needs two generic workers and the pedagogue role offers a framework to develop this. This is supported by the model of working that pedagogues utilise, which takes a holistic view and works with children and families in a collaborative way across traditional disciplinary boundaries. They argue for the introduction of a pedagogue and pedagogue assistant role. All pedagogues would be graduates and have training incorporating leadership and management and assistants would be trained to at least level three (BTEC/Diploma standard) and approximately an equal ratio of each would be appropriate. Pedagogues and assistants would work across education, children's services, residential and social care and this would promote integrated and collaborative working. It is acknowledged that this would require a radical shift and this would bring challenges. For example, relationships between the roles and established professions, career progression and pay and conditions would need to be addressed. Aspects of these approaches are clearly more evident in some of the developments seen in the sector and it is important not to assume that simply mirroring structures that are successful in other countries will be right for the UK. However, it is possible to draw out some key issues from the discussion that have relevance to the drive for workforce development in the UK:

■ There is a push for more and more integration at local level, but there are still a number of central government departments that fund and contribute to the organisation of children's services. The introduction of the Sure Start Unit has achieved a more co-ordinated response but from this other bodies, such as those that make up the CWN, have been established. To achieve integration at a local level a more integrated approach at national level, for example through a Ministry for the Family, has the potential for significant benefits by offering direction in an integrated and co-ordinated way.

■ A number of developments have occurred in training but there are still clear boundaries between different professions. To embed an integrated approach as the universal standard, providing a common foundation across professional boundaries followed by pathways geared towards specific routes would allow a common core of skills and specific professional requirements to be part of all training. This approach would also fit well with introduction of the pedagogue role and facilitate movement across professional boundaries. There would need to be careful consideration of the core curriculum to ensure that relevant professional body requirements were addressed but this could also promote a deep and meaningful level of dialogue between the professional bodies to undertake a fundamental review of the skills, knowledge and competencies (many of which will be common across professions) needed to function effectively.

- The current approach to service delivery is about integration, information-sharing and working across traditional professional boundaries. A fundamental question emerges from this: why continue to train professionals in all of the traditional roles? There will undoubtedly be a need for specific roles but past approaches should inform, rather than continue to dominate, the roles needed to achieve current aspirations.

- A fundamental concern in the UK is the low value that is often attached to early childhood and education services. It is not uncommon to find that practitioners with lower levels of qualifications work with the youngest children. This does not value children as it should and does not provide the opportunity to develop the skills of those working in these services to the full. The IQF and workforce review are a good start in addressing these issues, but to address the longstanding view of caring roles not being valued, this will need to go hand–in–hand with a complete review and reward package that aligns new responsibilities and roles with appropriate remuneration.

- Since 1997 there has been a significant level of funding injected into child and family services. However, much of this funding has been targeted at specific areas, has only been guaranteed for short periods of time or tied to a raft of targets. An example of this is the recent transformation fund that was targeted at enhancing the skill level of the early childhood workforce. However, there was a requirement to spend much of this money very quickly and it was only initially guaranteed for two years, which makes forward planning difficult. It is clearly right that public money comes with accountability, but a coherent and consistent funding stream, which allows each local area to decide on their priorities, has the potential to deliver and achieve more within current funding levels. There could then be an expectation on local services to justify their decisions to contribute to a broad aim, such as the government commitment to reduce child poverty.

Conclusion

This chapter has outlined the key changes that are taking place within the workforce. There is currently more effort to bring a coherent approach to early childcare and education services then at any time in the recent past. The developments that are planned to raise the skill level of the workforce, develop an integrated approach to qualifications and enhance the professional standing of the sector are extremely positive. However, there are a number of fundamental issues that remain, which have the potential to impact on the aim of achieving a world-class workforce in the child and family sector. A number of key issues have been outlined that would undoubtedly place significant short-term challenges for the sector as a whole. The path that these changes would lead the sector has already been partly travelled, but with many services and organisations walking in the same direction on different pathways. Therefore, this highlights that rather than a change of direction, the challenge ahead is to combine investment and efforts to travel together on one path. If this challenge is seized it has the potential to reach the desired destination – a truly world-class workforce.

Recommended reading

Anning, A., Cottrell, D., Frost, N., Green, J. and Robinson, M. (2006) *Developing Multiprofessional Teamwork for Integrated Children's Services*. Maidenhead, Berkshire: Open University Press

Reports and discusses a range of issues from an in-depth research study of working in multiprofessional teams from the perspective of service providers

Baldock, P., Fitzgerald, D. and Kay, J. (2005) *Understanding Early Years Policy*. London: Paul Chapman

Provides a useful overview of policy in child and family services and gives the context for many current approaches to multi-agency working

Department of Health (2004a) *National Service Framework: Children, Young People and Maternity services*. [online] Last accessed 15 March 2007 at URL: http://www.dh.gov.uk/en/Publicationsandstatistics/Publications/ PublicationsPolicyAndGuidance/DH_4089100

Outlines government position and aspirations for developing responsive and effective services to support children's development

HM Government (2006a) *Children's Workforce Strategy: Building a world-class workforce for children, young people and families. The Government response to the consultation.* London: DfES

Provides an overview of government aspirations for developing the children's workforce

In addition there are a number of informative web-based resources that will provide useful background information and an overview of recent developments from reliable sources, including:

Children's Workforce Development Council
Department for Children, Schools and Families
Department of Health
National Children's Bureau
Office of the Children's Commission (separate sites for each country of the United Kingdom)
OfSTED
SureStart

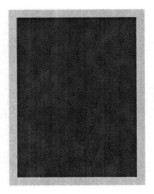

References

Abbott, D., Townsely, R. and Watson, D. (2005) 'Multi-agency working in services for disabled children: what impact does it have on professionals?', *Health and Social Care in the Community*, 13, pp. 155–63

Acheson, D. (1998) *Independent Inquiry into Inequalities in Health*. London: The Stationery Office

Action for Sick Children (2007) [online]. Last accessed 14 February 2007 at URL: http://www.actionforsickchildren.org/

Adams, K.S. and Christenson, S.L. (2000) 'Trust and family–school relationship. Examination of parent–teacher differences in elementary and secondary grades', *Journal of School Psychology*, 38, 5, pp. 477–97

Anderson, R., Brown, I., Clayton, R., Dowty, T., Korff, D. and Munro, E. (2006) *Children's Databases: Safety and Privacy*. Foundation for Information Policy Research [online]. Last accessed 5 March 2007 at URL: http://www.fipr.org/childrens_databases.pdf

Anning, A., Cottrell, D., Frost, N., Green, J. and Robinson, M. (2006) *Developing Multiprofessional Teamwork for Integrated Children's Services*. Maidenhead, Berkshire: Open University Press

Bachmann, M., Husbands, C. and O'Brien, M. (2006) *National Evaluation of Children's Trusts: Managing Change for Children through Children's Trusts*. Norwich: University of East Anglia/National Children's Bureau

Baldock, P. (2001) *Regulating Early Years Services*. London: David Fulton

Baldock, P., Fitzgerald, D. and Kay, J. (2005) *Understanding Early Years Policy*. London: Paul Chapman

Batty, D. (2003) 'Dying in vain', *Guardian*, 23 January 2003

Bawden, A. (2007) 'Together we can do this', *Guardian*, 16 January 2007 [online]. Last accessed 8 March 2007 at URL: http://education.guardian.co.uk/egweekly/story/0,,1990762,00.html

Beaumont, D. (2005) 'Developing a combined baby record: using clinical governance to overcome the barriers', *Journal of Neonatal Nursing*, 11, pp. 22–7

Bertram, T., Pascal, C., Bokhari, S., Gosper, M., Hakerman, S., John, K. and Nelson, C. (2002) *Early Excellence Pilot Project Third Annual Evaluation Report 2001–2*. London: DfES/HMSO

Boddy, J., Cameron, C., Moss, P., Mooney, A., Petrie, P. and Stratham, J. (2005) *Introducing Pedagogy into the Children's Workforce (Children's Workforce Strategy: A Response to the Consultation Document)*. London: Thomas Coram Research Unit

Brandon, M., Salter, C., Warren, C., Dagely, V., Howe, A. and Black, J. (2006a) *Evaluating the Common Assessment Framework and Lead Professional Guidance and Implementation in 2005–6*. Research Brief RB740 April 2006. Annesley, Notts.: DfES Publications

Brandon, M., Howe, A., Dagley, V., Salter, C. and Warren, C. (2006b) 'What appears to be helping or hindering practitioners in implementing the Common Assessment Framework and Lead Professional Working?', *Child Abuse Review*, 15, pp. 396–413

Brent Borough Council (1985) *A Child in Trust – The Report Of The Panel Of Inquiry Into The Circumstances Surrounding The Death of Jasmine Beckford*. London: HMSO

Brindle, D. (2004) 'Clash of cultures', *Guardian*, 19 May 2004

British Medical Association (BMA) (2006) *Child and Adolescent Mental Health – A Guide for Healthcare Professionals* [online]. Last accessed 15 March 2007 at URL: http://web.bma.org.uk/ap.nsf/Content/Childadolescentmentalhealth~Multiagency

Brown, K. and White, K. (2006) *Exploring the Evidence Base for Integrated Children's Services* [online]. Last accessed 4 March 2007 at URL: http://www.scotland.gov.uk/Publications/2006/01/24120649/1

Bruce, T. and Meggitt, C. (2002) *Child Care and Education* (3rd edition). London: Hodder and Stoughton

Bryant, B., Harris, M. and Newton, D. (1984) *Children and Minders*. Oxford: Grant McIntyre

Bryson, J. M., Crosby, B. C. and Middleton Stone, M. (2006) 'The design and implementation of cross-sector collaborations: propositions from the literature', *Public Administration Review*, 66, S1, pp. 44–55

Cameron, C. (2003) 'An historical perspective on changing child care policy', in Brannen, J. and Moss, P. (eds) *Rethinking Children's Care*. Buckingham: Open University Press

Chalmers, H. and Aggleton, P. (2003) 'Promoting children's health through health care: a rights based approach', in Brannen, J. and Moss, P. (eds) *Rethinking Children's Care*. Buckingham: Open University Press, pp. 146–62

Chandler, T. (2006) 'Working in multi-disciplinary teams', in Pugh, G. and Duffy, B. (eds) *Contemporary Issues in the Early Years* (4th edition), London: Sage

Children1st (2006) *History* [online]. Last accessed 17 January 2007 at URL: http://www.justgiving.com/charity/history.asp?FRSId=11971

Cleveland Inquiry (1988) *Report of the Inquiry into Child Abuse in Cleveland 1987*. London: HMSO

Cummings, C., Todd, L. and Dyson, A. (2004) *Evaluation of the Extended Schools Pathfinder Projects*. London: Department for Education and Skills [online]. Last accessed 6 March 2007 at URL: http://www.dfes.gov.uk/research/data/uploadfiles/RR530.pdf

CWDC (Children's Workforce Development Council) (2006a) *Early Years Professional National Standards*. Leeds: CWDC

CWDC (Children's Workforce Development Council) (2006b) *Clear Progression: Towards an Integrated Qualifications Framework*. Leeds: CWDC

CWDC (Children's Workforce Development Council) (2007) *Background to Pedagogues* [online]. Last accessed 22 February 2007 at URL: http://cwdcouncil.org.uk/projects/pedagogues.htm

Dali, C. (2002) 'From home to childcare: challenges for mothers, teachers and children', in Fabian, H. and Dunlop, A. (eds) *Transitions in the Early Years: Debating Continuity and Progression for Young Children in Early Education*. London: RoutledgeFalmer, pp. 38–51

Day, C., Hall, C. and Whittaker, P. (1998) *Developing Leadership in Primary Schools*. London: Paul Chapman

Department for Education and Employment (1998) *Meeting the Childcare Challenge*. Sudbury, Suffolk: DFEE Publications

Department of Education and Science (1967) *Children and their Primary Schools* ('The Plowden Report'). London: HMSO

Department for Education and Skills (2002) *Early Excellence Centre Pilot Project: Third Annual Evaluation Report 2001–2* [online]. Last accessed 10 March 2007 at URL: http://www.surestart.gov.uk/doc/P0001373.doc

Department for Education and Skills (2004) *Healthy Living Blueprint for Schools* [online]. Last accessed 13 March 2007 at URL: http://www.publications.teachernet.gov.uk/default.aspx?PageFunction=product details&PageMode=publications&ProductId=DfES+0781+2004

Department for Education and Skills (2005) *National Evaluation of Children's Trusts: Realising Children's Trust Arrangements* [online]. Last accessed 1 March 2007 at URL: http://www.everychildmatters.gov.uk/_files/7AA130FBC3F2D0C8A2226426243AC0C7.doc

Department for Education and Skills (2006a) *National Evaluation of Children's Trusts* [online]. Last accessed 8 March 2007 at URL: http://www.everychildmatters.gov.uk/strategy/childrenstrustpathfinders/nationalevaluation/

Department for Education and Skills (2006b) *Fact Sheet: The Lead Professional*. Last accessed 1 March 2007 at URL: http://www.everychildmatters.gov.uk/resources-and-practice/IG00018/

Department for Education and Skills (2007a) *Quality Protects* [online]. Last accessed 7 February 2007 at URL:http://www.dfes.gov.uk/qualityprotects

Department for Education and Skills (2007b) *Statutory Framework for the Early Years Foundation Stage*. Nottingham: DfES

Department for Education and Skills/Department of Health (2004) *Every Child Matters: Change for Children in Health Services*. London: DfES/DoH

Department for Education and Skills/Department of Health (2006) *Options for Excellence: Building the Social Care Workforce of the Future*. COI

Department of Health and Social Security (1976) *Fit for the Future: The Report of the Committee on Child Health Services*. Volume One. London: HMSO

Department of Health and Social Security (1982) *Child Abuse: A Study of Enquiry Reports 1973–1981*. London: HMSO

Department of Health (1989) *Children Act, 1989.* London: HMSO

Department of Health (1991) *Child Abuse: A Study of Inquiry Reports 1980–1989.* London: HMSO

Department of Health (1991) *Working Together Under the Children Act.* London: HMSO

Department of Health (1999) *Working Together to Safeguard Children.* London: HMSO

Department of Health (2000) *Framework of Assessment for Children in Need and their Families.* London: HMSO

Department of Health (2003) *Tackling Health Inequalities: A Programme for Action* [online]. Last accessed 15 March 2007 at URL: http://www.dh.gov.uk/en/ Publication-sandstatistics/Publications/PublicationsPolicyAndGuidance/ DH_4008268

Department of Health (2004a) *National Service Framework: Children, Young People and Maternity services* [online]. Last accessed 15 March 2007 at URL: http://www.dh.gov.uk/en/Publicationsandstatistics/Publications/ PublicationsPolicyAndGuidance/DH_4089100

Department of Health (2004b) *The NHS Improvement Plan: Putting People at the Heart of Public Services.* London: HMSO

Department of Health (2006) *Extended Schools and Health Services Working Together for Better Outcomes for Children and Families.* Bristol: DoH/Care Services Improvement Partnership

Department of Health and Social Security (1974) *Report of the Committee of Inquiry into the Care and Supervision Provided In Relation to Maria Colwell.* London: HMSO

Department of Health and Social Security (1980) *Inequalities in Health (the Black Report).* London: HMSO

Dunn, J. (2005) 'Daddy doesn't live here any more', *The Psychologist*, 18, 1, pp. 28–31

Editorial (to Long *et al.*) (2006) 'Standards for education and training for interagency working in child protection in the UK', *Nurse Education Today*, 26, pp. 179–82

Edwards, A. and Knight, P. (1997) 'Parents and professionals', in Cosin, B. and Hales, M. (eds) *Families, Education and School Differences.* London: Routledge

Eilbert K. W. and Lafronza, V. (2005) 'Working together for community health – a model and case studies', *Evaluation and Program Planning*, 28, 185–99

Every Child Matters (ECM) (2007) *About ContactPoint* [online]. Last accessed 8 March 2007 at URL: http://www.everychildmatters.gov.uk/ deliveringservices/contactpoint/about

Every Child Matters: Change for Children (2007) *Setting Up Multi-Agency Services* [online]. Last accessed 30 January 2007 at URL: http://www.everychildmatters. gov.uk/deliveringservices/multiagencyworking

Fitzgerald, D. (2004) *Parent Partnerships in the Early Years.* London: Continuum

Fitzgerald, D. (2007) *Coordinating Special Educational Needs: A Guide for the Early Years.* London: Continuum

Frost, N., Robinson, M. and Anning, A. (2005) 'Social workers in multidisciplinary teams: issues and dilemmas for professional practice', *Child and Family Social Work*, 10, 3, 187–96

Galilee, J. (2005) *Learning From Failure: A Review of Major Social Care / Health Inquiry Recommendations*, 21st Century Social Work [online]. Last accessed 22 January 2007 at URL: http://www.socialworkscotland.org.uk/resources/pub/ SummaryofMajorSocialWorkInquiryRecommendations.pdf

Glass, N. (1999) 'Origins of the Sure Start local programmes', *Children and Society*, 13, 257–65

Haigh, G. (2006) 'How far should schools extend?', *Times Educational Supplement*, 20 October 2006

Halsey, K., Gulliver, C., Johnson, A., Martin, K. and Kinder, K. (2006) *Evaluation of Behaviour and Education Support Teams*. London: DfES

Hampshire County Council Information Network (2007) *Social Services Committee – Special Sub-committee 16th May 1986 Item 3 A Child in Trust – Report of the Director of Social Services* [online]. Last accessed 10 January 2007 at URL: http://www.hants.gov.uk/scrmxn/m00266.html

Hanvey, C. (2003) 'The lessons we never learn', *Observer*, 26 January 2003 [online]. Last accessed 19 January 2007 at URL: http://www.observer.co.uk

Hill, M. and Tisdall, K. (1997) *Children and Society*. Harlow, Essex: Prentice Hall

HM Government (2004) *Every Child Matters: Change for Children*. London: DfES

HM Government (2005) *Common Core of Skills and Knowledge for the Children's Workforce*. DfES: Nottingham

HM Government (2006a) *Children's Workforce Strategy: Building a World-class Workforce for Children, Young People and Families. The Government Response to the Consultation*. London: DfES

HM Government (2006b) *The Lead Professional: Practitioners' Guide*. London: The Stationery Office

HM Government (2006c) *Working Together to Safeguard Children*. London: The Stationery Office

HM Government (2006d) *The Common Assessment Framework for Children and Young People: Practitioners' Guide*. London: The Stationery Office

HM Treasury (2003) *Every Child Matters (Green Paper)*. Norwich: The Stationery Office

HM Treasury (2004) *Child Poverty Review* [online]. Last accessed 12 March 2007 at URL: http://www.hm-treasury.gov.uk/spending_review/spend_sr04/ associated_documents/spending_sr04_childpoverty.cfm

Hopkins, G. (2007) *What Have We Learned? Child Death Scandals Since 1994* [online]. Last accessed on 12 March 2007 at URL: http://www.communitycare.co.uk/Articles/2007/01/11/102713/what-have-we-learned-child-death-scandals-since-1994.html

Hudson, B. (2005a) 'Information sharing and children's services reform in England: can legislation change practice', *Journal of Interprofessional Care*, 19, 6, pp. 537–46

Hudson, B. (2005b) 'Not a cigarette paper between us: integrated inspection of children's services in England', *Social Policy and Administration*, 39, 5, pp. 513–27

Hunter, B. (2006) 'The importance of reciprocity in relationships between community-based midwives and mothers', *Midwifery*, 22, pp. 308–22

Hurst, H. (2006) 'An integrated life: creating integration from the heart out', *Integrate: The Newsletter of the British Association of Early Childhood Integration*, 7, pp. 6–7

INTEC (2005) *Lead Professional Good Practice: Guidance for Children with Additional Needs*. Cambridge: Institute of Technology Cambridge

Jackson, B. and Jackson, S. (1979) *Childminders: A Study in Action Research*. London: Routledge and Kegan Paul

Jeffree, C. and Fox, G. (1998) 'Managing self and others', in Taylor, J. and Woods, M. (eds) *Early Childhood Studies*. London: Arnold

Johnson, S., Dunn, K. and Coldron, M. (2006) *Mopping Qualifications and Training for the Children and Young People's Workforce (Report 4)*. London: DfES.

Johnson, P., Wistow, G., Rockwell, S. and Hardy, B. (2003) 'Interagency and interprofessional collaboration in community care: the independence of structures and values', *Journal of Interprofessional Care*, 17, 1, pp. 69–83

Jordan, L., Reyes-Blanes, M.E., Peel, B.B., Peel, H.A. and Lane, H.B. (1998) 'Developing teacher–parent partnerships across cultures: effective parent conferences', *Intervention in School and Clinic*, 33, 3, pp. 141–7

Kennedy, I. (2002) *Bristol Royal Infirmary Inquiry* (the Kennedy Report) [online]. Last accessed 12 March 2007 at URL: http://www.bristol-inquiry.org.uk/ final_report/report/report_footnote_info_.htm

Keyes, C. (2002) 'A way of thinking about parent/teacher partnerships for teachers', *Journal of Early Years Education*, 10, 3, pp. 177–91

Keyser, J. (2001) 'Creating partnerships with families: problem-solving through communication', *Childcare Information Exchange*, 10, 3, pp. 44–7

KPMG LLP (UK) (2007) *Evaluation of the Manageability of the Corporate Assessment and Joint Area Review Process*. London: Ofsted

Laming (2003) *Report of the Inquiry into the Death of Victoria Climbié*. London: HMSO

Larson, C.E. and LaFasto, F. (1989) *Teamwork*. London: Sage

Library Association (2007) *Early Years Advocacy Pack* [online]. Last accessed 8 February 2007 at URL: http://www.la-hq.org.uk/directory/prof_issues/early01.html

Lloyd, G., Stead, J. and Kendrick, A. (2003) 'Joined-up approaches to prevent school exclusion', *Emotional and Behavioural Difficulties*, 8, 1, pp. 77–91

Long, T., Davis, C., Johnson, M., Murphy, M., Race, D. and Shardlow, S.M. (2006) 'Standards for education and training for interagency working in child protection in the UK: Implications for nurses, midwives and health visitors', *Nurse Education Today*, 26, pp. 11–22

Marsh, C. (1994) 'People matter: the role of adults in providing a quality learning environment for the early years', in Abbott, L. and Rodger, R. (eds) *Quality Education in Early Years*. Buckingham: Open University Press

Mcwilliam, R.A., Tocci, L. and Harbin, G.L. (1998) 'Family-centered services: service providers' discourse and behaviour', *Topics in Early Childhood Special Education*, 18, 4, pp. 206–22

Ministry of Health (1959) *The Welfare of Children in Hospital* ('The Platt Report'). Central Health Services Council. London: HMSO

Mooney, A., Moss, P., and Owen, C. (2001) *A Survey of Former Childminders.* DfES Research Report RR300 Thomas Coram Research Institute, Institute of Education, University of London

Morrison, T. Lewis, D. and Howarth J. (2005) *From Area Child Protection Committee to Local Safeguarding Children Boards: An Audit and Preparation Toolkit* [online]. Last accessed 12 March 2007 at URL: http://www.rip.org.uk/publications/champions/champions seven/champions7.asp

Moss, P. (1987) *A Review of Childminder Research.* Thomas Coram Research Unit, Institute of Education, University of London

National Association of Hospital Play Staff (NAHPS) (2007) *National Association of Hospital Play Staff Milestones* [online]. Last accessed 16 February 2007 at URL: http://www.nahps.org.uk/Milestones.htm

National Audit Office (2007) *Joining Up to Improve Services* [online]. Last accessed 10 February 2007 at URL: http://www.nao.org.uk/publications/nao_reports/01–02/0102383main.pdf

National Childminding Association (2007) *NCMA History* [online]. Last accessed 16 March 2007 at URL: http//www.ncma.org.uk/#1035X0

National Council for Voluntary Youth Services (2007) *News Release 30th January 2007* [online]. Last accessed 5 March 2007 at URL: http://www.ncvys.org.uk/pdfs/News_release_talking_trusts.pdf

National Evaluation of Sure Start (NESS) (2007) [online]. Last accessed 16 March 2007 at URL: http://www.ness.bbk.ac.uk/

Ofsted (2006a) *The Annual Report of Her Majesty's Chief Inspector of Schools 2005/6.* Norwich: The Stationery Office

Ofsted (2006b) *Extended Schools: A Report on Early Developments* [online]. Last accessed 12 March 2007 at URL: http://www.ofsted.gov.uk/assets/4158.doc

Organisation for Economic Co-operation and Development (2006) *Starting Strong II: Early Childhood Education and Care.* Paris: OECD

Percy-Smith, J. (2006) 'What works in strategic partnerships for children: a research review', *Children and Society*, 20, 4

Pithouse, A. (2006) 'A common assessment for children in need? Mixed messages from a pilot study in Wales', *Child Care in Practice*, 12, 3, pp. 199–217

Plowden Report (1967) *Children and their Primary Schools (Central Advisory Council for Education).* London: HMSO

Powell, J. (2005) 'Multiprofessional perspectives', in Jones, L., Holmes, R. and Powell, J. (eds) *Early Childhood Studies: a multiprofessional perspective.* Maidenhead, Berkshire: Open University Press

QCA (Qualification and Curriculum Authority and Department for Education and Employment) (2000) *Investing in Our Future: Curriculum Guidance for the Foundation Stage.* London: QAA/DfEE

Quill, D. (2006) *Response to the DfES consultation on Budget Holding Lead Professional pilots.* Leeds: CWDC

Read, M. and Rees, M. (2000) 'Working in teams in early years settings', in Drury, R., Miller, L. and Campbell, R. (eds) *Looking at Early Years Education and Care.* London: David Fulton

Robertson, J. (1952) *A Two Year Old Goes to Hospital* (film)

Rodd, J. (1994) *Leadership in Early Childhood.* Bucksingham: Open University Press

Rodd, J. (2006) *Leadership in Early Childhood* (3rd edition). Maidenhead, Berkshire: Open University Press

Rowntree, N. (2006) *Education News: Extended schools – Support for Parents Causing Concern.* Children Now 8 November 2006 [online]. Last accessed March 12 2007 at URL: http://www.childrennow.co.uk/news/index.cfm?fuseaction=details& UID=ec1c2ebd-af87–4118-be1c–59f291defcf7

Rushmer, R. and Paliss, G. (2002) 'Inter-professional working: the wisdom of integrated working and the disaster of blurred boundaries', *Public Money and Management,* 23, 1, pp. 59–66

Ryan, M. (2006) *Safeguarding (Champion for Children Research Briefing for Councillors) Research in Practice.* October 2006 [online]. Last accessed 9 March 2007 at URL: http://www.rip.org.uk/publications/documents/champions_docs/ champions7.pdf

Schaub, A. and Altimier, L. (2006) 'Tenants of trust: building collaborative work relationships', *Newborn and Infant Nursing Reviews,* 6, 1, pp. 19–21

Schein, E. (1985) *Organizational Culture and Leadership.* San Francisco, CA: Jossey Bass

Sherif, M. (1966) *In Common Predicament: Social Psychology of Intergroup Conflict and Cooperation.* Boston: Houghton-Mifflin

Shribman, S. (2007) *Making it Better: For Children and Young People.* London: Department of Health

Sloper, P. (2004) 'Facilitators and barriers for co-ordinated multi-agency services', *Child: Care, Health and Development,* 30, pp. 571–80

Smith, A. and Langston, A. (1999) *Managing Staff in the Early Years.* London: Routledge

Smith, M. K. (2004, 2005) 'Extended schooling – some issues for informal and community education', *The Encyclopedia of Informal Education* [online]. Last accessed 6 March 2007 at URL: www.//infed.org/schooling/ extended_schooling.htm.

Smith, M., Oliver, C. and Barker, S. (1998) *Effectiveness of Early Years Interventions – What does the Research Tell Us?* Comprehensive Spending Review: Cross-Departmental Review of Provision for Young Children, Volume 2. London: HM Treasury

Smith, P. K., Cowie, H. and Blades, M. (2003) *Understanding Children's Development* (4th edition). Oxford: Blackwell Publishing

Stuart, C.C. (2003) *Assessment, Supervision and Support in Clinical Practice.* Edinburgh: Churchill Livingstone.

Sure Start (2000) *Providing Good Quality Childcare and Early Learning Experiences through Sure Start.* London: DfEE

Sure Start (2007a) *History of Sure Start* [online]. Last accessed 15 March 2007 at URL: http://www.surestart.gov.uk/surestartservices/settings/ surestartlocalprogrammes/history/

Sure Start (2007b) *Local Programmes* [online]. Last accessed 15 March 2007 at URL: http://www.surestart.gov.uk/surestartservices/settings/surestartlocalprogrammes/

Sylva, K., Melhuish, E., Sammons, P., Siraj-Blatchford, I. and Taggart, B. (2004) *The Effective Provision of Pre-school Education Project: Findings from Pre-school to End of Key Stage One*. London: Sure Start

Taylor, J. (1998) 'Child health', in Taylor, J. and Woods, M. (eds) *Early Childhood Studies*. London: Arnold

Tillema, H. and Orland-Barak, L. (2006) 'Constructing knowledge in professional conversations: the role of beliefs on knowledge and knowing', *Learning and Instruction*, 16, pp. 592–608

Tuckman, B. (1965). 'Developmental sequence in small groups', *Psychological Bulletin*, 63, pp. 384–99

University of East Anglia (2005) *Children's Trusts: Developing Integrated Services for Children in England*. DfES Research Brief RB617 Feb 2005

University of East Anglia (2006) *Managing Change for Children through Children's Trusts/DfES* [online]. Last accessed 5 March 2007 at URL: http://www. everychildmatters.gov.uk/_files/6F8E352B46D8BD089680941098BF95FD.doc

Utting, W. (1997) *People Like Us: The Report Of The Review Of The Safeguards For Children Living Away From Home*. London: HMSO

Valios, N. (2007) *The Bigger Picture on Children's Trusts*. Community Care Feb. 2007 [online]. Last accessed 6 March 2007 at URL: http://www.communitycare.co.uk/ Articles/2007/02/06/52883/childrens-trusts.html

Ward, L. (2006) 'Databases could be danger to young, says study', *Guardian*, 22 November 2006

Warmington, P., Daniels, H., Edwards, A., Leadbetter, J., Martin, D., Brown, S. and Middleton, D. (2004) 'Conceptualising professional learning for multi-agency working and user engagement'. Presented at British Educational Research Association Annual Conference, University of Manchester, 16–18th September 2004

Wenger, E. (1998) *Communities of Practice: Learning, Meaning and Identity*. New York: Cambridge University Press

Wexler, P. (1996) *Critical Social Psychology*. New York: Lang

Whalley, M. (2001) 'Working in teams', in Pugh, G. (ed.) *Contemporary Issues in the Early Years* (3rd edition). London: Paul Chapman

While, A., Murgatroyd, B., Ullman, R. and Forbes, A. (2006) 'Nurses', midwives' and health visitors' involvement in cross-boundary working within child health services', *Child: Care, Health and Development*, 32, 1, pp. 87–99

Wilkin, A., Kinder K., White, R., Atkinson, M. and Doherty, P. (2003) *Towards the Development of Extended Schools* (DfES Research Report 408). London: DfES.

Index

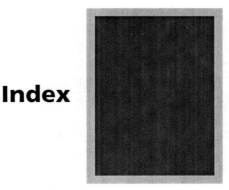